First published 2001 by Prowler Books,
part of the Millivres Prowler Group,
116-134 Bayham Street, London NW1 0BA

A catalogue record for this book is available from the British Library

ISBN 1 873741 57 X

Printed and bound in Finland by WS Bookwell

STILL WATERS

Jack Dickson

PROWLER BOOKS

Prologue

The waters of the loch shone silver in full moonlight.

Two men stood on the shore. The visitor from Maryland, USA held an expensive palm-cam. The other unscrewed the top of the whisky bottle and held his breath.

'Just about here, the old guy said?' The American pressed his eye to the video camera's viewfinder and trained it on the loch's still surface.

'You don't want to pay any attention to Hamish.' Archie took a slug from the bottle and passed it right. 'He lays it on a bit thick at times.' He moved his attention from the American's broad shoulders to the tantalising bulge in those baggy Dockers. A systems analyst. On his first visit to Scotland. With a family – and with interests other than those of the usual tourist.

'A sighting is a sighting.' Jeff Bowen, of Maryland USA, continued to pan the video camera over the dark loch, ignoring the whisky.

'Indeed it is, my friend.' Archie stared at the man's crotch. The guy was up for it: those sly glances and lingering smiles at dinner were more than just stereotypical American sociability. 'But maybe it's better to show a little discretion in these matters...'

Jeff lowered the palm-cam and regarded his Scottish host curiously.

'The beastie's a wee bit shy.' Archie winked, nodding to a thickly wooded area just behind them. He extended the whisky bottle again.

This time Jeff took it and smiled, slipping the video recorder back into his pocket. 'You're the native. You're calling the shots.' He raised the bottle to his lips and drank deeply.

Archie stared at the firm jut of the American's chin. Silhouetted in moonlight, he could see the dark shadow of beard growth which dotted his skin and spread down over the man's adam's apple. Already half hard, his prick flexed against his stomach. Archie frowned, glanced at his wrist then placed a hand on Jeff's strong arm.

The signal was read in an international language which needed no words. The American lowered the bottle. His eyes locked with Archie's. Somewhere behind them, an owl hooted.

Without breaking the eye lock, Jeff sat the half-empty bottle of whisky on a rock. He tentatively raised his hand and stroked Archie's cheek.

Archie's prick flexed again. Blood was flooding into the thick length of desire as he leant towards the hand, rubbing himself against Jeff's palm. His own hand was moving up over the American's biceps, cupping the rounded muscle and enjoying its swell.

'What about your...' The voice was low, husky with need. 'Your wife?'

Archie turned his face, kissing the flat of Jeff's palm. 'What about yours?'

The American's face flushed. 'I – er, we –'

'This is just between us.' Archie talked through the man's awkwardness, running his hand up over Jeff's shoulder and stroking the back of his crew-cut head. 'I love my wife, you love yours. What harm are we doing?'

Jeff's moan was low. He moved closer, resting his head on Archie's shoulder. 'Christ, I want you.'

As his fingers continued to massage the soft bristles on the back of the man's lowered head, Archie glanced at his watch a second time. 'Not here.' He started to move forwards, guiding the American towards the shelter of the trees.

'Yes! Here!' Jeff twisted away.

A jolt of panic stopped the breath in Archie's lungs. He stood there, half aroused, half appalled, as the American fell to his Dockered knees and began to tug at the belt of Archie's jeans. Jeff's movements were stumbling and rushed, fuelled by a desire ignored for too long. The touch of the man's fingers sent shivers over Archie's balls and stiffened his prick further.

'I want your jism in my mouth! I want to feel it slide down my throat, hot and salty.'

The words made Archie's stomach churn with longing. His balls clenched. The hair on the back of his neck stood on end. He was closer to coming than he wanted to be; closer to a lot of things. Archie glanced from the lowered, crew-cut head out over the mirror-smooth surface of the loch. No breeze tonight. Not so much as a ripple stirred the still, murky waters.

As Jeff ground his face into the straining fabric at his crotch, Archie's eyes swept to the far side, past the dark shadow which was all that was visible of Boleskin House, and along the rocky shoreline to the small hotel he owned and managed with Morag. Almost two a.m. One tiny light was visible.

A frown tugged at Archie's lips, then he gasped as the fumbling American eventually got the belt free and began to unzip. Balmy night air ruffled the soft fuzz on his belly. With a groan of victory, Jeff wrenched Archie's jeans and underpants down over his thighs and thrust his face into his host's musky crotch.

Archie moaned. His eyes narrowed. His hands rested on the American's shoulders. His knees bent and he began to undulate against eager-if-inexperienced lips. Dark stubble rasped over his balls. Soft, analyst's hands slipped around to clutch at his arse-cheeks.

Archie's fingers curled into fists. His undulating focused into solid thrusts. He wanted to force himself between the man's lips and fuck his face till he shot sticky wads straight into the American's stomach.

Jeff was nuzzling over his shaft, kissing and licking the stretched cock skin. He could feel the man's breath hot on his stomach. Archie's mouth opened in a groan while the other's lips remained firmly closed. He scowled, frustration taking over from the previous fear he would come too quickly. 'Suck it – take it in your mouth and suck it!' The whispered demand was harsh, urgent.

Jeff groaned but nuzzled on, one hand leaving Archie's arse and fumbling at the front of his own trousers. But Archie grabbed the

American's neck, forcing his face upwards and away from his prick.

A pair of shining eyes, half aroused, half terrified, met his. 'I'm sorry – I can't do this.' Jeff ducked from Archie's grip and began to stagger to his feet. An owl hooted again, somewhat closer.

Archie flinched and forced a smile. 'It's just nerves.' He wrapped his arms around Jeff's shoulders, pulling him against his own muscular body. A virgin – a fucking virgin! The flirting, the come-ons: the guy was more inexperienced than he'd thought.

The moon slipped behind a cloud and the silvery loch faded into an ominous gloom. The American's hands rested on his waist. He buried his face in Archie's neck. 'I want to – honest I do. It's just –'

'It's okay.' Archie ran a hand over Jeff's head, scowling at the great expanse of water behind them. Trapped between their bodies, his exposed prick continued to stretch. Despite the man's apparent cold feet, he could feel the outline of Jeff's arousal strong against his. Pulling his eyes from the dark loch, Archie began to kiss his neck. 'We don't have to... do anything. We can just cuddle.'

His lips tracked a line up towards Jeff's ear. The American shuddered. Archie felt the tremor spread from the American's body to his. He continued to kiss the man's neck, rubbing his face over the bristly skin while one hand roved down Jeff's back. Blowing down from the hills, a soft breeze played against his bare arse-cheeks. Archie's prick was now a thick, throbbing length sandwiched between his stomach and another married man's belt.

As he stroked and kissed, Archie began to grind himself against the buckle of that belt. He wrenched Jeff's plaid shirt free of the back of his jeans, slipping both hands up to caress the bare, warm skin.

The American groaned. His hands crept lower, tentatively resting on Archie's quivering arse-cheeks.

Now it was the host's turn to moan. Jeff's head swivelled left, catching Archie's mouth with dry, eager lips. Then they were hauling at each other's clothes. Buttons popped. Fabric ripped. Archie thrust his tongue between Jeff's lips. His hands swept up over the man's chest, cupping and massaging the firm flesh of his pecs. Jeff was groaning into his mouth, gripping and kneading Archie's arse.

Slowly, they sank to their knees, never breaking the kiss. Jeff's fingers were now probing the hairy crack between Archie's arse-cheeks.

Archie felt the American's nipples stiffen against his palms. He stared at Jeff's closed eyes, then lowered his gaze. Freed from the Dockers, Jeff's prick rose sturdily from his bushy groin. Thick and circumcised, the meaty red glans glistened slick with desire. Already moist, Archie's mouth watered further.

He wanted that prick in his mouth. He wanted to run his tongue around the rim of that magnificent head, to draw it deep between his lips and feel it bang off the back of his throat.

The owl hooted again. Two short, eerie hoots, this time.

One lesson he had learned over the years: flexibility was all. Archie pulled himself together. There would be other opportunities. Tonight, this hearty American would suck on his first prick. And it would be a Scottish prick. Leaning back against a rock, Archie reluctantly broke the kiss.

No need for guidance this time. Sitting back on his heels, Jeff lurched forward, lowering his mouth, still wet from the kiss, over the head of Archie's drooling cock.

Their joint moans drifted up into the night. Archie spread his thighs, allowing the American greater access. Jeff's hands delved between Archie's legs, cupping his bollocks. As a frantic mouth gripped his shaft in a velvet vice, Archie stared beyond to the loch and tried to think of something else.

Jeff's tight lips slipped into a hurried descent. Freed from its thick covering of foreskin, the sensitive glans bumped against the roof of the American's mouth. Archie winced and glanced at his watch. He wanted this to last. This had to last.

His hands lightly gripped the sides of Jeff's head. 'Easy, easy...' Archie slowed the pressure of the man's mouth, controlling the pace to a speed which would give them both more pleasure. He stared down at the top of the American's head.

Jeff's fingers clutched at the back of his thighs. The American was breathing through his nose, sending delicious shivers over Archie's balls with every exhalation. The rock dug into the base of Archie's spine. He continued to guide the man's head, groaning as Jeff's tongue snaked across his tender glans. The pace was becoming less frantic. The man was learning.

Archie blinked in the darkness, glancing down to where Jeff's cut prick twitched and shuddered as if some invisible mouth was caressing its length. The ministrations to his own shaft were pushing him closer to the edge. Muscle trembled in Archie's thighs as he thrust down then up between eager lips.

But while he was completely immersed in the encounter from the waist down, his ears were attuned to any change in their surroundings. The owl hoots had faded. Over the occasional scurrying of the night bird's prey, the only sound was the soft lap of the water on the rocky shoreline.

Then he heard it. Distant at first, then closer. The barely detectable whoosh of something very large moving steadily through water. A shudder shook Archie's body. Instinctively, he moved his hands to Jeff's ears.

On his knees, the American was lost in his task. His breathing came unevenly. He snuffled noisily, his mouth crammed with Highland prick.

Archie continued to fuck the man's face, his attention moving from where Jeff was now wanking his own length to the no-longer still surface of the loch.

Eyes closed, hearing further dampened by sweat-slicked palms and thoroughly otherwise engaged, the tourist was oblivious to everything.

Archie tracked the dark shape's progress, watching as it broke the surface mere yards from where he stood. The breath stopped in his lungs. Warm sweat cooled on skin suddenly icy. His balls clenched, part fear, part passion. He fought the latter, the muscles in his thighs iron and braced against the delicious feel of another man's mouth on his shaft.

Then the immense dark shape dived abruptly.

Archie gasped. Something deep inside him relaxed and was immediately seized by another tension. Fingers tightening around Jeff's ears, he bucked with his hips and shot between the American's lips.

Over the fizz in his ears and the force of his own orgasm, he could hear vague choking sounds, then the fleshy rasp of fist on shaft as Jeff hurriedly and noisily came seconds later. Archie's legs gave way. He slipped from the rock, his hands moving to hold the jerking, shuddering American against his own pleasure-racked body.

As they both knelt there, spent and panting, the large almost-silent shape made its way back to the murky depths of Loch Ness.

Chapter One

Another faculty party.

Professor Michael St. Clair drained his spritzer, nodding to a couple of late arrivals who were handing bottles to a beaming Richard. Another boring faculty party. He glanced at his wrist – at least another hour of this – then watched his partner of ten years, Dr Richard Rodgers, mingle with assorted students and staff from the university's marine palaeontology department.

Richard was in his element, chatting with the Dean, flattering Mrs Dean and generally playing the host with the most. Any minute now, Michael knew he'd be dragged into some tedious exchange on grants, financing or tenure, none of which he was in the mood to discuss at the best of times.

Now? Michael shifted position. The crotch of his well-cut trousers brushed against the back of the armchair, reminding him that the hard-on he'd had for the last thirty minutes showed no sign of going away. A vague smile twitched his lips as he imagined Mrs Dean's horror at the sight of his very obvious erection: it would almost be worth discussing university business to see that.

'All set for tomorrow, Professor?'

A slightly accented voice at his side made Michael turn. He stared, trying to place the glossy-haired man who was holding a can of ginger ale and beaming at him 'Er, almost: just a bit of last-minute packing to do, Mr – ?' He groped for the fellow's name, his eyes instinctively running over slender shoulders encased in white cotton.

Professorial absent-mindedness was graciously overlooked. The man stuck out a hand. 'Rajiv Azad.' He nodded to where Richard was now laughing at one of the Dean's lame jokes. 'Dr Rodgers suggested I introduce myself, since we will be working together for the next seven days.'

'Nice to meet you, Rajiv.' Michael gripped warm fingers, squeezing slightly. One of Richard's overseas postgrads: he should have known. Holding Rajiv's hand a little longer than was strictly necessary, Michael thought of the irony that, considering his professed lack of interest in matters physical, Richard still managed to secure the most handsome male students for himself, while Michael only ever got women and the occasional mature learner.

'Doctor Rodgers is a wonderful teacher. I am very honoured he has chosen me to accompany you on this field trip.'

At the far side of the room, a door opened.

'Your stance on the existence of palaeontologically significant life in Loch Ness is well-documented, but a little blinkered if I may say so, Professor St. Clair, sir,' Rajiv babbled on. Michael was no longer listening. His attention had been taken by one of the university porters, who was unceremoniously thrusting a package plus a set of keys at one of their other guests.

'Yes, yes – will you excuse me?' He released Rajiv's hand, making his way across the crowded room. He was yards from door when a palm touched his arm.

'Michael! Come and say hello to –'

'Sorry, can't stop – I think I've parked my car in a reserved spot.' He pushed past Richard and the Dean, his eyes focused on the porter's departing head and shoulders. 'Back in a second.'

'But –'

The disappointment in Richard's voice failed to register, as did the surprise and vague disapproval in the eyes of Dean Hearns and his wife. Michael moved on swiftly though groups of chatting students. All his attention was focused on the back of a blond, French-cropped head which sat above a pair of appealingly broad shoulders.

A very familiar French-cropped blond head.

And the chase was on.

The solid slap of Doc Marten sole on stone led him down steep twisting stairs and out into the quadrangle. Framed on four sides by pillared aisles, the square offered a variety of exits.

Michael paused, listened then turned right and began to walk briskly in the direction of the car park. The head of his cock pushed against the fly of his well-cut trousers.

Jim? Brad? Some one-syllabled name or other. Michael had encountered the young porter quite a few times, over the past months, and now wished he'd paid more attention to the name-tag which was pinned to the man's well-developed, uniformed left pec. He smiled to himself: it was amazing the details which helped someone linger in the mind. It was not Jim/Brad's bleached hair nor his well-muscled form which had initially made the impression.

Only recently employed by the university, Jim/Brad had been assigned the initial rank of post-delivery boy. The mail was always late, invariably mixed up with someone else's. This was almost as much a tradition at St. Aloysius College as the May Ball or punting down the Isis. But under Jim/Brad's guidance the internal mail system plumbed new depths of inefficiency.

Michael veered left at the end of the pillared aisle, turning into the cloisters. Less well-lit than the quadrangle, one flickering sodium light illuminated the dark space. Michael quickened his pace.

When the mail did finally arrive, it was delivered without knocking, usually in the middle of a tutorial and without as much as an apology. Michael slowed. His hand moved to his groin and he repositioned his bollocks, which were pressing uncomfortably against the root of his swollen cock, before picking up the pace again.

Ahead, he could still hear the fall of the porter's booted feet on the ancient stone. Michael quickened his pace.

Jim/Brad was wordless to the point of rudeness. He stared blankly at whoever talked to him, a lazy scowl which bordered on the confrontational fixed to his sulky face – exhibiting the same attitude, in fact, as ten minutes ago, when handing in whatever it was he had handed in to Richard's rooms – not so much as a knock, let alone the deference which should be accorded senior university teaching staff.

Michael squared his shoulders. He didn't expect forelock-tugging, but civility cost nothing. A frown twitched his lips and his cock flexed against the fly of his trousers. Sullen, sulky and probably very stupid – God, it was so appealing!

As he turned right, along another dark corridor and across another quadrangle towards the stairs, Michael's blood-starved brain was filling with fantasy scenarios.

Jim/Brad, the young wayward porter, receiving a stiff talking to by the stern, older professor. Jim/Brad sullen and aggressive, but eventually penitent, apologetic and eager to make amends in the presence of an older, dominant man. The stern professor deciding that words were not enough, delivering a more corporal lesson in manners.

Jim/Brad loosening the trousers of his porter's uniform, hauling them down along with his underpants until they bagged around his knees. Jim/Brad standing there, blushing and stammering while the stern professor sat in a strong chair and beckoned. Jim/Brad making his undignified way across the room, reluctantly positioning himself over the stern professor's knees.

The feel of warm flesh against his thighs. The sight of another man, draped across his lap, vulnerable and a little fearful. The stern professor raising one sturdy palm then bringing it down hard on the wayward porter's firm white buttocks and –

A loud boom made him jump. The university clock began to strike. The tolling bell cleared Michael's mind. He stopped abruptly and looked around himself. The area was dimly lit. An unpleasant, slightly mildewed smell drifted into his nostrils. As his eyes acclimatised to the gloom, he stared at a wall green with moss. Where the hell was he? Michael slowly turned. Eventually, he identified his surroundings. Somehow, he'd ended up in the basement area which, although well-used by the Aloysian monks who had inhabited this part of the university 600 years ago, now only housed the underfloor heating units and the boiler room.

Michael sighed. His ears strained in the darkness. Apart from the distant drip of water, nothing. He'd lost Jim/Brad somewhere along the way. Worse still, as the clock struck eleven, it dawned on him he'd been away from Richard's bloody party far longer than he'd intended. Michael frowned: there would be accusing, hurt looks followed by the usual interrogation if he returned to the faculty rooms now. May as well go home – he could pretend to be asleep: with a bit of luck, what with the approaching field trip, Richard would have forgotten all about his disappearance by morning.

Feeling more than a little peeved, and now nursing a bad case of frustration, Michael got his bearings and set off back towards the stairs which led up to ground level. It was one thing to be berated when one strayed: quite another when nothing had actually happened.

He was on the third stair when he heard the footsteps. Michael paused. So did the footsteps. Michael turned. Nothing. He turned back and continued upwards. Sound travelled strangely, down here. As he re-emerged into the quadrangle, pausing to light a cigarette, he caught sight of a shape ducking behind one of the pillars, a short distance away. He started: the match went out and Michael smiled at his own ability to spook himself.

End of summer term always brought a little high-jinks, and this was most likely some stoned undergraduate making his way back from a party not unlike the one Michael had just left.

He struck another match, strolling across to the pillar as he raised the flame to the end of his cigarette. Inhaling deeply, he glanced behind the stone structure. Nothing.

A short burst of laughter and the trundle of wheels from the far side of the quadrangle drew his attention. Michael moved in against the wall, narrowly avoiding a group of four young men in evening dress as they raced past, chasing a fifth balanced precariously on a skateboard.

He smiled and walked on, envying their sense of fun and freedom. Soon he was back at the front of the building. A little ahead he spotted his car, and instinctively patted his pockets.

Bugger it: he'd left the keys in Richard's rooms. But it was a pleasant night, and only a 30-minute walk. Then a flash of light caught his eye, just behind the car park. Michael peered. Amidst the trees, a French-cropped blond head gleamed orange beneath the sodium street light. Coincidence?

Michael suppressed a grin. With as much of a stride as his aching balls would allow, he drew on the cigarette and set off again. The chase was back on. Only this time, hunter and hunted had swapped roles.

Four storeys up, Richard watched the tall, smoking figure saunter off across the courtyard. Removing his reading glasses, he rubbed tired eyes and bit back a frown before turning once more to his departing guests. 'Professor St. Clair will be sorry to have missed you, Dean. I know he wanted to talk to you about next year's timetable.' He helped the Dean's wife on with her coat and smiled apologetically at her husband. 'But there are a few last minute details to organise for tomorrow's field trip.'

Dean Hearns nodded curtly and ushered his wife towards the door.

'So glad you could come.' Richard called after them, managing to hide his annoyance at having to make excuses for Michael once again. 'We'll send you a postcard from Scotland!'

Dean and Mrs Hearns moved through the doorway. His face sore from smiling, Richard allowed his lips to relax. He knew Michael hated the social niceties one was forced to go through at this sort of occasion, and he didn't blame him for making an excuse to leave early. What hurt was the total lack of interest in his responsibilities. They were a team. Partners – at least, they were meant to be.

As the door closed behind Dean and Mrs Hearns, Richard looked to where Rajiv Azad was standing alone, examining volumes in a tall bookcase while the bulk of the other students were well on their way to leglessness courtesy of the free wine. Rajiv worked hard. Quiet and reserved, he was an eager student and a joy to teach. He had a fine future in research.

Richard's eyes narrowed and he scanned for the other postgrad who was to make up their party of four on tomorrow's field trip. Lionel was also bright. He had a fine mind but lacked Rajiv's dedication

An abrupt gale of laughter from the huddle of students around the drinks table distracted Richard's meditations. In the middle, surrounded by half the university rugby First Eleven, a stocky man wearing what looked like a jockstrap over his face was attempting to clamber on to the table while balancing a full bottle of Newcastle Brown Ale on the palm of each hand.

Yes, Lionel lacked Rajiv's dedication, and his sense of decorum. But Dr Rodgers couldn't help smiling as Lionel, to the accompaniment of a mounting chant, ascended the table. It was impossible not to like Lionel Banks. Jovial, ale-swilling Lionel who headed the college rowing team, captained the First Eleven, enjoyed a full social life and still somehow managed to work on his doctoral thesis.

Lionel would end up teaching: he had the knack for communication which the more studious Rajiv lacked, and his sporting prowess would ensure him plenty of job offers if he ever decided to give up the student lifestyle and settle into adulthood.

Tearing his eyes from where the stocky redhead was now juggling with the bottles, Richard began the clearing up process. His mind remained on Raj and Lionel, as he swept empty cans and wine-boxes into bin-liners. The pair reminded him so much of himself and Michael, more years ago than he cared to remember.

A dashing Mike St. Clair, the youngest man to receive a professorship. Drank like a fish and flirted with everyone. Drove fast cars and wrestled naked for the college grappling club.

Bookish Richard Rodgers. Academic slogger, with a love of his subject and a sexuality he would rather have ignored.

So alike, in their chosen field of research. Their sense of humour. Love of Japanese food. So different, in temperament. And other areas?

Richard pulled his mind away from this line of thought. All couples had problems. Ten years together was no flash in the pan – nor any mean feat. Relationships took as much work as any doctoral thesis: work and effort and constant attention. So he felt a little neglected – hurt even, that Michael had thought nothing of walking out of what was an important faculty occasion. So they were going through a rocky patch. So Michael had a higher sex-drive than he did – so what?

Relationships were more than just sex...

Richard moved on, picking up paper plates and overflowing ash-trays. So, they had different needs in life. But those very differences were what had attracted each to the other, all those years ago. Different strokes. Different strengths. Different goals?

'Can I be of assistance, Dr Rodgers?'

The polite voice at his elbow pulled Richard from his over-analysis of the situation. He turned and found himself staring into Rajiv Azad's deep brown eyes. 'Guests don't –'

'I would like to think I am more colleague than guest, Dr Rodgers.' Raj gently but firmly took the bin-liner from Richard and began to clear the top of the mantelpiece. 'And it is quicker if I help, no?'

With a smile, Richard relented. 'Thank you, Raj.' All these thoughts of Michael – problems or not – had made him eager to break up the party and get home.

On the far side of the room, a conga line was forming, with Lionel – now sporting the jockstrap as a makeshift, one-cup brassiere – at the head.

As he and Raj worked steadily, neatly avoiding the weaving line of drunken, carousing men, Richard knew that one thing firmly distin-guished himself and Michael from Raj and Lionel: while the Iraqi postgrad seemed to have no romantic attachments at present, there was no doubt he was straight. And Lionel's girlfriends were legion, if university gossip was to be believed.

Despite the arrival of the Third Millennium, relationships like his and Michael's were still too infrequently acknowledged. Suddenly, Richard needed to be with Michael. He needed to know they were a couple. He needed to know that, despite everything, he had some-thing other than work to come home to.

'Would you mind terribly locking up for me, Raj?' Richard fumbled in his pocket for the keys to the faculty rooms. 'I know I can trust you, and I've just remembered I –' He broke off, surprised at the expression of near-pleasure which adorned his research student's face.

Raj executed a small bow. 'I would be honoured, sir.' He glanced disapprovingly at Lionel as the conga line swayed past again. 'It will be my pleasure to look after matters for you.'

Richard thrust his keys into a pale-palmed hand. 'Thanks – see you tomorrow morning? Five a.m. sharp?'

Raj nodded. 'May your dreams be pleasant, Dr Rodgers.'

'Er – thanks, Raj.' And with that, Richard grabbed his battered sports jacket and hurried from the room.

Michael thrust his hands into his pockets and began to whistle non-chalantly.

He wondered if the so-called hunter knew that the prey was all too aware of what was going on. Part of Michael hoped so – he liked a game where everyone knew the score. On the other hand, it would be most satisfying to turn the tables on his sullen stalker at the last minute.

On the long walk home – all the longer, due to several detours Michael had taken – his erection had grown from half-hard to its full, stout seven inches. Several times he had almost stopped, turned to face his tracker in some secluded part of the road or in one of the many small copses he had cut through on the elaborate winding walk. But he had resisted the temptation: teasing himself was one of his pleasures. Teasing another added a extra frisson to the evening's sport. Postponement was the name of this game. Postponement. Anticipation. Control.

As he approached the small pied-à-terre he shared with Richard, Michael glanced at his watch: half-eleven. If he knew Dean Hearns, his partner would be having the arse bored off him for a good hour yet. Plenty of time. Plenty of time to see just how far Jim/Brad was pre-pared to take this.

With a jaunty air, Michael pulled house keys from his pocket and jogged up the stairs to the front door. He didn't glance behind. He did-n't need to: if Jim/Brad was ever forced to hunt for a living, discreet tracking would not be his strong point.

As he secured the latch back, ensuring the door would open easily if pushed, it suddenly dawned on Michael he was taking a big risk. Jim/Brad could be some homophobic maniac: Professor St. Clair was not in the habit of hiding his sexuality. But he was also a powerfully built man: Mike had, after all, wrestled during his student days. On the other hand, physique was little defence against a knife. Or a gun.

As the reality of the situation sank in, Michael was shocked to find his prick throbbing harder than ever. Danger gave the whole thing a further edge. But he was not completely stupid. Michael turned casually and stared at the low hedge which separated the house from the street. 'Are you coming up, or what?'

Only silence greeted his question. For one fleeting moment, Michael wondered if he'd imagined the whole thing. Then, slowly, a bleached blond head rose from behind the hedge, followed by broad shoulders and chest. Brushing leaves from the front of his porter's uniform, Jim/Brad stared at him, a little sheepishly.

Michael grinned and stepped to one side. One hand moved to caress the very obvious bulge in the front of his well-cut trousers. The other held the door open.

Like a little lamb, the previously sullen Jim/Brad trotted meekly up the stairs and into the flat. But the door had barely closed behind them when the lamb became a lion. Jim/Brad lunged at Michael, lips parted in longing.

The force of the kiss knocked the professor of marine palaeontology on to the hall carpet. Something tinkled alarmingly to the left of his head. Michael stuck out an arm to steady the small cabinet which housed Richard's prized collection of hand-blown glass animals.

Jim/Brad beat him to it, knocking the entire cabinet on to the floor as he covered Michael's body with his own and began to tear at his clothes.

The sound of smashing glass loud in his ear, Michael groaned, returning the urgency of the kiss. He pushed his tongue into the younger man's mouth, tasting the vague bitterness of lager and wondering vaguely if the porter had been forced to resort to Dutch courage.

He could feel Jim/Brad's erection grinding against his hipbone. Michael thrust up, arching his back and wriggling out of his own shirt while simultaneously hauling at the buttons of the porters' uniform jacket. Somewhere at the back of his mind, he half-wished the man had kept the uniform on. But his body was in charge now – or, more accurately, his prick. Michael grabbed the porter's arse-cheeks. He pulled the man down on top of him, grinding upwards and deepening the kiss. Then he rolled.

As he did so, Jim/Brad's hands moved to the front of Michael's well-cut trousers. Nimble fingers soon had the fly down and Michael gasped as his cock and balls were cupped in a warm palm.

His gasp was echoed by a long, baritone groan which resounded deep in the blond porter's chest. Now on top, Michael sat up and leant back, grinning down at the half-naked man who held his prick. Jim/Brad's eyes were shining, the pupils swollen with lust. His normally sullen features contorted further into an irresistible sneer of longing. The transformation made Michael's prick flex against the younger man's fingers. Already scarlet skin flushed further. Jim/Brad bucked up off the floor in another lunge.

Michael placed a palm on the broad chest. A few fair hairs fringed tantalisingly erect nipples. He would have loved to suck on those hard pink buds. But after nearly two hours of postponement – longer if one counted the weeks of anticipation which had begun the first time Jim/Brad had unceremoniously dropped a pile of mail on Michael's desk – other matters needed to be taken care of.

In one swift movement, the professor moved from his position on top of the panting blonde porter and hoisted trembling thighs over his shoulders. The suddenness of the action made Jim/Brad grunt. Then grunts became low growls as Michael spread two firm arse-cheeks and thrust his face into the man's downy crack.

The porter made a grab for Michael's cock. Michael inhaled deeply and raised the man's legs further. He didn't need a hand-job. He was already mere minutes from coming, and the musky smell of another man's body would push him over the edge. Rubbing his cheeks and nose up and down the moist crack, Michael felt his bollocks tighten. Somewhere just above the crown of his iron-grey head another tightening was detectable. Plus other movement.

Michael thrust his tongue into Jim/Brad's young body, only distantly aware of the jerks and moans as the porter began to wank himself towards orgasm. He fucked steadily, pushing past the tight sphincter and drawing the taste of another man into his mouth.

Around them, tiny dismembered glass animals tinkled and crunched as the two men rolled again. Now Jim/Brad was on top, straddling Michael's sweating face.

Michael groaned. The porter's bollocks hit the bridge of his nose. Warm arse-cheeks pressed around the sides of his face. Blood pounded in his ears. Breath caught in his lungs. He was suffocating in the man, drowning in the hot musky stink. What a way to go! As he thrust ever upwards, the man on his face thrust down, wanking himself more furiously. Part of Michael wanted to watch Jim/Brad come. Another, greater part wanted to tongue-fuck the porter until –

His orgasm took him by surprise. He gasped into Jim/Brad's crack, feeling the familiar clench and rush as his prick flexed violently. Then something warm and wet hit the skin on his back and a roar of release cut through the sound of pounding blood.

Followed swiftly by the sound of a door opening.

And a shocked gasp.

Chapter Two

The hall was in an uproar. Clothes lay strewn everywhere. The display cabinet had been overturned and sat in a sea of crushed crystal which sparkled in the overhead light. But that was the least of it. The blood drained from Richard's cheeks as he stared at the naked stranger.

The expression on the blond boy's face changed from ecstasy to one of complete horror. He leapt up. 'Um – er – I –'

Richard looked down at the sprawled, spunk-splattered form of his partner. Shock gave way to a simmering fury.

Mike gave a low laugh. Slowly, he turned over on to his side to look at the boy, who was now hurriedly dressing. 'Hey! What's the hurry? We –'

They stared at each other.

Irrationally, Richard felt a burning behind his eyes. Fury was spilling over into hurt. Dragging his gaze from the well-muscled, sweating body, he tried to pull himself together.

He knew this sort of thing went on. He'd known for a few years now that Michael had other lovers. His mind flashed back to the first time he'd found condoms in the pocket of Mike's jacket, while searching for car keys.

Just because he had little interest in sex, there was no reason Michael should remain celibate – and at least he was being sensible about it. Richard clenched his fists, fighting back tears.

Michael was now clambering to his feet. Somewhere behind, the door opened then banged shut as the semi-dressed boy, carrying his boots, fled from their house. Their house. Their hall. Their carpet.

Richard was well aware of the illogicality of it, but that was what hurt. He could handle Mike's cruising, the furtive encounters in cottages and clubs: at least, in the abstract. But to be brought face to face with it in their home, to walk in on the man with whom he had spent the last ten years of his life, flushed and invigorated from an encounter with a younger and very handsome boy... Something warm and salty rolled down his cheek.

'This wasn't meant to happen.'

Richard scowled, pushed past Mike and ran upstairs.

'Listen – I'm sorry.' Mike was running after him. 'Let's talk about this.'

Richard sprinted faster. At the top of the stairs he grabbed the handle of the bathroom door. Plunging inside, he drew the bolt behind himself.

The handle rattled. 'Baby, please.'

'Go away!' He didn't want to hear it.

'He's nothing – just some kid I –'

'Go away!' He didn't care.

'Richard, please open the door. We can sort this out.'

'Fuck off!' Chest tight, tears now coursing down his cheeks, Richard flattened himself against the door. 'Just – fuck off!'

The harsh edge to his voice shut Michael up. The handle ceased to rattle. Abruptly, the strength left Richard's legs. His knees buckled and he slid slowly down the door. As he sat there, crouched and hurting, Richard listened to the slow pad of bare feet moving away. When he was sure his partner was well out of earshot, he gave in to the unbearable tightness in his chest.

Richard sobbed his heart out: part in anger at the humiliation of it all, part grief at something he and Michael had obviously lost. But the larger part was fear: fear and dread of what he had been expecting for some time now. That casual sex would not be enough. That the warmth, friendship, affection – and love? – which characterised their relationship would be eventually outweighed by the lure of pastures new. That Michael would leave him for a younger, more virile man.

Slowly, Richard hauled himself from the floor and staggered over to the basin. He turned on the tap, dousing his face in icy water in the vain hope of pushing the deep-seated fear back to where it had come from. As he turned to grab a towel, he caught sight of himself in the mirror. Forty six. Five foot ten. Losing it a bit on top, but not yet grey.

Richard peered critically. His neat beard and moustache were still the same dark brown they had been when he and Michael first met. His eyes were the same – a little more creased, but one couldn't expect to look like a teenager forever.

His gaze moved downwards. Richard scrutinised the rest of his body. He'd put on a bit of weight, but not much. Instinctively he turned sideways, patted, then sucked in his gut. At one time, Michael had adored that same, slightly chubby body.

'Gives me something to hold on to in bed at night – you can't cuddle skinny men.'

Richard sniffed. A small smile twitched his lips. They had enjoyed some fine times. But somewhere along with way, his sex drive had slackened off. Twice a day had slipped to twice a week. Then twice a month. With a sigh, Richard tried to remember when exactly he'd become more interested in curling up beside Michael in bed at night than fucking his lean, muscular arse. Just before the conference on new data analysis techniques in Madrid? After he'd been awarded tenure and his teaching timetable had suddenly increased? When Michael had secured his professorship?

As he exhaled, something tugged at his brain. For so long he and Mike had been academic equals, following parallel but very different research paths. Richard frowned into the mirror. Where Mike was the pragmatist, the accepted face of marine palaeontology, Richard had found himself drawn more and more to the esoteric fringes of the science. Where Mike trod a well-worn path, Richard was forging new ground, considering the inconsiderable: theorising, postulating and allowing other sciences to influence his thinking.

But who got the papers published? Who was asked to appear on TV pop-science programmes? Who was in danger of becoming the Carol Vorderman of marine palaeontology? And who received the professorship, when Dr Richard Rodgers's theories – although unproven as yet – were by far the more progressive?

He sighed. Could it be professional envy that was stopping his dick getting hard for the tall, distinguished man whose naked body could still make his heart skip a beat? Richard scowled at himself. Of course not!

A soft tap at the window made him jump. He spun round, just in time to see a broad, hairy-wristed hand slip in through the small skylight at the top and undo the latch at the bottom.

The plane of glass swung inwards to reveal Michael perched on top of a ladder. He smiled tentatively. 'If you won't come out, then I'll have to come in.' Now dressed in sweat pants and a vest, Michael moved a trainered foot from one of the rungs on to the window sill.

Richard continued to scowl. 'You'll kill yourself, you madman – it's a 20-foot drop out there!' He quickly moved an array of shaving-gear and cologne from the shelf above the bath and stretched out a hand. Strong fingers grasped it and Michael slowly made his way into the bathroom.

They stood there, looking at each other. Michael took in Richard's red-rimmed eyes. His rugged face creased with concern. 'Honestly, I didn't mean to bring him back here – that's the last thing I wanted. It was a mistake – it'll never happen again.'

As his partner talked on and apology followed on ever-more-sincere apology, Richard's mind returned to his worst fear. Better to call it quits now than be left, at some future point. Better to leave Michael before he left him. Better to avoid facing the unfaceable possibility that he was unbearably jealous of his partner's academic success.

'Am I forgiven?'

Mike's penitent voice edged into Richard's brain. He refocused on the man who stood before him. Swallowing hard, Richard screwed up all his courage and met Michael's eyes. 'I think we want different things, these days.' The shock in his partner's clear blue eyes made his heart thump, but Richard knew what he had to do. 'We're just making each other unhappy, continuing on like this.'

Michael sat down heavily on the side of the bath. 'What do you mean?'

Richard couldn't look into that apprehensive face so he stared at the floor. 'I think we should go our separate ways.'

On the other side of campus, another difficult conversation was in progress.

'You all packed for tomorrow, Raji?' Completely smashed, Lionel beamed drunkenly at the small Iraqi man and quickened his pace to keep up.

'Yes.'

Another one-word answer.

'Have you been to Scotland before?'

'No.'

Lionel was running out of questions. At least eight pints of Newcastle's finest ale made him brave. And gave him wind. He belched loudly. 'Why don't you like me, Raji?'

'I do not dislike you.'

Progress, of a sort. Lionel tried to focus on the side of the Iraqi man's angular face. 'I would have helped you clear up the mess back at old Rodgers's rooms – you only had to ask.'

'You are disrespectful.' Rajiv's lips tightened further.

Lionel belched a second time. 'Okay, okay – Dr Rodgers.' Rubbing his face, Lionel sighed. He never knew what to say to this man. With his rugby mates, or women, he was the life and soul of the party. But there was something about Rajiv Azad which either struck Lionel dumb or twisted his tongue into knots and almost guaranteed he'd say the wrong thing.

The two postgraduate students walked in silence for a while. Lionel noticed they had long since passed the turning for Rajiv's rooms. Where was the fellow off to?

Rajiv turned his head imperiously. 'I have business to attend to. Why are you following me?'

'Hey, I'm just walking – taking the night air before bed. No law against that, is there?' Lionel grinned, marvelling at the way Rajiv's swarthy face seemed to dance before his eyes.

Then his reluctant companion stopped completely. Rajiv withdrew a set of keys from his pocket. 'Please go home. I must return these to Doctor Rodgers and he does not want a drunken boor cavorting on his doorstep.'

Had Lionel been sober, he would not have let this pipsqueak get away with that remark. But he was drunk – and when Lionel was drunk he loved the world. He staggered in front of Rajiv, determined to make the best of this opportunity. 'What about a night-cap, back at my rooms – to toast the field trip? We'll have the place to ourselves – my roommate's already left for the summer.'

A horrified expression creased Rajiv's face. 'I am Moslem – I do not drink alcohol.'

Lionel slung an arm around the fellow's narrow shoulders and clasped him in a bear hug. 'Come on – just a quick one. I won't tell Allah if you won't!'

A sharp elbow caught him abruptly in the stomach. One minute he was crushing Rajiv against his chest, the next the man had become smoke and was slipping easily out of Lionel's well-muscled arms.

'You are a disgrace! I trust you will conduct yourself in a more proper manner when we travel to Scotland as representatives of the university. Go home and sleep!' He walked quickly away.

Winded and pushed to the ground, Lionel lay there writhing. 'I'm sorry – come back! It was a joke. I have soft drinks too – do you like tea? I have tea. I have –' He suddenly realised he was shouting into an empty quadrangle. Feeling a little foolish, he slowly staggered to his feet and stared towards where he had last seen Raji.

Fuck him!

Lionel had tried to be nice, but if this was the way Mr Oh-so-proper Rajiv Azad wanted to play things, so be it. As he walked back to his rooms, the night air began to clear his head – and fill his cock. Lionel groaned. Brewer's droop wasn't a problem he ever encountered: in fact, he was always randy as hell after a good piss-up. Why hadn't he gone into town with Jim and the lads, gone to a club and picked himself up a bit of cunt? Why had he wasted good fucking time, trying to talk to that swotty git?

Something at the back of Lionel's ale-fuddled mind knew why.

Something which only allowed Lionel to consider such an option when the excuse of too much booze was there to rely on.

By the time he reached his rooms, Lionel was already fumbling with the fly of his jeans. Christ, he needed a wank – and he needed it now. Charging through the doorway, he ran straight to his room and locked the door behind himself, even though he knew his flatmates had gone home for the summer. Surrounded by *Baywatch* posters and souvenir rugby programmes, Lionel fell to his knees. He groped under the bed amongst dog-eared copies of *Playboy* and *Fiesta*, scowled then hurled them over his shoulder.

Where was it? Were was the magazine with the she-males?

Even thinking the word make Lionel's nipples tingle. He continued to rummage, pushing other publications aside until his fingers made contact with the somewhat crumpled object of his search. With a cry of triumph he wrenched it free and threw himself on the bed. Lionel hurriedly flicked for his favourite shot, then placed it open on his chest while he wrenched down his jeans and boxers.

His prick was already half hard. His broad palm slick with sweat, he seized the thick member, caressing himself slowly while grabbing the magazine with his other hand.

The picture was entitled Billie. Lionel wondered if the model was Bill or Wilhemina in real life. He moaned, taking in the beautiful almond eyes set in a face the colour of polished bronze.

Billie's hair was black and glossy, cut in a boyish bob. It flicked the tops of narrow shoulders and urged Lionel's goggling eyes down to small, pert breasts.

He'd always been a tit-man. Big, overblown busty blondes had been his weakness – Lionel's prick flexed against his clammy palm – until one of the rugby team had brought back this magazine from a trip to Amsterdam, amongst the usual selection of women-with-women, women-with-dogs and women-with-root-vegetables.

Lionel stared at Billie's breasts. Tiny, brown, almost prepubescent mounds perked cheekily up at him from the well-worn centrefold. He was panting now. The head of his prick pushed past the last millimetres of foreskin, stretching itself towards the cheap, shiny paper.

Jack Dickson

Billie's stomach was flat. Ridges of hard muscle were just visible beneath the smooth skin. As his eyes moved lower to the lighter, shaved area which heralded Billie's pubes, Lionel began to caress himself more roughly. Billie's cock was slim and elegant. It jutted up from the bottom of the page, seven proud inches of unashamed masculinity framed by a gleam of hipbone.

Lionel moaned louder. His brain rebelled at the contradiction, while his body responded more strongly than ever. His damp fist paused at the head of his swollen prick. A rough thumb swept over the gaping piss-slit, catching the oozing droplets of clear arousal and slicking them back down over his straining shaft.

The magazine had been passed round a post-match locker-room. The rest of the team hooted and laughed, finding the mixture of male and female in Billie and her exotic companions odd and freakish.

Lionel's breathing was shallow and harsh. He could no longer hear the rasp of fist on cock flesh. His mind reeled with possibilities. Billie stroking his cock while Lionel sucked on those pert breasts. Billie's pouting lips moving down over Lionel's shaft. Lionel kissing and licking every inch of that slim, polished body.

Abruptly, his bollocks drew up against the root of his hard prick. Lionel's spine arched up off the bed and he was fucking his fist, pushing the thick flexing shaft up into curled fingers. The she-male magazine slipped from his chest. Lionel shoved his free hand up beneath his rugby jersey and began to pull roughly on his erect nipples

He had no idea what Billie looked like from behind, but he'd fucked women up the arse before. Tighter than cunt – different feeling. The sensation of curving his groin around plump arse-cheeks had done strange things to his mind. As he moved closer and closer to orgasm, Lionel wondered vaguely if a man's arse felt different from a woman's. The fantasy in his mind cranked up another gear and he was kneeling behind Billie, fingers around those gleaming hipbones and pushing deep into that warm, she-male arse.

Before he could stop it, a taboo image thrust itself into his mind. Lionel gasped. Arse-cheeks leaving the bed completely, his fingers moved from his nipples to fumble at the entrance to his own body. As the first tremors of orgasm sent a clenching through his bollocks, Lionel's sweaty index finger thrust itself into his arse.

Billie was inside him. Billie's pert breasts pressed against his spine. Billie's shaved pubes rasped against his big hairy arse while Billie's slim, elegant cock gave Lionel Banks, captain of the college rugby team and stud-about-town, the fucking of his life.

The first thick wad of spunk tore loose from his slit.

Lionel roared his release. Feet planted firmly on the bed, his head and shoulders reared up. Then his body crashed back down on to one thick finger, burying the digit deep in his arse.

The second wave shook his already trembling frame more violently, intensified by the penetration. Lionel squeezed his eyes tightly shut, horrified and aroused and not wanting to see the smouldering, arrogant fantasy eyes which had appeared before him.

Billie might be fucking him, but it was Rajiv Azad's dismissive gaze which painted itself on his retinae.

'Give me another chance – come on. It's just sex – I can stop whenever I want.'

They had moved from the bathroom to the lounge. On the couch, Richard sighed and looked at his now-pacing partner.

'These hands will never touch another man's body, if that's what it takes.' Michael's voice was growing increasingly desperate.

Richard narrowed his eyes. 'You mean it?'

'Of course I mean it!' His partner stopped pacing, strode over to the couch and crouched in front of Richard. 'I don't want to lose you, baby. That's the last thing I want.' Professor St. Clair grabbed Richard's knees and squeezed them.

Dr Rodgers's brown eyes narrowed sceptically. Extravagant gestures were easy – as were words. Could he believe Mike? Did he even want to believe him?

Michael gazed up, beseechingly. 'Please?' His right hand began to move from kneecap along the inside of Richard's thigh.

Richard stood up. 'Why deny yourself what you obviously need?' He walked to the window, just in time to see the slight figure of Rajiv

Azad trotting quietly up the front steps. 'And if it is as... casual and meaningless as you claim, why do you do it at all?'

'Because –' The voice was close.

Richard watched the small Iraqi man quickly slip what looked like a set of keys through the letterbox then trot back down the steps and off towards the student accommodation.

' – because –'

He was vaguely touched by the gesture: there had been no need for Raj to return the keys that night. But the action was symptomatic of the same attention to detail the man exhibited in his academic work.

' – because I think – if I just give it time, you'll want to have sex with me again.'

The pain in his partner's voice made Richard spin round.

Michael's rugged face was crimson. 'I miss you – I miss having sex with you. My pickups are fun, but I want you. I know you've gone off me, in that department, but maybe your interest can be rekindled if you –'

The unfinished sentence dangled between them, heavy with innuendo. Richard's eyes widened.

Michael grinned, knowing he had the man's attention. 'You should try it. Anonymous, casual sex can be –'

'Me? Have sex with – other people? Whose names I don't know?' The very thought made him ill.

Michael laughed heartily. 'You sound like someone's maiden aunt, instead of the sexiest, most desirable man I've ever met.'

Now it was Richard's turn to blush. He was suddenly aware of a stirring in the crotch of his trousers – whether from the compliment or the concept of cruising he had no idea. He did know he wanted to get off this particular topic as quickly as possible. 'You're serious about trying celibacy?'

'Deadly – how about the field trip?' Michael crossed his heart with a flourish. 'These hands will touch no man's body for seven full days – on one condition.'

Richard waited.

Michael walked over to the couch and sat down. 'You get yourself a bit of casual fun.'

'I can't.'

'Yes you can – you still wank. I've seen you.'

Richard's blush deepened. 'I don't mean I can't, in that sense – I just don't want to. It's not me. You know I've never been one for that sort of thing. The idea does nothing for me.' His cock twitched inside his trousers and he knew he was lying about something.

'Perhaps it's time you reassessed yourself, baby.' An edge of tease had entered Michael's voice. 'How can you make judgements about something you've never tried?'

Richard looked at the man he loved. Maybe it would be worth it – maybe he could just grab some local and hurriedly suck him off. With supreme effort, Richard brought his rational mind to bear on this very irrational subject. Think of it as a scientific experiment. Two subjects. Each reversing their normal proclivities in a semi-controlled environment for a strictly limited period. What was there to lose if he made a complete fool himself with some stranger? 'Well... all right.'

Michael leapt to his feet and cheered.

'But I'm not promising anything. I will, however, make myself open to the possibility of an emotion-free encounter.'

Michael rushed over and hugged him. 'Don't make it sound so clinical. There are emotions involved and it will be good for you to feel what I feel for yourself.'

Richard wrapped his arms around Michael and nuzzled his neck. And if nothing else, the week's experiment would give them both time to decide if they had any future together.

Burying his face in Richard's warm neck, Michael suddenly frowned: what was he letting himself in for? A week without a fuck? He'd go out of his mind!

And neither man was aware of the small, coffee-skinned figure, beyond the living room window, who was watching their embrace with a slowly sinking heart.

Chapter Three

Insistent buzzing pushed itself into a dream in which he was watching Mike get fucked by a faceless blond boy in a porter's uniform, while something warm and damp closed around his own cock.

Breathing heavily, Richard woke from an uneasy sleep, barely three hours after his head had hit the pillow. His left hand uncurled from around his shaft, arm lunging towards the bedside table to switch off the alarm. The illuminated digits read 4.02 a.m.

Richard swung his legs over the edge of the bed. He sat there for a minute, rubbing the sleep from his eyes and hauling his mind from the remnants of the dream. Outside, dawn was edging up beyond the spires of the university.

They had a long drive ahead of them, and an early start was necessary if they were to reach Drumnadrochit this side of midnight.

Despite the lack of sleep, Richard felt well rested – almost invigorated. He continued to sit there, watching the sky pinken behind the college roofs. Glancing down at his crotch, he was horrified to see a lob of Morning Glory languidly curving up from his thick dark pubes. He shuddered, half-surprised at the effects of the dream, half-fancying an early wank, back in beside Mike.

He turned, switched on the bedside lamp and stuck an elbow in the approximate area of his partner's kidneys. 'Come on – rise and shine.'

From beneath the duvet, a grunt. The Mike-shaped mound stirred slightly. 'Go away.'

Richard elbowed again. 'Come on.' He stood up, grabbed a dressing gown from the foot of the bed and strode into the kitchen. 'Mike!' Richard fired up the espresso machine, shouting over his shoulder.

Nothing from the bedroom.

Richard sighed, listening to the hiss of water over ground beans. 'Mike!' He turned, and the thin fabric of his dressing gown brushed against the head of his lob. A second shudder shook his body. Then more buzzing. Different buzzing.

'What the hell's going on out there?' A roar of irritation, from the bedroom.

Both glad of the distraction of the doorbell which had finally stirred his partner into consciousness and taken his mind off his own early morning hard-on, Richard strode from the kitchen into the hall.

He had no idea who would call on them at 4.11 in the morning. But he did know he owed them thanks.

Turning the key, Richard opened the front door and found himself staring into the eyes of Rajiv Azad. Dressed in neatly pressed jeans, a bright yellow waterproof jacket and holding a rucksack over one shoulder, the postgraduate student bowed briefly.

'Good morning, Dr Rodgers. I hope you will pardon my forwardness, but I am here to offer my services as regards the loading of the car in which you are so kindly conveying me north.'

Richard swayed slightly under the verbal onslaught. What on earth was the man doing here? They'd arranged to pick up Raj and Lionel in the main quadrangle at 5 a.m.

'I am ready, willing and able. Please feel free to take advantage of me.' Rajiv's eyes strayed from Richard's to a point over his shoulder.

Suddenly aware of his hard-on, Richard gripped the revers of the dressing gown, pulling them closer together. 'Thank you, Rajiv – that's very kind of you, but...' He followed the Iraqi man's gaze, just in time to catch a glimpse of Michael's firm white arse as he stumbled across the hall into the kitchen.

Richard frowned and turned back. 'Sorry, Rajiv – as you can see, we're still in the process of getting up.'

'It is no trouble, Dr Rodgers.'

Richard blinked, watching his star postgrad carefully place his rucksack just inside the door.

'I am sorry to have disturbed you so early, but now that I am here, I may as well make myself useful.' Rajiv eyed the large pile of tents, sleeping bags, ground sheets and general provisions which had kept Richard up into the early hours of that morning.

Richard smiled as a blast of Radio 1 echoed through from the kitchen, signalling that Mike was now at least on the road to being awake. 'Thank you, Raj.' He lifted his car keys from the hall table and held them out.

The small man flushed with pleasure. Richard's fingers brushed smaller, more slender digits as he dropped the keys into a waiting palm. 'It's just over there, the one with the...'

'I know which car is yours, Dr Rodgers.' Rajiv bowed again. 'Please leave this to me.'

Before Richard could intervene, Rajiv was moving swiftly towards the first tent. He grabbed the long nylon-covered bolster, threw it over one narrow shoulder and grabbed the other. Richard blinked. The guy was stronger than he looked.

'Where's the milk?' A whine from the kitchen. 'Rick, you know I can't drink black first thing in the morning.'

Richard turned towards the sound of the voice. 'Use the powdered stuff.' He turned back, smiling. 'Give me a minute to get dressed and I'll help you.'

But Rajiv was already staggering towards Richard's Volvo estate, car keys gripped between small white teeth and a tent on each shoulder.

Richard's smile broadened. 'Thanks, Raj – we'll be with you in about ten minutes, tops.' He left the front door opened and walked back into the kitchen.

Ten minutes became 20. Then 30, by the time Dr Rodgers had packed for Professor St. Clair, who had, predictably, forgotten to do it last night and needed even more caffeine than usual to get going at that hour.

Meanwhile, Rajiv Azad had rearranged the field trip equipment a second, then a third time. He'd also trotted round to Lionel's rooms, when the other student had not appeared in the quadrangle by quarter past five. Finally, at quarter to six, the four men stood behind the open boot of Richard's Volvo estate. He sighed. Mike lit a cigarette. Lionel leaned against the side of the car, looking like death warmed up.

Rajiv Azad's disappointment was palpable. 'I have tried four times, Dr Rodgers.' He extended one long finger to the meticulously packed car. 'There is nowhere else to put our recording equipment except in the back passenger seat, and if it is put there, only enough room remains for two passengers – one in the back, one in the front.'

Mike grinned. 'You can sit on Lionel's knee, eh?'

Rajiv looked horrified and the stocky captain of the First Eleven raised hungover eyes from the ground for the first time.

'No, we can't overload the car, anyway.' Richard stepped in. 'I didn't really want to take a second vehicle, but it looks like we'll have to.'

'It's no problem. I'll follow you up on the Harley.' Mike was sounding brighter already.

Richard looked at him and Professor St. Clair grinned and shrugged. 'I know it's been a while, but she was serviced two months ago and I still have my leathers.'

A shiver brushed over Richard's skin – a shiver which had nothing to do with the cool morning air.

'Two minutes – give me two minutes and we can all leave at the same time.' Mike turned and jogged towards the lockup garage at the end of the small row of pieds-à-terre.

'Prof St. Clair has a bike?'

Rick heard the surprise in Lionel's voice. Despite himself, he smiled. Mike's vintage Harley Davidson had been a present to himself on receiving his professorial seat.

Mike had always loved bikes. He'd owned an ancient Norton, decades ago in their student days. Richard had many fond memories of trips up to Forest Hill, his arms wrapped round his partner's waist, the smell of the leather and the diesel in his head as he perched on the pillion and pressed his face to the back of the battered biker jacket.

But Mike had barely ridden the Harley three times in the past two years. And then, it had been on his own, driving to God knows where to do God knows what with God knows who.

A roar of horsepower followed by a cloud of blue-grey exhaust blasted from inside the lock-up doors and refocused Rick's attention. A flock of sleeping starlings rose from the tops of nearby trees, their roost disturbed by a series of heavy revs. The early morning quiet exploded into sound as the powerful Harley's front wheel appeared from between the lock up doors. Then the handlebars. Richard tore his eyes from the broad figure in leathers who sat astride the massive machine and glanced at his two companions.

Lionel was goggling, bloodshot eyes wide in admiration. Rajiv coughed in the cloud of exhaust, one neat hand in front of his mouth.

His helmet balanced on the seat in front of him, Professor Michael St. Clair steered the Harley round in a semicircle, one leathered hand twisting the throttle theatrically.

Richard laughed and walked over as his partner brought the machine to a halt.

'Can you take my rucksack?' Michael roared over dying revs.

As the sound receded, so did the years, and they were both in their early twenties again. Mike wild but brilliant, wearing biker's boots to tutorials and arguing with the head of the palaeontology department. Richard half-appalled, half in love with his tall, grinning, disruptive fellow student.

'Eh?' Mike lowered the engine's revs to a quieter rumble, removed one hand from the Harley and grabbed the rucksack from the ground. He thrust it at Richard, then pulled on his helmet.

Rick stared at the slim leathered pillion between his partner's strong legs and suddenly envied it. His arms took the rucksack but his mind was elsewhere, led by the stirring in the crotch of his well-cut tweed trousers. On the fringes of his vision, he saw Mike glance at his wrist.

'Ten hours, you think?'

Richard nodded.

Beneath the scarlet crash helmet, Mike grinned. 'I'll do it in eight.' He reached out one hand, ruffled Rick's hair affectionately, then pulled the visor down into place. Kicking the foot prop back up, Professor St. Clair steered the now-roaring Harley round. He raised a gloved hand in salute.

'Drive safely!' Dragged back to the here and now, Richard shouted into the machine's wake. But Mike was off, leaning back on his seat and guiding the Harley into the distance.

The three of them stood there. Richard was vaguely aware of Lionel's awed voice, asking about HPRs and maker's numbers. Then a less vague instruction seeped into his ear.

'Dr Rodgers, should we not be leaving too, if we are to avoid the traffic?'

Richard turned, blinked back into the present. 'Yes, thank you for reminding me, Rajiv.' He extended a beckoning arm to both Lionel and the smaller, dark-skinned man. 'Now does anyone have a travel-sickness problem?' Lionel was still a little green around the gills. 'If so, then they should sit in the front with me.'

'I have familiarised myself with our route, Dr Rodgers.' The Iraqi postgrad talked smoothly through him, producing a folded map from the pocket of his bright yellow waterproof. 'It would be my pleasure to be your navigator.'

A small frown twitched Richard's lips. He continued to look at the stocky captain of the First Eleven rugby team. 'Are you okay?'

'I'm fine, fine.' Lionel ran a hand over his closely cropped hair. 'I'll probably sleep this off on the way up, if that's okay with you, Doc.' The man smiled blearily.

Richard chuckled at the title. Doc – so this was what they called him, when he was out of earshot?

Rajiv was tutting. 'That is most disrespectful of you. Apologise at once, please.' He lowered his map and glared.

'Christ, lighten up, eh?' Lionel rolled his eyes and hoisted his sports bag over one shoulder. 'The Doc doesn't mind, do you Doc?'

Richard was surprised how much he liked it, in truth. He laughed. 'Although technically this field trip is university work, I think we can all relax a bit. First names are fine with me, and I'm sure Mike won't mind.'

The small Iraqi man's disapproving face creased with confusion.

'Cheers, Doc!' Lionel had wandered over to the Volvo. He gripped the door to the back seat, hauled it open and slid into the car.

Richard moved to lift his own bag but a small brown hand beat him to it. 'Allow me, Dr Rodgers.' Rajiv Azad lifted the rucksack and moved round to the driver's door. Richard followed, watching in bemusement as Rajiv opened the door, held it there and passed him the car keys. Only after he was safely seated and belted into place did Rajiv Azad close the door and return to the passenger side of the car.

Minutes later, they were moving smoothly through the deserted streets of Oxford and heading towards the motorway.

The wind blasted his body.

Peter Fonda.

Mike twisted the throttle and watched the speedometer tick towards 65.

Dennis Hopper.

Seven a.m. and the M1 was empty. Just him, the Harley, and snaking miles of road.

Easy Rider.

The Wild One.

Mike grinned, thinking of Marlon Brando in jeans and Muir cap. Watching the old black-and-white film at 15.

He'd spent weeks pestering his mother for Levi 501s after that.

He wanted Brando.

And he wanted to be Brando.

He practised the sneer in the mirror, an unlit cigarette dangling from one side of his mouth.

Whatchoo rebelling against, son?

What ya got?

Mike threw back his head and howled into the wind.

He was rebelling against the fact they never had any money, never mind how many jobs his mum took on. Rebelling against where they lived, the father who had walked out on them when Mike was six months old.

He was rebelling against the hormones which raged through his 15-year-old body. Rebelling against the girls who eyed him and giggled in the playground.

The miles sped by.

Mike cranked up the throttle and watched the needle pass 70. Then 80. The M1 joined the M4. The Harley roared up the motorway, dominating what little traffic there was. Mike wove in and out of the outside lane, back to the middle when he'd overtaken the few cars and lorries on the road at this hour on a Sunday morning.

Rebelling against rules. All the rules. Grabbing hold of each and breaking it to his will. Including the rule which demanded he get a girlfriend.

The minutes sped by, then the hours. Mike slowed the Harley at Gretna Services, guiding the huge machine past parked lorries and containers. He'd often drive out to service stations like this, around the Oxford area, in his car. A throwback to his teenage years, when he'd discovered how to get sex? Mike grinned. Maybe – maybe it didn't mater.

The smell of diesel mixed with the ripe musk of a man's unwashed balls. Stale sweat. The meaty stench of an older body. All he'd known was sucking the cocks of men twice his age in the cabs of lorries and the back seats of hire-coaches was the only thing that made him feel really alive at 15. And it still worked.

Now they were his own age, or a little younger. Sometimes he sucked them off. Sometimes they did him. A few times, he even got a fuck out of it.

Tossing the ignition keys into the air and catching them, Mike tucked his helmet and his gloves beneath one arm and strode across the lorry park.

In the cafe, he ate a full breakfast of double egg, bacon, sausage, black pudding, beans, mushrooms and fried bread. Beside truckers and container drivers, Mike washed it all down with a steaming mug of tea and met the eyes of one haulier in particular for the fourth time.

He smiled into his tea. Not this time. Not this trip.

The breaker of all the rules would keep his own. If it meant he and Richard had a future, Mike could lock his cock up in the sweaty crotch of the leathers and make sure it stayed there for the next seven days.

He sipped his tea, caught the eyes of the truck driver again. And held it. Mid 30s, a bobble hat pulled low over his face, two days' worth of dark growth smudging the jaw line and upper lip. Big lips. For a guy.

Mike watched the trucker pull another cigarette from his packet, shove it in his mouth with badly bitten, nicotine-stained fingers. Those big lips clamped around the filter, holding it there while the guy flipped the top of a Zippo and held the flame beneath the tip.

Inside the leather trousers, his cock flexed. Mike groaned into his tea. Moth-like, he continued to stare. But when the trucker flipped the Zippo shut and glanced across the cafe, Mike shook his head almost imperceptibly. The guy shrugged but the corners of those big lips sloped into a smile of regret.

Mike scowled with irritation. This was going to be harder than he initially thought. It took every shred of self-restraint to turn down the man's very blatant offer. But Professor Michael St. Clair drained his mug, grabbed his helmet and gloves and got up from the table.

And as he paid the cashier, a pair of narrowed eyes bored into the back of his biker's jacket.

Mike had half-hoped the stop to eat would give Richard's Volvo time to catch him up.

At 2.30 he crossed the border into Scotland. The road was a little busier. He kept within the speed limit now, leaving the motorway and joining the A74. By 3.30 he was skirting Glasgow, on route for the Erskine Bridge. The smells were different up here. Despite the presence of more cars and the increasing urbanisation, the air had changed. Mike flipped up the visor and drew great lungfuls of it into his body.

He'd missed the Harley – he hadn't realised quite how much. There was something about the combination of so much power throbbing between one's legs, the speed, the wind around one's body and the vulnerability of a mere two wheels beneath one. The freedom. The danger. The risks. All the same constituents as good sex.

Mike drove on, his body tingling. He was still half hard from the guy in the cafe. Trapped between his hairy stomach and the worn suede of the inside of the leathers, his shaft throbbed in sync with the vibration from the engine which shuddered against his arse and balls.

On the Harley, he skirted Loch Lomond and felt the air change again. Fresher. A breeze from the water stung his cheeks. Mike drove on to Balloch, then across Scotland to join the M9.

It was approaching four in the afternoon when the motorway slimmed down to become the A9, the road which would take him all the way to Drumnadrochit. The sun, which had been lurking behind thin cloud all day suddenly stepped out. Mike smiled. The road ahead was winding but deserted. He checked his mirror. Same behind – no traffic, no cops or speed trap cameras. He'd been a good boy for nearly 500 miles.

The smile broadening into a grin, he released the throttle. His leathered knees against the side of the pillion, thighs gripping the quilted leather of the Harley's seat, Mike leant back and loosened the throttle completely.

With a smooth roar, the Harley soared forward.

Centrifugal force hurled Mike back harder against the back of the seat. And he was flying. The needle tipped 80. Ninety. Man and machine were one, eating up the miles. Tearing up tarmac. Burning rubber. Mike only just managed to resist the urge to wrench off his helmet and feel the wind in his hair.

The speedometer needle hovered just above 110. Mike was in a world of his own, at one with the Harley and speed and the road and his cock. He leaned right, curving the bike around a sudden corner. As man and machine dipped down to take the bend, a figure appeared out of nowhere.

In the middle of the road, a man in a T shirt, waving his arms. Mike clenched his teeth and only just managed to avoid him. He only just managed to right the Harley afterwards. But he did. Fifty yards up the road he did a smooth U-turn and, more than a little annoyed, drove back towards the figure, his speed now a more manageable 40.

What the hell was this idiot playing at?

Chapter Four

In the back seat of Doc Rodgers's Volvo, Lionel changed position for the umpteenth time and drifted in and out of a light doze.

The car was warm, the journey smooth. Soothed by the motion of the vehicle, Lionel leant his head back against the seat and tried to close his ears.

'You are an excellent driver, Dr Rodgers.'

His head jerked. Lionel groaned, turned to rest the side of his face on the back of the seat.

'And no power steering, you say?'

One ear was filled with the steady rumble of the Volvo's engine. The other, however, could still hear. Lionel groaned again.

'It's not too bad, and you get used to it.' Dr Rodgers laughed. 'Turning the wheel of this tank is about the most exercise I get these days.'

'You look very fit to me, sir.'

Lionel slumped sideways, cradling his head in his and trying to get away from Rajiv's insistent babbling.

For the first 100 miles, the Iraqi had read the bloody map, insisting on naming every B road between Oxford and the North. When old Rodgers had been forced to tell him, politely but firmly, to put the thing away because he was starting to complicate what should be a relatively straightforward drive, the guy had started on the car.

How old was it? How long had Dr Rodgers owned it? What was the mileage? When had it last been serviced?

Jack Dickson

'You are naturally muscular, I think.'

Lionel moaned. After the car's complete history, Rajiv had switched seamlessly to the purpose of the field trip. Then back to the car. Now, apparently, his questioning was taking a more personal turn.

'Um – well, er… thank you, Rajiv.'

Even through a layer of arms and the pounding hangover, Lionel could hear the unease in the older man's voice. He sighed – more audibly than he'd intended.

It served as a welcome distraction. 'Okay, back there?'

Lionel managed to mumble something and curled his body more tightly against the well-padded object to his right. Then a shriek pierced his ears:

'The equipment! Your are leaning on the equipment!'

Lionel reared up, every bone in his dehydrated, alcohol-sodden body jarring. The Volvo swerved beneath him, then righted itself as Dr Rodgers fought to regain control.

'Get off it! Get off it before you damage it!' Rajiv continued to shriek, now turning round in the passenger seat and making a grab for Lionel's shoulder.

Hauled from his semi-doze, the captain of the First Eleven gazed blearily at the furious, dark-skinned face.

'It's okay, Rajiv.' Doctor Rodgers was placating now, his head swivelling between the back seat and the road ahead. 'The equipment is quite robust.'

Lionel's unfocused eyes swam between the panicky dark face and the back of Dr Rodgers's head.

'It's put up with more than that, over the years.'

He frowned. Rajiv continued to glare at him. Lionel rolled his eyes. 'Lighten up, eh?' But he took off his jacket, balled it up beneath his head and slumped left against the window, away from the apparatus. The small Iraqi man's gaze continued to smoulder. Lionel scowled. His head was thumping now.

'Yes, do… um, lighten up, Rajiv. Get your map back out – I think we're approaching a junction.'

Lionel closed his eyes. Stupid bugger. Stupid, swotty, irritating little bugger. He drew up his knees, trying to get comfortable against the glass, but he could still feel those eyes.

And the start of a hard-on he couldn't ignore.

A good two hundred miles further on, Michael secured the Harley's footstand, hauled off his helmet and walked back towards the man who had almost been responsible for his first accident in 25 years.

A frown narrowed his eyes. He was angry – very angry. And as soon as earshot would permit, he had no qualms about giving free reign to that anger. 'What the hell do you think you're doing? You could have killed me.'

'Sorry – sorry. But I had to. You're the first sign of life I've seen in two hours. My fan belt's gone, my mobile won't work with all these damn hills.' The figure, which Mike could now see was male and not under-endowed in the basket department, waved a T-shirted arm to a blue Proton, which sat, bonnet up, on a small grass verge. ' So if you could give me a lift to the nearest garage or phone box…'

Mike glanced briefly at the car, then returned his attention to the worn denim which clung to the man's crotch like a second skin.

'I'd really appreciate it.'

There was something about denim. You could keep your spandex and lycra, your torn shorts and brief Speedos. Nothing showed off a man's equipment like worn, sixteen ounce, indigo-dyed denim. Years of wear, years of stretching and straining over what was obviously a substantial package drained the colour from the fabric and drew the eye.

As if in sync, the blood was draining from Mike's weather-beaten face, pounding its way into his own cock.

'Thanks for stopping, and sorry if I frightened you.'

As he stared at the heavily creased V of the man's thighs, the accent rolled itself around in Mike's head, a soft, Highland burr.

He'd worked with a Glasweigan palaeontologist a few years back. The guy's voice could cut glass, it was so harsh and guttural. This was different: deeper, but more lilting. Almost Irish-sounding. Mike's eyes continued to drink in the outline of the man's cock, drifting down to the bleached-in creases which covered his bollocks while the accent circled in his head.

'Kieran, by the way. Kieran McLeod.'

The buzz of the guy's consonants made Mike's cock twitch beneath the leathers.

'Um – are you okay?'

The question cut through his haze of arousal. Mike's head jerked up. He took in the man's face for the first time – and his outstretched hand. He grinned. 'Mike.' He hauled off one leather gauntlet, grabbed the guy's fingers in a solid grip. 'Mike St. Clair. Good to meet you, Kieran.'

Early 30s. Short, ginger hair, with the accompanying skin tone and an appealing covering of freckles. A small goatee beard. Green eyes. A firm mouth, and an equally firm handshake. Mike held the man's hand slightly longer than necessary, feeling the warm palm against his own. The firm mouth twitched into the start of a smile. Mike met those green eyes briefly. Kieran McLeod's index finger moved almost imperceptibly against his. Mike grinned. Then the grin froze and he remembered his promise to Richard. His own small smile slipped into a frown.

The other man picked up on it straight away. The hand was withdrawn. But an expression of semi-amusement hovered around the creases at the corners of Kieran's McLeod's eyes. Then those eyes moved to the helmet beneath Mike's left arm. 'Do you have a spare?'

Seven days. Seven short days. Just a week. A week without sex. He could do it. He could do it easily.

Mike stepped back and extended the helmet. 'Ever been on a Harley?'

Kieran McLeod took the red and black helmet and grinned. 'No, but I can hum "Born To Be Wild." '

Mike laughed. A sense of humour and a nice package. What a waste. What a fucking waste – literally. But he could do this. He could do it easily.

Mike draped a fraternal arm around Kieran McLeod's shoulders. 'Okay, my friend – get ready for the ride of your life. There's got to be a phone box or a garage around here somewhere.' As they both walked up the middle of the deserted road, back towards the bike, Mike knew it was the only kind of ride he was liable to get for the foreseeable future.

He couldn't remember passing any garage or service station in the last 100 or so miles. So they rode onwards, in the hope that the landscape would even out and enable Kieran to call the AA on his mobile, or that they would encounter some sort of habitation which either possessed a normal phone or a mechanic.

The Harley throbbed between his legs. Now helmetless, the wind blasted Mike's face, driving his hair back over his head and stinging his cheeks. Behind, on the pillion, Kieran McLeod's arms were tight around his waist. It felt good to have another body behind his. The man's knees shadowed Mike's knees. His thighs curved parallel to Mike's. Mike could feel the man's hands, just above the waistband of his leathers. He smiled. Despite the bravado of the earlier joke, he could also feel the man's slight fear.

Bikes were marvellous. Exhilarating. The combination of speed and power made you feel like the world was yours for the taking. Mike leant left, lowering the Harley to smoothly take a sharp bend. He righted the powerful machine between his legs and thought of the man at his back. Mike slowed a little, shifting position astride the quilted leather pillion. Then he straightened his arms out fully, bracing them on the Harley's high wide handlebars – and thrusting his arse against Kieran McLeod's crotch.

He felt, more than heard, the man's response. Even through the heavy leathers, even through the roar of the wind and the way it was buffeting his body, Mike was aware of the thrusting lob of Kieran McLeod's hard-on, pushing through that wear-whitened denim and up into the crack of Mike's arse.

The arms around his waist tightened. Mike twisted the throttle and leant back further. He could feel the hard outline of the helmet against his shoulders, and knew the man was clinging on for dear life while simultaneously responding to the feel of Mike's arse against his crotch.

The Harley roared forward, pushing him back further still. The sound of the engine filled Mike's head, the way he wanted this virtual stranger's cock to fill his arse. They rode like that, tearing up the miles, framed by steep hills and a darkening sky.

Mike's own cock throbbed against his stomach, in time with the engine, held there thick and pulsing by the tightness of the leathers. Despite the coolness of the air, his body was drenched in sweat. And he knew from the pressure of the arms around his waist that Kieran McLeod was having a hard time of it too.

Finally, out of the blue – or rather, out of the falling dusk – the familiar red outline of a phone box appeared ahead. Almost with a sense of disappointment, Mike slowed the Harley, curving smoothly to a halt just in front of the slightly surreal looking iron and glass structure. He switched off the engine.

Kieran dismounted without a word and strode towards it. Mike watched the man's tight buttocks as he did so, groaning inside and taking the opportunity to stretch his own legs. Eyes never leaving the slender outline in the phone box, Mike adjusted his cock, easing his balls into a more comfortable position. Usually the Harley left them numb and slightly frazzled, but today he felt every change, every twitch and clench in the heavy sac which now nestled at the root of his hard cock.

Mike leant against the bike and repeated what was becoming his mantra. I can do this. I can do this easily.

Minutes later, a grinning Kieran emerged from the phone box. 'Fifteen minutes – they're sending a mechanic straight off.'

Mike tried a smile he didn't feel.

Kieran wandered over. 'Thanks for the lift – thanks a lot. Christ knows how long I would have been waiting there, if you hadn't stopped.'

Mike nodded and painted a smile in place. I can do this. I can do this easily.

Kieran ran a hand through his sandy hair. 'I feel like I should... buy you a drink or something.'

Mike shuddered, an image of his mouth sucking the spunk from this ginger-haired god's cock strong and hard in his mind. He gritted his teeth and pushed it away, his smile becoming more of a grimace.

Kieran McLeod looked at him curiously. 'You up here on holiday?' He smiled. 'I couldn't help notice your accent.' Then the smile slipped. 'Christ, sorry – I've already taken up too much of your time.' He sighed. 'Hope I've not made you late for anything.'

Mike had lost the power of speech. The soft lilting voice was doing strange things to his cock. He could listen to Kieran McLeod all day – and he knew he needed to get as far away from this tempting prospect as possible. Mike groaned.

Kieran's head tilted. 'Are you okay?'

Apart from the worst case of blue balls he'd had in years? Mike managed a nod. 'Hope your Automobile Association mechanic turns up soon.' He knew his words were curt. He saw the confusion in Kieran's green eyes. Then Mike turned and stalked back to the Harley, thrust the helmet in place and drove off before his body got the better of him.

'Historically, this land belonged to the MacDonald clan.'

Dr Rodgers continued to do his impression of a nodding dog.

'Their arch enemies were the Campbells, with whom they feuded for hundreds of years.'

His neck hurt from the driving. Richard had been tempted, two hours back, to ask for volunteers to take a turn at the wheel. But Lionel didn't seem in a fit condition to do much apart from sleep. And he wasn't sure Rajiv could even drive.

'This whole area was dominated by the clan system.'

His ears were sore from the man's voice. But at least he had discarded the map for a guidebook.

'Many fierce and bloody battles were fought, over land. For example –'

And it was mildly interesting. But as Rajiv's eyes dipped to his guidebook again, Richard's mind returned to Michael, out there on that damn Harley. He knew the man. He knew him all too well. Words were easy. No sex with anyone, for the next seven days. Richard had no doubt that last night, when they had made their pact, Mike probably meant it. But that was then. This was now. Richard doubted that Mike had even got as far as the first service station without indulging in a bit of cruising. In his leathers, with his eyes dancing from the ride, Mike would draw men like flies. He sighed, and didn't blame them. Mike could still turn him on. In leathers. Naked. In his battered tweed jacket with the elbow patches. In the old sweats he worked in at home, hunched bare-chested and absorbed over the desk in their study.

'We are just passing Loch Mhor, on our right. Dr Rodgers, take the left fork here and we can drive along the banks of Loch Ness.'

Rick turned the wheel in a dream. But there was so little time, these days. His teaching schedule had been particularly heavy, this past year, and what with his own research, there just weren't enough hours in the day to accommodate a sex life as well as a professional one.

'What's that over there, Raji?'

The voice of the third member of their little troupe pulled his mind from things he could do nothing about. Richard's head flipped round, to where Lionel was pointing. A large structure had appeared on their right, just visible behind a tall fence and in breaks in a thick bank of trees. Richard peered, slowing the car.

'Yes, what is that Raji? It looks fairly modern.' He wound down the window, waiting for fresh air to flood into the car, from the large body of water which he couldn't see yet, but knew had to be there. Unless Rajiv's map reading was totally inept.

'Ah – um, yes – that will be...'

While the small Iraqi flicked frantically through the guidebook, Richard slowed the car to a halt on a small grass verge. This would be as good a place as any to stretch their legs. As he engaged the hand brake and unbuckled his seat belt, he noticed for the first time that no breeze at all was coming in through the open window.

'That's Boleskin! Boleskin House!' Lionel was already out of the car when Richard opened the driver's door, still pointing beyond the tall trees.

'You are correct.' Rajiv's slightly peeved voice followed, as they all got out and wandered over for a closer look.

Boleskin. Boleskin... The name was vaguely familiar. In the still, dusky air, Richard slapped an insect away from his neck and looked at Lionel.

'Aleister Crowley owned that, for a while.' The captain of the Rugby First Eleven was smiling broadly. 'I used to date a girl who was really into him.'

Richard nodded indulgently, eyes flicking between Lionel and Rajiv. The latter looked distinctly put out at the former's sudden knowledge on the subject.

'Do what thou wilt shall be the whole of the law.' Lionel grinned, rubbed his hands. 'Man, she was a wee cracker!'

Rick laughed.

Rajiv frowned, raising his eyes from the guidebook. 'Yes, indeed – Mr Crowley was an explorer of the black arts. A most intriguing and odd fellow.'

Lionel slapped his thighs. 'Well, thanks to him I got some of the best fucks of my life – Rhona was her name. Yeah – Rhona. She liked shagging in the open air – excuse my French, Doc.'

Richard waved a dismissive hand and smiled encouragingly. He liked the way this stocky, uninhibited lad talked so easily about his exploits.

'Only thing was – when we came, we were all supposed to think about what we really wanted most in the world. Give our – um, orgasm up to the Dark Gods, or something.' Lionel sniggered. 'What I wanted most, at that point, was another suck on Rhona's juicy tits.'

Richard chuckled.

Rajiv tut-tutted and blushed. He cleared his throat theatrically. 'Well, we –'

'Who lives in the place now, Raji? I know Robert Plant or someone bought it in the Sixties, but he sold it soon afterwards.' His face took on a darker cast. 'No one can live there for long: there are –' Lionel's voice dropped to a whisper '– restless spirits in the place, ancient gods who Crowley called up but failed to return to the nether regions.' He rolled his eyes and laughed wickedly.

A shiver ran down Richard's spine.

Rajiv frowned. 'Do not mock things you do not understand.'

Richard was surprised at his tone, but Rajiv's nose was soon back in the guidebook. 'Boleskin is now owned by Jim Tyson, whoever he might be.'

Richard's laugh of surprise sent the shiver back to wherever it had come from. 'Jix? Jix Tyson?' He looked at Rajiv.

The smaller man nodded. 'Yes – I presumed the Jix was a misprint.'

' "Stairway To Hell", right Doc?' Lionel grinned and adopted an air-guitar-playing stance.

'From the *Infernal Machine* album.' Richard smiled and nodded. 'I thought old Jixy was long dead, just another Seventies acid casualty.'

Lionel laughed. 'Like Keith Richards, Jix Tyson should have kicked the bucket years ago. He no longer records, but his stuff has been discovered by a new generation of fans.' Lionel winked. 'Maybe he's made his own pact with Crowley's ancient gods, eh?'

Richard shivered again, staring beyond the trees to what he could glimpse of the house. Rajiv was now reading a history of the structure's architecture, what bits had been added when and where. Lionel was humming the riff from Stairway to Hell. But Richard's mind was spinning back 25 years, to a 15-year-old boy with a bad haircut. A rock legend. And his first, fumbling sexual experience.

Chapter Five

Less than 50 miles away, Mike was trying to keep his mind on the road ahead. Sandwiched between warm leather and his sweat-slicked stomach, his prick had other ideas. A vague arousal which had been simmering all day had been brought to the boil by his encounter with the slim, ginger-haired motorist.

Mike clenched his teeth and twisted the throttle more vigorously. The bike beneath him roared and only served to send a sudden sharp spasm of need up into his balls. His cock flexed, now fully erect and itchy inside his leathers. Mike scowled. He'd tried to will the damn thing away for the last half an hour. When that didn't work, he'd filled his mind with mathematical calculations and formulae, trivia, bits and pieces of rubbish to distract himself. The throbbing ache deep in his balls won out over Newton's more obscure laws of physics every time. And seemed to defy most of them.

Even his own personal mantra – I can do this. I can do this easily – only served to draw attention to what he couldn't have, and make him want it all the more.

There was nothing else for it. Mike eased back on the throttle, indicated and drew into the side of the road, just in front of a small copse of trees. Richard hadn't mentioned anything about not wanking.

Mike dismounted, grabbed the Harley's T-shaped handlebars and pushed the huge machine into the copse. He was breathing heavily, partly from the effort, partly from the rhythmic shudders which quivered up his shaft each time his cock came in contact with the worn nap of the leathers.

Wanking wasn't betrayal.

He wrenched off the helmet, sat it on the pillion and started to pull off the heavy leather bikers' gauntlets. Then he paused. Wanking wasn't sex with someone else. And Richard hadn't insisted on celibacy. Removing one of the thick hide gloves, Mike kept the other on and unzipped the leather one-piece, drawing the metal tab right down to his crotch. He was naked beneath.

Hidden by the trees, but able to see the road, Mike shrugged his shoulders free of the warm hide. The cooling evening air erected the thick covering of chest hair. His nipples sprang to attention. A shudder of pleasure made him gasp.

Easing his arms free of the top half of the biker's one-piece, Mike felt the weight of the leather as it crumpled around him. The upper half of the second skin bagged around his hips, dragging the zip down further.

Mike moaned and looked down at his pubes. Framed by the silver V of the zip, the top three inches of his erection sprouted up from its bristling nest of salt-and-pepper hair. The flesh was swollen and angry, the thick head barely held in check by the sliver of tightly-stretched foreskin.

Mike's balls clenched, somewhere out of sight. As he stared at his cock, the member strained for release, engorging further and pushing itself against the teeth of the zip. Mike winced, feeling the bite against his shaft.

A mere 15 feet away, cars whizzed past. The road was busier now, traffic making its way up to the Highlands and back down towards central Scotland.

Blood buzzed in his ears. Mike leant back against the trunk of a tree, hearing nothing but the fizz in his head, unaware of the rough bark against his shoulders, feeling only the tight clench somewhere in his arse and the chill of the evening air on his skin.

With his ungloved hand, he pushed the leather one-piece down further, freeing his cock and balls. The metal dragged deliciously over his swollen sac. Mike gasped, gripping his shaft in his gauntleted fist. His back arched against the tree. His leathers hung from the tops of his thighs in soft, worn folds.

Mike gripped more tightly, dragging his hand down to the root. He watched seven inches of engorged flesh glide up through the soft leather of the bike glove. His thighs quivered. His bare shoulders moved against the tree trunk. Mike widened his stance, planting his booted feet a yard apart. The movement only served to tighten his balls. His arsehole clenched.

Over the roar of the traffic, Mike's moans increased. He swept his fist back up the length of rigid flesh, caressing himself more roughly. He hauled at his cock, pulling the tight skin up and over the thick, purple head. Mike's knees buckled. He ran his fist back down his length then pushed up again, feeling the second skin of leather covering his. Familiar. And not familiar. Alien... and second nature.

The smell of his sweat, his crotch and the odour of old leather filled his head. His own hand. Another's hand. A stranger's hand... the fist of some nameless man.

Richard's fingers tightening around him. Richard's breath on his neck. Mike groaned and fucked the gauntlet more steadily. His skin flushed cool then hot again as a new covering of perspiration flowed from his pores. Somewhere in the distance, he could smell carbon monoxide from the passing vehicles. Closer to home, the stink of his own body mingled with the perfume of the trees and the woody aroma of bark.

Mike's head lolled forward, the ungloved hand moving to brush his right nipple. He groaned and wanked himself furiously, hips and fist working in perfect sync. Muscle in his thighs quivered. His nipples felt unbearably itchy. He wanted to claw them from his chest.

Sweat trickled down from the thick mat of hair across his pecs, moving slowly down the furrow which bisected his abs. His eyes stung. His short, close-cropped hair crawled with a thousand tiny insects. His arse muscles spasmed, his hole clenching and unclenching as his fist moved faster and more urgently.

Tension which had been building all day suddenly focused, narrowing to a point just beneath his balls. Mike squeezed his eyes shut. Patterned on the inside of the thin skin, images of himself and countess faceless strangers strobed before his eyes.

His hand worked the sensitive head of his cock, tightening and drawing more clear need from the now gaping piss slit. The worn nap of the gauntlet was damp with it. Mike was breathing through his mouth now, his lips loose and open, where everything from the waist down was a twisted, torqued mass of tension.

The final clench took him by surprise. Mike reared back. His head flew up, eyes blinking open at the force of the release. As his balls spasmed, pumping spunk up through his cock and over the leather gauntlet, Mike's knees gave way. He slumped to the ground, thrown forward by the jerking of his body.

He stared, his gaze unfocused and glassy, towards the nearby road. His cock spurted again, another slitful of warm milky spunk oozing over his knuckles... and he caught green, semi-amused eyes from the passenger seat of a passing AA rescue van.

Richard steered the Volvo past the small village of Easter Boleskin and along the narrow B road which circled the loch. He glanced at Lionel, now considerably more alert and sitting in the passenger seat at his side.

Either the fresh air, the leg stretch a few miles back or the doze seemed to have revived Lionel. He and Rajiv had swapped places and, Dr Rodgers had to admit, the easy, ensuing silence which had characterised the journey since was most welcome. As if on cue, a long exaggerated sigh came from the back seat.

Richard tightened his hands on the wheel. Rajiv hadn't been pleased when Lionel beat him to the front seat. He seemed to have taken it as some sort of personal slight. Richard released the wheel briefly and wound down the window further, amazed at the stillness of the air outside. They had made good time and, even with the head start, Mike shouldn't arrive too much ahead of them. But even though Rajiv had been very helpful, as far as map-reading was concerned, Rick wasn't about to give into whatever silly rivalry he was trying to stir between him and Lionel.

Another sigh from behind. Richard groaned inside and glanced again at the captain of the rugby First Eleven. Lionel continued to gaze out of the window, lost in the huge dark body of water and his own thoughts.

Richard turned his eyes back to the road. There was a lot of competition in academia. That was par for the course. As far as research grants were concerned, he and Mike were up against every other marine palaeontology department in every other university, the length and breadth of the country. Funding for trips like this had to be fought for, tooth and nail. The same was true for postgrad research. Richard knew, as far as the renewal of both Lionel and Rajiv's scholarships were concerned, the final word rested with him, as course director. But whereas Lionel seemed laid back and phlegmatic about exactly what he was doing next academic year, all the flattery and helpfulness from Rajiv seemed slightly suspect.

Richard didn't want to think that Rajiv was trying to ingratiate himself in the hope of securing favour, but what other explanation could there be?

Another deep sigh from the back seat.

Irritation creased Dr Rodgers' brow. He was just about to utter an uncharacteristically sharp word, when:

'I had no idea it would be so... beautiful.'

Richard's eyes raised themselves to the rear-view mirror. In the back seat, the small Iraqi man gazed out of the window at the loch. Rick smiled. He'd barely noticed the scenery so far. 'Very different from Oxford, I know, Raji.'

Another sigh slipped from between the postgrad student's full, almost girlish lips. 'Very different from anything I have ever seen. There is a great... peace about the water. Oddly, the nearest comparison I have is the desert.'

Dr Rodgers's gaze lingered on Rajiv's face. He nodded, surprised at the insight. 'Yes – the whole area has a vastness, don't you think?' His eyes returned to the road ahead.

'Does it have any pubs, though?' A grumble from the passenger seat.

Richard laughed heartily. There was something distinctly attractive about Lionel's ability to ground everything.

In the back seat, Rajiv tut-tutted.

'Not sure about pubs, Lionel.' Eager to avoid yet more verbal sparring, Richard turned his gaze to the side of the loch. 'But there seems to be everything else.'

Three sets of eyes skimmed across the dark water to the extravaganza which decorated the opposite shore. A hotel, a huddle of B&Bs, two campsites, a caravan site and what seemed to be a miniature Jurassic Park featuring a large, Nessie-shaped bouncy castle were clearly visible even at this distance. Richard sighed, noting the distinctive golden emblem of a well-known fast food chain. The clans may have long since stopped feuding, but a MacDonald presence seemed to be unavoidable, wherever one went these days. Rajiv sighed disappointedly.

'Oh excellent – so we're not quite in the back of beyond after all.' Lionel, on the other hand, was sounding distinctly brighter. 'And that hotel's bound to be licensed.' A frown of worry creased the stocky man's broad forehead. 'This isn't one of the dry areas of the Highlands, is it Doc?'

From the extent of the other commercialism obvious around the Loch Ness Visitor's Centre, Richard somehow doubted there was much evidence of strict Scottish Presbyterianism here. He shook his head. 'Shouldn't think so.'

'Man, that's a relief.' Lionel rubbed his hands together and grinned. 'Okay! Last one to pitch his tent buys the first round, eh Doc?'

'I would have thought you'd have had enough alcohol, after last night.' Rajiv's disapproving tones drifted from the back seat. 'That was a disgraceful exhibition.'

Richard steered the Volvo around the head of the loch, past the lock which joined the darker body of water to the Caledonian Ship Canal and down towards the small village of Drumnadrochit. He smiled at the memory of the captain of the First Eleven, a jockstrap on his head, leading a conga of capering men around his study at last night's end-of-term social.

'Christ man, lighten up, eh?' Lionel's response was good-natured.

'Why I expect anything else from someone who so frequently takes his Lord's name in vain I have no idea.' Rajiv snorted.

'Don't you ever relax, pal?' Lionel laughed.

Richard concentrated on the road, peering at signs and trying to locate the turn-off for the campsite which he knew was a mile or so along from Drumnadrochit itself.

'Don't you ever do anything except drink?' Rajiv countered swiftly, his voice low but still irritated.

'Hmmm... let me think.' The reply was slow, laid-back. Richard knew Lionel was playing with his colleague, teasing him mercilessly.

'Oh yeah, in between getting pissed I fuck quite a lot.'

Richard's eyebrows shot up. It took all his strength not to laugh out loud. He glanced left, in time to see Lionel turn in his seat and wink at Rajiv.

'That's what's wrong with you, pal – you're not getting any!'

Rajiv's face was a mask of horror. 'My body is a temple.'

'Well maybe it's time to let the congregation in, eh?' Lionel roared at his own joke and slapped the back of the seat.

Richard gripped the wheel and looked away before the laughter became too much to hold in check.

'I refuse to talk further with you, while you are in this mood.'

'Fine by me. But I hope you know what you're doing. That temple of yours can turn into a prison, overnight, if you don't watch it.'

There was no answer form the back seat.

'You'll let me buy you a drink, eh Doc? A thank you for putting up with us.' Lionel continued, in banter-mode.

Richard glanced in the rear-view mirror. He hoped Rajiv wasn't taking all this too much to heart. But when he met his student's glowing brown eyes, Dr Rodgers was shocked by the intensity which burned there.

Lionel was glad to get out of the car. He'd never been as glad to get out of anywhere in his life. No sooner had Doc Rodgers turned off the ignition than Lionel bounded out of the Volvo and trotted round to the boot. Wrenching it open, he delved in and began to haul the tents and sleeping bags out.

The camping area the university had booked was a little apart from either of the main sites. Lionel noticed a jetty, and the small, battered looking motor launch which was docked there – presumably to give them access to the loch, day and night.

He cleared the boot in ten minutes flat, leaving Doc Rodgers and bloody Rajiv to unload the more delicate research equipment.

This was going to be a 24-hour-a-day job. He knew that. Working in shifts of two, one pair on the water, the other either sleeping or recording the results of the ultrasonic sounding.

Lionel's eyes narrowed. He closed the boot, grabbed a rolled tent in each hand and marched over to a small clearing. He barely noticed Doc Rodgers and Rajiv carrying the equipment past him to the jetty. He barely heard whatever it was his postgraduate supervisor shouted over to him. He barely saw the darkly beautiful hills beyond, or the serene stillness of the deep body of water. Lionel scowled, dumped the tents on the ground and crouched beside them.

Irritating little prick! Maddening, stuck-up, patronising little bastard! He tore at the bag which encased the first tent, hauled it free and spread the fabric out on the ground. The poles came next. Lionel jammed them together, crawled into the flat envelope of nylon and jammed the supports into place. This was going to be a nightmare.

Lionel clenched his teeth, crawled back out of the tent and grabbed a handful of pegs. The large wooden hammer came next. Grabbing the first guy rope, he stretched it out, pushed a peg into the loop and brought the mallet down violently on its head.

Seven days – smack! Twenty four hours of each of those seven days – smack! Lionel pounded the peg into the hard ground, each blow sending shivers through the hard-on he'd been trying to ignore for the past three hours. When there was nothing left to hit, he moved round to the opposite end of the tent and repeated the processes.

He hoped to God he got paired with either the Doc or Professor St. Clair.

The sides came next. He tugged taut each guy rope in turn, hammering the pegs into the ground and transforming the floppy rectangle of double-proofed nylon into a structure suitable for sleeping in.

He'd even do the sweeps of the loch on his own – anything to avoid further exposure to that prat Raji.

Lionel checked the ropes, then started on the second tent. If that car journey was anything to go by, they'd just fight all the time. He clenched his fist around the mallet and brought it back down furiously on the tent-peg. And the more they fought, the brighter Rajiv's eyes burned. And the harder Lionel's cock became. He moaned, aware of the way his crouched position was forcing his knob up against his stomach.

He'd go mad. He'd go stark staring bonkers if he had to spend any time at all with the bugger.

Staggering to his feet, Lionel surveyed his handiwork. Erected in record time – and that held true for both the tents and himself. As he stood there, staring at the tents, the sound of an approaching bike seeped into his ears, along with the worst thought yet. Only two tents.

The Doc and old Sinclair were a couple – everyone knew that. Lionel moaned. So who was he going to be sharing with?

Chapter Six

Michael slowed the Harley to a smooth halt just behind the Volvo. A frown twitched his lips. How on earth had Richard managed to get here before him? Dismounting, he pulled off his helmet and looked around for the rest of the party.

The chunky Geordie kid was standing in front of one of the already-pitched tents, staring at it rather disconsolately. Richard and the Iraqi postgrad were nowhere to be seen.

With a sigh, Michael drew off his gloves, placed them on the Harley's pillion along with the helmet and strode across. 'You made good time.'

Lionel jumped, as if stirred from some personal dream.

Mike grinned. 'Ready to start your onslaught on the local female population?' The kid's reputation as a cocksman was legendary. He winked then scanned the area, unzipping the neck of the one-piece leathers and peering down towards the loch. 'Where's everyone else?'

"Um... Professor St. Clair? Can I do the shifts with you?'

The Geordie kid's voice pulled Mike's eyes back. He cocked his head. 'That's really Richard's province, er – ?' Leo? Lance? What the hell was the guy's name again?

'Lionel.' It was thoughtfully supplied.

Mike laughed. 'I can name every genus of ammonite, but give me a face and I'll get it wrong every time.'

The Tynesider grinned, looking almost back to his usual, hearty self.

'Where's Rick? And the...?'

'Rajiv and Doc Rodgers are down at the boat, Professor.' Lionel's head swivelled.

Mike followed his gaze. Five hundred yards away, he could just make out two figures: one on deck, the head and shoulders of the other appearing periodically from the hatch which led down to the small cabin.

'I'm willing to do extra shifts, even – on my own. Or with either you or the Doc.'

Mike had stopped listening. He ran a hand through hair sweaty from eight-odd hours beneath a helmet. Inside the leathers, spunk from the wank had crystallised to a powdery web. He needed a wash – and he needed it before Rick came back. 'Any idea how far we have to walk to find... facilities around here?'

'A couple of hundred yards back, there's showers and toilets at the main campsite, gentlemen.' The answer came from behind them.

Both Mike and Lionel spun round.

A well-built, red-haired giant in T shirt and jeans beamed at them. 'And please feel free to use any of the hotel amenities.' He stuck out a hand. 'Archie Campbell, gents – campsite owner and hotelier. On behalf of myself and my wife Morag, welcome to Drumnadrochit!' Mike caught a twinkle in a hazel eye.

Mike winced as his cock flexed abruptly. Matted pubic hair dragged in the suddenly stretching foreskin. He winced again but covered it with a smile and grasped the offered hand. 'Mike St. Clair.'

'Your reputation precedes you, Professor – I know who you are.'

He caught the hazel eye again. Fingers tightened around his. Mike found himself grimacing again, this time more from the strength of this redhead's grip than the discomfort in his groin. 'Good to meet you, Mr Campbell.'

'Ach, call me Archie!' The redhead squeezed one last time then turned to the postgrad student. 'And this is Dr Rodgers?'

Lionel laughed. 'No such luck – Lionel Banks.' He stuck out his hand. 'Common-or-garden variety research student.'

This time, Mike saw Archie Campbell wince at the rugby player's strong grip. He smiled. 'Do you greet all your customers in person?'

The redheaded giant eased his hand free from Lionel's and managed a laugh. 'When they are attempting to disprove the existence of our monster? Always!'

Lionel chuckled.

Mike beamed. 'Ah, well I think Dr Rodgers may disagree with your assumption, Archie.' He caught and held the hazel eyes this time, wondering about the wife, wondering about –

'And what assumption would that be?' A cool voice from behind.

Mike spun round, an irrational shiver of guilt coursing over his body. 'Richard? This is Archie Campbell – he owns the campsite.'

'A pleasure, Dr Rodgers.' The hotelier again extended his hand.

Rick looked at it, then at Mike. 'What kept you? I thought you'd be here hours before us.'

Professor St. Clair felt his face redden. In the background, Archie was nodding and chatting with the two postgrads, but all Mike saw was the accusation and hurt in his partner's eyes. The misplaced accusation.

He moved forward, steering Rick towards the tents. 'Sorry, I had to stop and help someone – this guy. His fan-belt was fucked and I...'

'And it wasn't the only thing that ended up fucked, I bet. I knew it!' Richard's voice was an angry whisper. 'Can't you keep it in your pants for seven hours, let alone seven days?'

'I never touched him!' Mike hissed back, the blush of guilt deepening to the scarlet of anger. 'If you must know, I gave him a lift to a phone box then waited a bit with him, to make sure the AA turned up.' Best not to mention the wank – not when his partner was in this mood.

'Quite the Good Samaritan, aren't we?' Richard turned to walk away. And tripped over one of the guy ropes.

Mike sprang forward, grabbed his arm. 'Watch, baby – you'll hurt yourself.'

'Get your hands off me!' Rick staggered upright, wrenching his arm away from Mike. 'Go back and find your motorist in distress – or that big ginger-haired fellow, there. You and he were having quite a little laugh at my expense, weren't you?'

'Everything okay, gents?' As if on cue, Archie Campbell's powerful voice called over to them.

Both Richard and Mike pulled themselves together a bit. This was unprofessional – most unprofessional. 'Fine, Archie – just an… academic difference of opinion.' Professor St. Clair tried a laugh.

Academic was the word for it. Despite the blatant offer from the lorry driver and the potential with green-eyed Kieran McLeod, Mike had remained true to their agreement. And it irritated him greatly that Richard had such scant faith in his word.

'Good, good – nothing like a bit of debate, is there?'

Mike glanced to where the hotelier was now standing between Lionel and Rajiv.

'Now, you must all be hungry after your long journey. Please be my guests for the evening, up at the hotel. Morag does a lovely Scotch Woodcock.' Archie Campbell smiled.

Mike glanced at Richard. 'What about it?' His voice was low. He put on his best, most appealing expression. 'A hot meal, then a shower, eh?'

Richard's expression was stone. 'You go, by all means. I have work to do.'

Mike rolled his eyes. 'Christ, even you've got to eat.'

'I'll have a sandwich later.'

Mike moved, standing between Rick and the waiting threesome. He held sulky eyes with his. 'I really did just stop to help that bloody guy with his car – I had no idea it would take so long.'

The eyes remained hard for a second. Then Richard sighed and rubbed both hands over his face. 'I know – I'm just a bit on edge, after the journey. Rajiv babbled for at least three hundred miles… then he and Lionel started sniping at each other.'

'Poor you.' Mike laughed sympathetically. 'You'll feel better after you get something hot inside you.' He winked suggestively.

Rick managed a grin, his hand moving to rub Mike's shoulder through the worn leather. 'Seriously – I need some time on my own, get my head cleared. And I do want to get all the equipment set up, for later.'

The slightest touch from the man he loved did more to stretch Mike's scummy cock than all the lorry drivers in all the transport cafes countrywide. 'Okay – if you're sure.' He covered Rick's hand briefly with his, then moved away. 'We'll only be an hour or so.'

Rick smiled and nodded beyond to Rajiv and Lionel. 'Bring them back intact, won't you?'

Mike laughed. 'Intact and ready for seven days' work.' He looked one last time into his partner's eyes, then turned. 'Okay, as the senior academic here, I suppose it falls to me to buy the first round!'

Mike strode to join the trio. He tried not to think about how much he wanted Richard, right now, as he smiled and nodded and they made their way along the small path towards what he presumed was Archie Campbell's Land Rover.

Richard watched them go. He did believe Mike. At least, part of him did. But niggling doubts, both about fidelity and this ridiculous bargain of theirs, plagued his brain.

As the Land Rover, with Mike in the front beside the redhead, Lionel and Rajiv sitting in the rear, sped off towards the distant hotel, Richard turned and strolled past the tents back down to the jetty. He pushed thoughts of Mike with other men from his mind and tried to focus on the reason they were here at all.

The soles of his shoes clattered along the old but solid decking of the small pier. The motor launch he had hired for the week was of similar heritage: it had definitely seen better days, but could still do the job. A small smile of self-depreciation twitched Richard's lips. A bit like himself, maybe?

He seized the boat's rail and clambered on board. Of course, the engine had yet to be put to the test. With Rajiv's attentive assistance, they'd got the echo-sounding equipment safely installed in the small wheel house. The cabin below now housed spares, back-up batteries as well as a bunk, a small stove and enough coffee to last each two-man team through the gruelling twelve-hour shifts.

The vessel swayed beneath him. Richard glanced up at the small illuminated cruise boat which, with its cargo of tourists and sightseers, was making its way down the middle of the loch. The motor launch swayed again, buffeted by the large vessel's wash. In its wake, a frisson of professional excitement made Richard shiver.

During the day, Loch Ness was very much like any other loch. The ferry, various private yachts, the odd speedboat and even jet-skiers skimmed across its cold, glassy surface. Despite the fact that most of the so-called 'monster sightings' had taken place during daylight hours, indicating that Nessie was far from shy, something told the marine palaeontologist that, under cover of darkness, it became a very different place.

Richard waited until the cruise boat was further down the loch before making his way round into the wheel house. It would be during the night hours that, if they were to find anything, they would find it. Withdrawing the keys from his pocket, Dr Rodgers stuck the ignition into place, turned and pressed the starter.

One splutter, then the satisfying vibration beneath his feet of a functioning engine, the sound of water churned by a propeller and the faintest whiff of diesel told him the motor launch was seaworthy. Or at least loch-worthy.

Leaving the engine to turn over gently, Richard moved back on to deck. He reached over, loosened the mooring ropes and coiled them on to the well-weathered wood. Around him, although it was still early evening, the sun was already sinking behind the steep hills of the Great Glen.

Richard ducked back inside, took the wheel and guided the vessel out from the jetty. For the first time since they'd arrived, the air around him stirred. A light breeze drifted in through the wheel house door, ruffling Richard's small beard and cooling his skin. Keeping close to the western bank, he followed the coastline slowly.

The echo-sounding equipment wasn't switched on, of course. The first official sweep would not begin until midnight – a good four hours yet. This was merely an exploratory voyage to ensure everything was in working order. And to give Rick some time on his own. With his first love.

As the motor launch chugged along, he laughed softly at himself. At the age of six, he'd seen an artist's impression of 'Nessie' in an encyclopaedia. Ever since, he'd been hooked. The Great Glen, the huge glacier which had gouged it out of solid rock. The fault line which lay beneath this whole area. The fact that Loch Ness was linked to several other lochs in the region, by as-yet-unnavigated underwater tunnels – even maybe linked to the North Sea.

The myths. The legends. Water sprites. Kelpies. Darwinian throwbacks. Evolutionary anachronisms. Some great creature from the depths of the sea lured into the loch after the last ice age when its own kind were dying. Trapped here, unable to return to its home.

The motor launch chugged steadily onwards. Richard stared straight ahead. On the far, eastern bank, the craggy ruin of Urquhart Castle slipped by.

All scientific logic decreed the existence of any monster impossible. Too many variables. Too many sound reasons why, even if such a creature had ever inhabited these still, dark waters, it would have long since died. So what was the subject of so many sightings, over the years? Some kind of giant eel? A trick of the light? Floating logs, creatively interpreted by enthusiastic monster-spotters?

Richard mused on it all. He knew Mike laughed at him. And he wasn't the only one. Dr Rodgers's theories were held in scepticism if not open ridicule by the entire marine palaeontology world. But there was something here. And if he had to sweep this damn place himself, day and night for the next seven days, he'd prove that.

Dusk was falling. The forest-lined shore was a shadowy mass of tall Douglas firs and bushes. On the eastern bank, the headlights of a solitary car were the only breaks in the darkness. Instinctively, Richard's eyes swivelled along to the dark outline of Boleksin. He smiled.

He'd not thought about Jix Tyson in years – decades. Richard wondered where the guy was now. Like so many of its owners, his period of occupancy at Boleskin seemed to have been brief.

No one lived there, anymore... Something twinkled in the dark. No one? Richard peered left. Could be a street-lamp. But the entire circumference of the loch was in darkness, so that made no sense. Another car?

Richard pressed the starter. The engine cut out. The motor launch continued for a few yards. Then it stopped too. His eyes focused on the now brighter light. Not a car. Too high up.

The motor launch drifted gently, bobbing on the surface of the loch. Richard grabbed a pair of binoculars from the side of the wheel and stepped out on to the deck.

Through the dying light, he could just make out the rooftop of Boleskin, through the trees. And the source of light definitely originated there. He raised the binoculars to his eyes, adjusted the focus and stared. Was it possible the rock-star was actually living there?

Richard blinked, adjusted the magnification and continued to stare. It was clearer now. In one of the tops rooms, high in the tower which was visible through the thick bank of towering Douglas firs, a candle was burning. Richard shivered.

And it was definitely a candle, rather than light from an electrical source. The flickering pulse filled his eyes, and brought back memories of other candles, so long ago.

Richard lowered the binoculars and leant against the side of the wheel house.

Thirty years ago. A studious 15-year-old, with all the worldly experience of a pre-teen, Richard lived for books and school – even then. A credit to his parents. A lover of classical music, especially Beethoven.

His encounter with the work of Jix Tyson came about completely by accident. He'd been waiting to pay for a new recording of the Emperor Concerto, conducted by Solti and with Ashkenazy as soloist. The poster behind the cash-desk hadn't been there before. And when Richard glanced at it, stared into that haughty, arrogant face and scanned that emaciated, almost naked body, he knew he had to find out more.

In the crotch of his well-cut tweed trousers, 30 years on, Rick's cock twitched.

Solti went back in the racks. He spent all his pocket money for the next month acquiring the entire Jix Tyson back catalogue, including the *Uber Dog* album with the cover responsible for his interest in the first place.

It was a bonus that he liked the music. It was a bonus that Jix

Tyson was a media darling, pontificating on everything from politics to sexuality at every opportunity. He wore jeans so tight they left nothing to the imagination. Leather jackets with nothing underneath. Make-up and dresses which only served to enhance his raw, throbbing masculinity.

Jix Tyson bleached his hair and crawled around the stage. Jix Tyson simulated masturbation with a guitar in a way which would have made Hendrix blush. He strutted and he ground his hips, in bare feet or six-inch heels, and opened up another world for a fifteen year old whose only exposure to males was his studious father and the stupid, uncouth boys at school.

Richard bought every magazine, read every interview. He did his maths homework with Stairway to Hell thundering in the background, his eyes flicking between quadratic equations and Jix Tyson's full, pouting mouth.

In the middle of a loch, 30 years on and well past the infatuation stage, Richard sat the binoculars on top of a pile of ropes and smiled wryly.

When it was announced that Jix and his band were to play Hammersmith Odeon, he knew he had to be there. His parents were against it. The journey to London alone was a problem. Richard invented a school friend whose father would run both himself and the friend down, and bring them back. He'd been saving his dinner money for two weeks now anyway, to cover the price of the train ticket. Not that he felt like eating, anyway. All appetites focused in the growling need in the pit of his stomach. Fifteen, and never having been outside the small coastal town of Scarborough where he'd been raised, Richard Rodgers set off for his first big adventure. And, as it turned out, his first male-to-male sexual experience.

The gig itself was an anticlimax. Too busy,too noisy, too hot. His seat was behind a pillar, way at the back of the third circle. His beautiful idol was a tiny, platinum-haired dot at the front of a stage miles below.

His 15-year-old cock had been hard the moment he'd boarded the train to London. By the time the third encore of My Death had taken place, Richard's balls were practically blue. And he felt light-headed – mainly from not having eaten for three days. As the crowd around him slowly began to make their way from the auditorium, he followed reluctantly in a daze of frustration and lust. He couldn't just go home. He couldn't just walk back to Euston station and return to Scarborough as if nothing had happened. Not with Jix so close. So near. And yet so far.

Somehow, Richard found himself at the stage door, with a bunch of giggling girls waving their underwear and autograph books. The sensible jacket he'd been forced to wear now stuffed in to a rucksack, and dressed in a T shirt with the sleeves hacked off plus a pair of jeans he'd deliberately allowed his mother to wash at too high a temperature, he hung around in the shadows. Richard watched the girls flirt with the doorman. Then the security staff.

When Dick Dawson, Jix's bass-player appeared, Rick watched them rush forward and throw themselves screaming around his neck. His heart sank. He had no place here. Despite all the pontificating, his idol sported – along with the rest of the band – a string of beautiful girl-friends as long as your arm. Despite all the 'everyone is bisexual' spouting, despite the make-up, the dresses and the platinum hair, Jix Tyson was a ladies' man.

Chest tight, eyes stinging, bollocks aching, Richard turned away from the screaming, giggling throng and wandered back round towards the main road.

Half way down the alley, a tall figure in a full-length leather coat and wide-brimmed hat emerged abruptly from a concealed doorway – and slammed straight into the downcast 15-year-old. Richard stumbled, almost knocked off his feet.

'Ah – sorry, mate!' A strong hand gripped his bare arm, breaking his fall.

'No harm done.' Richard swayed, feeling the grip warm and tight around his skinny biceps. 'Sorry, I –' He looked up. The automatically polite response stuck in his throat. Without make-up and very pale, Jix Tyson's face swam before his eyes.

Richard swallowed hard. 'Oh my.'

On the deck of the motor launch, a 45-year-old doctor of marine palaeontology half-cringed at the memory of his own response to meeting his idol.

Jix Tyson's dark, sultry eyes narrowed in curiosity. 'You okay?'

The 15-year-old tried to nod nonchalantly. Then the face of the man he adored was swimming steadily in front of his eyes. Richard found himself sinking into a dark, deep pit. And as he collapsed in a dead faint, Jix Tyson laughed, scooped the boy up into his arms and carried him towards a waiting car.

He woke up on his side with something tickling his nose. He scrabbled with his hands beneath the soft fabric, hauling the fluffy blanket away from his face. Blinking, Richard took in his surroundings. He was lying on a huge bed. Alone. Richard moaned and sat up, trying to work out where he was and how on earth he'd got here. He remembered the gig. He remembered hanging around the stage door. His eyes scanned the room. Then his ears picked up on something. Voices. Low, but still audible.

Richard blinked, scanned again. He was definitely alone. In the wall opposite, a door caught his eye. A half open door. Dragging himself further up on the bed, he stared at it. 'Um – hello?' He found himself whispering, for some unknown reason.

No response from beyond the half open door.

Panic rose in his throat. Where the hell was he? What time was it? Scrambling out from beneath the blanket, Richard swung rubber legs on to the floor and staggered over to the door. Gripping it with shaking fingers, he eased it further ajar. The questions formed on his lips as he stared into the adjoining room. And remained there, caught in his throat.

Chapter Seven

Night had fallen around him. A gentle swell rocked the deck beneath his feet. Richard stood lost in thought and seriously aroused...

The adjoining suite, in what he was later to discover was the Earls Court Hilton, was a mirror image of that in which he'd woken up – with a few differences. Candles were dotted around the room, their flames flickering. There was a smell drifting up from an abalone shell in which a selection of dried herbs and incense smouldered. The voices he'd heard from the other room were coming from a small tape recorder which sat on the bedside table. Richard tried to make sense of whatever language drifted over, but the words were alien, the recording old and crackly.

And on the bed, amidst rumpled sheets, two figures. Two naked figures. One on its back. The other, face down, between its legs.

Richard bit back a moan. He stared straight into the narrowed, unseeing eyes of Dick Dawson. The man's features were contorted, his lips curled back in half-sneer, half sigh. His back arched up off the bed, head craning down to the hands which roved over his thick matt of chest hair. Beyond those hands, a shaggy platinum skull was moving slowly but steadily over the hidden area of the bass player's crotch.

Richard's cock flexed. He bit back a gasp, his circulation almost cut off inside the too-tight jeans. He watched the way Jix Tyson's head moved, watched his idol's hands play amidst the other man's chest hair, then descend to hard, tensed thighs.

Dick Dawson moaned, pushing his knees up under those hands and planting bare feet more firmly on the rumpled bed. From the tape recorder, the crackly voice was becoming more frantic. The words came quicker now, intoned and almost chanted. Like some incantation. A spell.

The entire scene had Richard completely entranced, and served to focus his attention completely on the two men on the bed. He knew he should feel he was intruding. He didn't. He knew he should slip back through to the other room and just leave. He couldn't.

Jix Tyson's hands were now moving over the outside of his bass player's thighs. Stroking. Caressing. Dick Dawson's back arched further. His arse left the bed and a pair of guitarist's hands slipped beneath.

Richard had no idea when he'd started stroking himself. Was it then? Was it later, when he moved sideways, his legs working by themselves independent of everything his brain was telling him? Was it when he stood side-on to the scene, watching the slick thick length of a man's cock slide seamlessly between Jix Tyson's pouting lips?

On the deck of the motor launch, Dr Rodgers's palms were sweating. A sudden breeze erected the hair on the back of his neck. He wiped his hands on the thighs of his tweed trousers and leant back against the wheel house.

The air in the hotel room that night was electric. The atmosphere crackled, more alive than any stage performance. Fifteen-year-old Richard Rodgers from Scarborough curled his fist around his own young cock, stroking himself in sync with the movement of his idol's lips.

Dick Dawson plunged himself deep into Jix Tyson's throat, returning each movement of his lover's mouth. His swollen balls slapped against the blond man's chin.

Richard shuddered, cursing his too-tight jeans. He'd managed to get his cock free, but his bollocks remained imprisoned, huge and sweating beneath the denim.

On the tape, the old, crackly voice was screaming now. Dick Dawson's body sheened with sweat. His fists tightened, one gripping rumpled sheets, the other buried in Jix's hair.

Even over the fervent exhortations from the cassette recorder,

Richard could hear both men. The slap of flesh on flesh. The wet sounds of cock fucking mouth. The growls from deep in the platinum-haired rock stars' skinny chest. The gasps and whimpers from the man who arched up off the bed, Jix Tyson's hands clenched around his arse-cheeks.

And he could smell them – and himself – the musk of their bodies joining whatever smouldered in the abalone shell to produce a powerful aphrodisiac.

Abruptly, a wind swept through the hotel room. The candles flickered violently. Richard gasped then felt his bollocks clench as a voice joined the pre-recorded shrieks. Dick Dawson was repeated something, his words low and hoarse, husky with need.

The sound registered with Richard, as unintelligible as the voice on the tape. Then his legs gave way. His cock flexed violently in his fist. He sank to a crouch, gasping as the spunk flew from his slit, splattering his hand and shooting on to the carpet.

On the bed, Dick Dawson was still intoning along with the crackly tape, despite an orgasm which was shaking his body.

The candles flickered again. Richard shot a second time, his fingers warm and sticky with his own come. He felt the thick ejaculate ooze down over his trembling knuckles.

On the bed, Dick Dawson was moaning now, the words still audible, the volume of the voice on the tape increasing until it dominated everything.

Then Jix Tyson was hauling his mouth from the dripping tip of his lover's still-jerking cock. He threw himself on to his back between the bass-player's thighs, his hand around his own curving cock which he now stroked violently. And his mouth was moving too, his lips slick with Dawson's spunk.

Richard's head was going to explode. The force of his orgasm had drained his body, but the smells, the noise and the strange wind which still whirled around all three of them had created another tension. In his mind. And this one was not to be as easily dismissed.

Mesmerised by the drag of Jix's fist up and down his thick curving cock, the alien words which flowed from his lips and the stink of the incense, something like panic suddenly flooded Richard's body. There was a sense he was intruding here. He knew neither man was aware of his presence. Nevertheless, adrenaline was pounding through his veins, stimulating the age-old flight or fight response from some unseen and unknown enemy.

Over the receding intensity of his orgasm, Richard's body was more alive than it had ever been. And before he knew what he was doing, he was on his feet once more, scrambling towards the door with his cock still half out of his too-tight jeans.

Thirty years on, he could still feel that panic, mixed with arousal and naked fear. On the deck of the motor launch, Richard continued to stare at the flickering candle in the tower room beyond the trees. Then he laughed. To this day, he had no idea what sort of bizarre ritual the man who had haunted his teenage years had been trying to enact, during what was really just a blow-job with his bass player.

Oddly enough, though, the following day Jix Tyson had announced that the Hammersmith Odeon gig would be his last. True to his word, he had never performed in public again. His recording career staggered on for a few years, collaborations with everyone from obscure Mongolian tribesmen to Zen Buddhist monks. He shunned publicity and refused to give interviews. He toured the world alone, followed by paparazzi until even they lost interest in whatever personal quest was driving the man on. His new work was slammed as self-indulgent and unintelligible. His past catalogue drifted out of fashion.

Richard dragged his eyes form the flickering candle and moved back into the wheel house. Probably just a caretaker or someone, making sure the place was aired.

But knowing Jix Tyson had subsequently purchased Boleskin went some little way to explaining what had happened, that night in the Earls Court Hilton. Not that it mattered. Richard knew he had a lot to thank the man for. His first sexual experience may have gone unnoticed by his two companions, but it was for ever emblazoned on Richard's mind.

Smiling, he pressed the starter once more and steered the chugging motor launch back round in the direction of the jetty.

'Now are ye sure I can't bring you anything else?'

Mike grinned and patted his stomach. The host with the most had been true to his word: a five-course meal and no sign of any bill. 'You know how to feed a man up here, my friend.' The guy was flirting with him.

Archie Campbell's hazel eyes twinkled. He grinned back. 'What about a refill then – a proper drink, this time?' He lifted Mike's glass. 'Just a wee one?'

He'd been doing it all evening, along with providing a rapt audience for Mike's personal theories on their loch sweeps and the general purpose of their visit to Drumnadrochit. Professor St. Clair shook his head. 'To be honest, whisky's not my tipple.'

'Ach, this is a lovely single malt. Brewed by the Benedictines, along at Fort Augustus. It'll slip down a treat.' Ignoring Mike's protestations, the ginger-haired hotelier tilted the bottle of amber liquid to Mike's glass. 'Smooth as silk.'

A bit like the guy's technique. As Mike moved his hand to take the glass, their fingers brushed. Not for the first time.

'There we go, Professor. If I'm not right, I'll… drink the loch dry!' Archie winked again.

Mike had been on mineral water all evening. He really wasn't much of a drinker, apart from the odd glass of wine. As he raised the whisky to his mouth, the crowded, previously noisy lounge bar of the Campbell Arms hotel fell silent. Mike glanced around.

On the opposite side of the table, four empty pint glasses and three stubby whisky tumblers stood before a now well-oiled Lionel Banks. At the rugby player's side, Rajiv was sipping ginger ale and eyeing his colleague disapprovingly.

Beyond, an assortment of locals, students and older tourists were watching him with a mixture of amusement and curiosity. From behind the bar, Mike caught the surly eye of Morag, Archie's wife, who stood polishing glasses.

'Come on, man!' The hotelier's cajoling tones seeped into his ear.

'The monks'll be most offended if ye don't at least try it.'

Mike laughed. 'Okay – slainte!' He downed the measure in one gulp.

'Slainte!' The Gaelic version of 'Cheers' resounded throughout the bar, in response to Mike's action.

Then everyone was applauding. Glasses clinked, feet stamped in approval. Mike smiled, enjoying the warm glow which drenched his throat and continued down his gullet. Smooth – very smooth. He opened his mouth, and was just about to thank his host when the whisky hit his stomach.

His jaw clenched. His eyes watered. Something detonated in his belly. Mike coughed. Then everyone was laughing and the cheering increased in volume.

Archie slapped his back heartily. 'Aye, smooth as silk – but with a kick like a mule. That's monks for you!'

As Mike tried to breathe, he was aware of the hotelier's warm palm lingering between his shoulder blades. Was there nothing the guy wouldn't do to engineer physical contact?

'Drink this, Professor – and don't let them tease you.' A female voice at his right side cut through the raucous cheering.

Mike refocused to see Morag Campbell, smiling and holding a pint glass of water. He took it gratefully, still unable to speak.

'Aye, my husband likes his sport, so he does.' Morag's calm, semi-amused eyes glanced from Mike to Archie and back again. 'But don't let him talk you into anything, you hear?'

Mike sat there, between husband and wife, and wondered if she knew. He'd never had so heavy a signal as he was getting from the gin-ger-haired giant. They smiled at each other. Mike squirmed a little, fighting the after-effects of the whisky in order to reassert himself in all this. He gulped down more of the water and finally regained the power of speech. 'Thanks, Mrs Campbell, I won't.'

'Morag?' A voice from the bar. 'What's a man got to do around here to get a drink?'

'Ach, hold yer wheesht, Donald MacDonald!' She roared her response.

Her husband's hand lingered, rubbing slightly. Then it was gone. 'Excuse us, Professor.' The warm palm briefly touched his shoulder. 'Work calls.' And with that, both Campbells made their way back across the lounge to the growing queue of impatient drinkers.

Mike watched them go, watched Archie's hand slip to his wife's arse. He smiled, shook his head to clear the last, lingering effects of the whisky. No – it was his imagination. He was so obsessed with keeping his side of Richard's bargain he couldn't think straight. Innocent, fraternal smiles and comradely backslaps were twisting into come-ons. He lowered his eyes to the two postgrad students across the table.

'Good stuff, eh Prof?' Lionel beamed happily, one muscular arm resting on the back of his companion's chair. He was definitely looking the worse for wear, despite the heavy meal – six pints and a good few complimentary shorts had seen to that.

Rajiv sipped his ginger ale demurely. He met Mike's eye. 'Since he has missed the meal, shall I request a... pussy bag, for Dr Rodgers?' His handsome face was all innocence.

Lionel exploded into giggles.

Mike fought hard to keep his face straight. 'A... what, Raji?'

Confusion creased the handsome face. 'A pussy bag. A... selection of food to take with us, in order that he does not miss his meal.'

'It's a doggy bag!' Lionel was spluttering now. 'Doggy bag!' His ruddy face was flushed both from the alcohol and his futile attempts not laugh out loud. 'I'm not sure what a... pussy bag would be, pal!'

'I am sorry – my mistake. A doggy bag.' Rajiv's eyes fell, his generous lips curling downwards in embarrassment. 'But I do think we should.'

'Aye, with my own eyes – and this very afternoon. Clear as day, I saw Nessie on the eastern bank.' A hoarse, Highland brogue cut through Rajiv's earnest request.

Every head in the room turned to the source of the statement. Mike narrowed his eyes. Across at the bar, in the middle of a huddle of gawking, camera-bedecked Japanese tourists, a small, grey haired figure was holding court.

'Was she big, sir?'

'How many legs did she have?'

'Did you get a photograph of her, sir?'

The tiny gnarled man laughed. 'Aye she was big – big as three double decker buses. Four legs, two flippers – and a long tail like a serpent. But Nessie's camera-shy, son.' The ancient, weather-beaten face turned to his third questioner. 'And why would I want a photy-graph anyway? Sure, I've seen Nessie almost every day of my life.'

'Now, don't you tease these gentlemen, Hamish.' From behind the bar, Archie Campbell grinned.

Hamish looked insulted. 'Since when is it teasing to tell the truth?' His dark eyes narrowed. 'Why would I lie?' His voice sank to a theatrical whisper. 'I know the truth.'

The truth? Mike sighed and rolled his eyes. The Campbell Arms was overbooked, three times over, all year round. Both camp sites were full to overflowing. The Nessie Heritage Trail was doing a roaring trade and on their way here, Mike had seen this same gnarled faker accepting money from a group of camera-laden American tourists, for what he knew was the same spiel.

'Nessie guards the loch –'

The huddle of Japanese were hanging on old Hamish's every word.

'Even St. Patrick saw her, after he'd driven the snakes out of Ireland. She's been here for thousands of years and –'

'And any large amphibian or reptile living in those waters would have long since died.' Mike couldn't hold his tongue any longer. 'If it was ever here at all.'

Every eye in the place moved to the Professor of marine palaeontology. The Japanese tourists looked distinctly put out. Hamish glared.

Mike laughed. 'You see what you want to see, my friend.' He winked at Hamish.

The old man scowled. 'Maybe – but you refuse to open your eyes in case it damages your precious reputation, son!'

Mike shook his head indulgently. 'As a scientist, I –'

'I know who you are. I've seen you on the television, son. Spouting off, with your big words and your clever arguments.' Hamish's eyes darkened. 'You don't convince me – and you'll not convince Nessie either.'

Mike folded his arms. 'Okay, where is she?' He threw down the gauntlet. 'Take me to where Nessie sleeps. Prove your point.'

'Neither me nor the beastie need to prove anything to the likes of you, Mr Professor St. Clair.' Old Hamish didn't falter. 'Open that closed mind of yours, son – and you'll see her. You'll see a lot of things.' His gaze returned to the now well-and-truly-convinced tourists. 'As I have.'

'You've seen... floating logs – swimming deer.' Mike wasn't about to let this drop. 'Maybe even seals. Dozens of scientific sweeps of the loch have failed to find any evidence of anything of any size.' He smiled. 'I have a vast body of scientific data to back up my opinion. What do you have?'

Hamish snorted. 'I have eyes to see. Ears to hear. And a soul that knows there are more things on heaven and earth than can be looked at with machines and microphones and... whatever.'

Two of the Japanese tourists applauded politely. Shouts of 'you tell him, Hamish!' broke out from the drinkers. It was all good natured, but Mike knew his point of view was far from popular, with locals and visitors alike. Bad for business.

Something about the whole Nessie thing rubbed him up the wrong way. Always had. And despite the glassy eyes of the captain of the rugby First Eleven and the knowledge he should get both his charges back to the campsite, Mike remained on his feet. He mentally squared up to Old Hamish, who had to be at least 80, judging by that heavily lined face. As the ancient local turned back to the bar to accept another drink from his Japanese admirers, Mike took a step forward.

'Okay, I'm opening my eyes. No recording equipment – nothing electrical at all. You take me to where you saw Nessie, friend, and if I see her too I'll –' he paused for effect '– I'll get you and your monster on television! Can't say fairer than that.' Mike grinned, rubbed his hands together and waited for the responding laughs.

Nothing. The place was deadly silent. Old Hamish continued to face the bar, his back to the rest of the room. Along with everyone else, Mike stared at the old man's grey hair and watched as Hamish calmly took the pint Morag had just drawn for him. He raised it to his lips, took a deep drink then wiped the froth from his lips with the back of a heavily veined hand. You could have heard a pin drop in the Campbell Arms.

Then, in his own time, and working the room like a pro, the old man finally responded to Professor St. Clair's challenge. 'You'll see her, son – and when you do, she'll change you. Mark my words.'

In the warm, busy bar, Mike shivered. Although he knew it was all just a show for the benefit of the tourists, there was something ominous in the tone of voice. Something almost threatening. In the wake of Old Hamish's assertion, no one spoke. Outside, even the birds had fallen silent.

'Ach, you're daft – the lot of you!' Morag's down-to-earth, common-sense voice echoed around the room. 'If I was Nessie I'd give you all a wide berth!'

Hamish snorted and continued to sip his pint. Mike smiled. The Japanese tourists giggled and bowed briefly. Slowly, conversation broke out amongst the drinkers and normality returned. Mike was still standing there, when a voice seeped into his ear:

'If you'd like, I can take you to where Old Hamish saw whatever he thinks he saw.'

Mike shivered again. This time, it was lust which trailed hot-cold burning fingers over his skin. He could feel Archie Campbell's breath on his neck. Glancing behind, he saw Lionel and Rajiv were standing up. The stocky Tynesider had one thick arm around the more slender man's shoulders, more for support than anything else. 'You guys manage back on your own?'

Lionel mumbled something.

The Iraqi postgrad student nodded efficiently. 'I think the walk is just what he needs.' He began to steer his charge towards the door.

Mike didn't turn. He didn't want to have to look at Archie Campbell's broad body. But he was semi-serious about this most recent creature-sighting. 'Okay, lead the way.'

Well aware he was lying to himself, Mike followed the hotelier in the opposite direction, into the Campbell Arms' kitchens and out through the back door.

Chapter Eight

'You are drunk again!'

Lionel felt Rajiv's arm curl disapprovingly around his waist. He laughed and pressed back against it. 'No, I'm not. I'm just –' They pushed through the doors out into the night and the air hit him.

His legs crumpled. He stumbled sideways, his arm heavy on the shoulder of the man supporting him. Lionel tried to regain his balance, but only succeeded in tangling his feet up with Rajiv's. Then they were both falling. And Lionel's face was in the man's neck. And there was nothing he could do about it.

Somewhere beneath him, he felt vague struggles. Even vaguer words of protest and gasps hovered somewhere just beyond his hearing. All Lionel knew was the feel of the body under his. The smell of it, combined with the souring stink of stale lager and cigarette smoke. That alien, exotic mix of whatever the guy washed his hair with and the heady, meaty odour of musk.

He moaned against the warm skin of the Iraqi's neck. His stomach churned with too much beer and too heavy a meal. His cock throbbed, erecting downwards to trap itself between his hairy thigh and the denim of his jeans.

'Get off me! Get off me!'

Lionel opened his mouth. 'Raji... Raji...' Lips parted on the cleanly shaven neck, his head full of the man while his cock thickened and ached against his thigh, the captain of the rugby team licked the warm skin.

A roar from beneath him. Before he knew what was happening, an impossible force was throwing him off and back on to the grass. 'Oi!' His arse hit the ground, his skull impacting solidly with the soft earth. Lionel's head swam. Gorge rose in his throat. 'What the hell – ?' By the time he'd managed to crawl on to his hands and knees and refocus his eyes, he found himself staring at a crouching, circling figure.

Lionel blinked. His jaw dropped. A fierce expression painted the man's face. Knees bent, his centre of gravity lowered, Rajiv continued to circle, arms akimbo in front of his body.

'I could have broken your neck easily.' His fingers splayed upwards, fanning out at shoulder height. 'But this is a warning. If you try to touch me again, I shall not hesitate to use my full skills to render you insensible.'

His cock thickened further, pushing painfully against the tight denim of his jeans. The captain of the First Eleven sat there, the arse of his trousers dampening on the dewy grass. The change in his colleague's body language took Lionel's breath away. Gone was the neat, almost prissy academic. In his place, a hard, muscular warrior swayed in front of the semi-stunned, well-pissed rugby player. No – not a warrior. Rajiv was moving like some strange animal, tilting his body and head.

His entire being seemed to be in motion, primed for action even when he paused in front of Lionel, something like a sneer on his handsome, dark-skinned face. 'You are drunk. So I make allowances. I think you are basically a good, if stupid man.'

Lionel continued to sit there and take words he would never take from anyone else.

Rajiv's right hand moved to the side of his neck, fingers brushing the area Lionel could still feel against his lips. 'But if you ever touch me again, in an... inappropriate manner, I shall not hesitate. Do you understand?'

Lionel's cock flexed violently. He winced, the smaller, slighter man's tone making his stomach churn and his balls tighten.

'Do you understand?' The voice was lower, almost a whisper. And all the more powerful for its lack of volume. Moaning inside, Lionel managed a pathetic nod.

Abruptly, Rajiv relaxed his stance. He thrust a hand down to Lionel. 'Now get up before someone trips over you.' Rajiv glanced over his shoulder to where a couple of girls were making their giggling way from the hotel, all eyes and nudges.

With a sheepish laugh, Lionel grabbed the extended hand and felt strong fingers curl around his and drag him to his feet.

'I did not hurt you, did I?' The previous harsh tone was gone, replaced by soft solicitation. The hand lingered.

The gentle enquiry sent a tremble through Lionel's body. Blood was pumping into his cock, leaving his brain at an alarming rate. He didn't know if he was coming or going. He only knew something had happened, on the ground – something which seemed to have corrected whatever was jarring between them and reasserting in its place a new equilibrium. Despite the ache in his balls and the strain of his swollen trapped cock, Lionel smiled. 'No, I'm fine – but you should try out for the squad, next term.'

The hand around his moved seamlessly away. 'Squad?'

'The team – the university rugby team?' Equally seamlessly, they both turned and began to walk in the general direction of the campsite. Lionel limped slightly, the pressure around his cock making every movement of his left leg a little uncomfortable. 'You'd be our secret weapon: you look like a hooker, but you've got the strength of a prop.'

'Hooker? Prop?'

Lionel laughed. 'A hooker is the smallest member of the team. It's his job to... hook the ball in the scrum, and pass it to one of the props.'

'Scrum? What is this...scrum?'

As they walked along what passed for a main street in Drumnadrochit, Lionel found himself detailing the ins and out of the game he loved to the most attentive audience he'd had in a long time. The effects of the alcohol seemed to vanish. His head was clearer than it had been in days.

Rajiv nodded, asked sensible questions in all the right places. By the time they left the village and the lights died behind them, it was

Lionel's turn to make enquiries.

Rajiv told him about the art of ground-wrestling. How he'd always been small, even as a child. How he'd been bullied by the other boys, both because of his size and his studious ways. How his culture valued self-control and respect above everything else. Respect for others. And respect for oneself.

His father found a teacher, an old retired trader from Jakarta, who was willing to take the young Rajiv on privately. In between studying the Koran and doing his school work, the eight-year-old had begun a different type of training. And not just physical. As Guro Lee helped develop his body and responses to an attack situation, Rajiv's mind developed at the same rate.

He learned how to argue his corner, debate points from both sides. He began to read the Sufi poets and delve more deeply into the religion in which he'd been raised. As the Indonesian Silate training focused Rajiv physically, with its strong emphasis on physics and body mechanics, his brain followed a parallel path.

By ten, he was moved to a class two years older. By 12, he was taking exams for his leaving certificate. At 14, Rajiv Azad's proud parents watch him become the youngest student to enter the University of Baghdad. And in the background, Guro Lee was there, his sombre face shining, his head nodding in encouragement. He remained there, through four years of study, to see his prize pupil graduate with honours at a time when his peers were only just starting their degree courses.

'And I have never used my body against another – I have never had to. So you see, it would be inappropriate from me to join your rugby team, regardless of how good I would be at the it. Guro Lee taught me that.'

Lionel barely noticed the darkness. He was entranced by Rajiv's story. 'Do you still keep in touch?'

'Guro died three years ago.'

'Ah... ' Lionel felt genuinely sad. 'Sorry, pal.'

'Do not be sorry. He was 91. His life was long and full. And he lives on in me.'

Lionel glanced at his companion. He could just see the outline of Rajiv's profile, through the dusk. There was indeed no trace of any mournfulness in the man's expression. In fact, a small smile was easing up the corners of his full lips.

Just at that moment, the moon appeared from behind a cloud and illuminated the area around them. For the first time since they'd left the Campbell Arms, both men paused and took in their surroundings. To their right, sparkles. Lionel blinked. Now bathed in a silvery sheet, the surface of the black loch glinted in moonlight like a huge mirror. They both moved at once, walking right to the rocky edge.

A little up, the jetty, two pitched tents along with the Doc's Volvo and Prof St. Clair's Harley Davidson bike were visible. No boat was moored. Lionel cocked his head. No sound of an engine. Nothing... just the faint slap of slow-moving water against the rocky shoreline.

'Fancy a swim, Raji?' The idea came from nowhere. Not waiting for a response, Lionel grinned and began to haul his polo shirt over his head.

A soft hand touched his bare arm. 'There may be currents.' A warning note drifted into the low voice. 'I know it looks calm, but beneath the surface there could be strong undertows.'

'And monsters?' Lionel chuckled. He balanced on one leg to remove his boot. 'What do you make of this monster stuff, anyway?'

Rajiv sat down on a nearby rock. 'Please do not go for a swim now. If you want, we can swim in the morning, but it is too dark and you are not familiar with the water.'

'And the monster might get me?' Lionel's grin broadened. He started on the other boot, then removed both socks and tossed them aside.

'I do not believe there is any monster, in the sense that elderly gentleman who was arguing with Professor St. Clair suggests.' Rajiv's voice was its normal, logical self.

Lionel's hands paused on the buckle of his belt, suddenly aware he was undressing in front of this man.

'But I concur with Dr Rodgers's thesis on this matter. Look at proteus. A creature which was only recently discovered by man, which lives at great depths and never sees light. Proteus has not evolved in over a million years.'

Lionel's hand shook slightly.

'Suspended in evolutionary animation, it is exactly the same as the fossilised remains of its ancestors. And even its own lifespan has yet to be accurately estimated by science.'

Lionel groaned. He knew Rajiv was totally absorbed in what he was saying and probably wasn't even looking at him. But his hard-on was steadily reviving. In an attempt to pull himself together and distract his mind, he began to counter argue. 'Proteus is – what? Six inches long?'

'What has size to do with it?' A low chuckle drifted over from the rock. 'We are talking about principle and precedent.'

Lionel clenched his teeth: the first time he'd ever heard the small Iraqi man laugh. Now – of all times. The sound made his stomach flip over and his cock thicken further. He wrenched the length of leather back through the buckle, unfastened it then fumbled with the fly of his jeans.

Rajiv continued. 'Proteus is a marine creature. There is speculation that there may be something about the marine environment which inhibits evolution.'

'Proteus is fresh water, not brine.' Lionel hissed the words and dragged down his zip. Still trapped against his thigh, his cock flexed violently. He moaned.

'It was been found in salt water pools too. It may be depth which is the rogue variable, rather than the composition of the water.' Rajiv's voice was calm. Unruffled.

Another rogue variable pulsed against the hairy skin of Lionel's leg.

'Something proteus shares with whatever lives in these dark waters. The loch is very deep in places.' A soft sigh escaped the Iraqi student's lips. 'Another reason why one should not swim in it, least of all at night.'

In truth, Lionel was steadily going off the idea of a dip anyway. But it was now a matter of necessity, not desire. His entire body trembled. The cooling evening air brushed against the thick hair on the

Tynesider's stomach. His balls clenched. His prick flexed solidly. He had to get rid of it. He couldn't sleep in a tent, a foot apart from this man with these six inches of need throbbing between them. And icy water would see to that.

'Just a quick plunge.' Lionel turned away, hauling down his jeans and underpants. Released from its denim prison, his cock sprang free, jutting up to slap off his stomach. He gasped.

'I'd rather you didn't, Lionel.'

He moaned at the use of his name. His balls drew up, tight and full at the root of him. Kicking his feet free of his clothes, he strode forward, picking his way past rocks on to the gravely sand. 'I'll only be a minute.' His voice was hoarse. Lionel cleared his throat and tried a laugh. 'Make sure the monster doesn't steal my Levis, eh?'

Another sigh from the rock. And somewhere in the distance, the soft chug of a motor launch. Lionel ignored both and stepped into the water. The chill around his ankles made him gasp but he walked on, feeling the icy loch close around his knees, then his thighs.

'It's lovely!' He shouted through chattering teeth and continued to wade out. 'Raji – you should have come in!' The floor of the loch sloped abruptly. His feet trod water for a few seconds. Then Lionel inhaled and dived.

He was a strong swimmer. Always had been. He'd swum the Channel as part of the university relay team, two years ago, his body greased and shivering. But this was something else. The water seemed unnaturally cold – even for Scotland. And it felt thick, almost viscous around him. Eyes open, Lionel blinked into the murky loch. He twisted his naked body, agile as a seal, and turned himself round, trying to push his way through the depths back up towards where the moon reflected on the surface.

His skin was numb in seconds. He could hold his breath for a good two minutes, but something about being down here was making him feel vaguely uneasy. Lionel swam onwards, ever upwards towards the moon. He was surprised the dive had taken him this deep. Twenty seconds passed. Half a minute. Then 40 seconds. Fifty. How had he got to this depth? No way that shallow dive had brought him this far down.

Lionel focused on the rippling moon above him, which seemed to back off the more he swam towards it. A minute. Eighty seconds. A minute and a half. His lungs tightened, muscle fighting the breath control. Panic tingled in his head, buzzing with the blood. Abruptly it dawned on him. He was swimming the wrong way!

Just as this thought burst into his mind, something long and black and slick passed just beneath him. Then air exploded from his lungs and he was twisting around, shooting towards the surface amidst a trail of air bubbles.

Richard heard the commotion 25 yards away as he tied the motor launch's mooring ropes to the jetty. Torch in hand, he jumped from the pier and ran along the side of the loch to its source.

The sight which met his eyes as he approached almost stopped his heart. Someone was lying on the small section of sand. He could see the whiteness of naked skin. Over the pale shape, someone else was crouching. Still running, Richard fumbled with the torch and managed to switch it on. He focused the beam. And illuminated the back of a glossy black head just above the collar of a sensible bright yellow rainproof jacket.

'Rajiv!' Richard ran faster. What on earth had happened?

The small Iraqi postgrad student seemed to be leaning over the naked body of another man. The torch beam jolted and jumped as he ran on, but Richard could see the figure on its back was male from the thick length of flaccid cock which lay between its splayed thighs.

In fact, Rajiv seemed to be kissing the man. As Richard covered the ground, running faster now, he watched Rajiv's head move, dip then raise itself up only to dip again.

He'd heard splashing and shouts, just as the motor launch's engine had cut out to allow docking at the short pier. He'd assumed it was locals, larking about. Or kids, skinny dipping.

Richard leapt over rocks, closing the distance between himself and the two men. 'Rajiv!' He slid on moss, stumbling, then sprinted on.

He was feet away from the two figures when the naked man on the ground began to cough and splutter. Rajiv was taking off his bright yellow jacket now, arranging it over the naked man's hairy chest. Richard saw the naked man's face for the first time and realised Rajiv had been administering mouth-to-mouth resuscitation. He saw Lionel heave himself up on one elbow and retch, spitting mouthfuls of water on to the dark sand while Rajiv looked on in concern.

Finally reaching them, Richard sank to a crouch beside the two men. 'What happened? Are you all right?'

Rajiv turned, blinking in the torch beam. 'This fool stupidly decided to go for a swim.'

More coughing and spluttering from Lionel cut the explanation short. 'I saw it.' The words were half-retched.

Richard leant forward. 'Are you all right?'

'Get that bloody thing out of my face, man!' A well-muscled arm batted the beam away.

Richard dropped the torch. It rolled, illuminating the silvery waves which lapped peacefully against the rocks. 'Are you okay?'

'I saw it – I fucking saw it!' Lionel was sitting up now, running a hand over his soaking cropped hair.

'What?' Richard and Rajiv spoke at once.

Lionel spat the last few mouthfuls on to the sand. 'I saw the bloody monster!'

Chapter Nine

Two miles away, around the other side of the loch, Archie Campbell pulled the Land Rover into the side of the road. 'We have to walk the rest of the way.'

Mike peered at the dark outline of the 14th-century Castle Urquhart, just a little ahead of them.

The hotelier turned off the ignition, slipped the keys into the pocket of his jeans and got out. 'Favourite place for beastie-sightings, this is – going back to the 1920s.'

Mike unfastened his seat belt and joined the red-haired giant at the side of the road. A smile played around his lips. 'Is it indeed.'

'Aye, it is that, Professor St. Clair.'

'Mike, please.' He grinned, following the hotelier across the road and down towards the ruins of Castle Urquhart. Archie had kept up a steady line of half-serious, half-teasing banter throughout the 15-minute car journey to this desolate spot. Mike liked the man's attitude: not quite cynical, but with a healthy dose of self-mockery regarding the existence or non-existence of the famed Nessie.

'Okay, Mike it is.' The redhead paused, just in front of a semi-crumbling red sandstone wall. His deep voice dropped to a whisper. 'Come on – it was just along here, from what Hamish was telling me.'

The grin broadened on Professor St. Clair's face. 'Okay, you lead the way.' He lowered his own voice to suitably hushed tones. Falling in behind the hotelier's broad outline, he could not decide what this guy's game was. Did he really think Mike was even remotely interested in some spiel the whole village of Drumnadrochit concocted for the benefit of their tourist trade? Or was this wild goose chase a continuation of the game he'd been playing with Mike, back at the Campbell Arms?

'Watch your footing.' A hiss from in front. 'The stone is a wee bit loose here.'

Mike chuckled and felt shingle crunch beneath his boots. He'd climbed Snowdonia, a few years back. There was nothing a bit of crumbling sandstone could show him. His eyes trained on the back of the ginger head, Mike walked on.

'Aye, a favourite spot this is.' Archie continued to whisper as they made their way deeper into the ruins of Castle Urquhart. 'Perhaps it's got something to do with currents – or maybe Nessie's home is around here somewhere. I'm not sure.'

Mike tried to keep his face straight. 'You may be right, my friend.' He choked back a snigger.

Then Archie disappeared from view.

Mike frowned. 'Hey, where are you?'

The ground sloped suddenly beneath his feet. Grabbing on to a stone ledge just above his head, Mike only just managed to keep his balance.

From below: 'Aye, that's it – feel your way down. It's a bit of a drop.'

The man's voice sounded miles away. Mike frowned, irritated that he'd been given no warning of exactly how much rock-face work was going to be involved in this little midnight stroll. The heels of his boots slipped, and he was soon picking his way down what felt like a sheer drop, clinging on by toes and fingertips alone.

'Down ye come, Mikey-boy.'

The affectionate term made him flinch. Then an owl hooted somewhere to his right and Mike gasped. His blood ran cold. His fingers lost their grip and he was pitching into darkness. 'Argh!' Legs flailing, he toppled backwards, his life flashing swiftly before him –

– and set foot on soft sand, a mere six inches below. Feeling more than a little sheepish, Mike wiped his hands on the thighs of his jeans and turned. Eyes acclimatising to the gloom, he saw Archie was frowning.

'Well, that'll have well and truly scared the beastie off – I thought you said you were an experienced hiker and mountaineer?'

Mike laughed. 'In daylight – not in the middle of the night when I have no idea where I am or where I'm going!' Highly convenient that his yells should have put paid to any chance of their seeing the monster. He smiled at Archie. 'Nessie can't be much of a... beastie, if a few shouts can put her off her stride.' He winked.

The owner of the Campbell Arms remained stony-faced. The frown played around his generous lips, tightening them into a hard line. In the light from the overhead moon, the freckles which dusted his pale skin seemed to shimmer.

Mike's cock twitched. He groaned inside. The atmosphere around them had changed. Gone was their semi-joking banter. Gone was the half-teasing expression and words. Now, two men stood in a rocky cove. In the darkness. Alone.

Mike's cock twitched again. His shaft was stretching, pushing its curving way towards his stomach. He clenched his fists and tried to pull himself together. How long had it been since he'd had another man – 24 hours? This was ridiculous – totally ridiculous. Mike turned and wandered over to where the loch was lapping softly against the edge of the sand. His mind was playing tricks on him. Or, if not his mind, his body certainly was. He was picking up signals everywhere – from everyone. Even this married hotel owner, who had brought him out here merely to perpetuate the Nessie myth and with no ulterior motive.

An owl hooted again, closer. Caught up with the slowly stretching foreskin, short pubic hair tugged as Mike's cock flexed. He winced. Then laughed. So obsessed with sex was he, even the night call of a bird was arousing. Another laugh drifted through the dark air. Then:

'Ach, I'm sorry, Mike – I shouldn't have dragged you all the way out here.'

Archie's voice was close. Professor St. Clair grinned but continued to stare out over the moonlit loch. 'No, I'm sorry.' He recommenced the banter. 'Maybe if I'd made less noise, Nessie could have been tempted up from the depths.' A low laugh, near his ear:

'Aye – all two double-deckers of her, with flippers and great tail!'

Mike chuckled.

Archie continued, his voice falling to a whisper. 'Old Hamish likes his whisky a wee bit too much – and there's no denying he lays it on thick for the tourists.'

Mike listened to the distant whoosh of waves on shale and ignored what his cock was doing.

'But what harm does it do, Mike? Who are we hurting, here?'

Professor St. Clair bit back his usual response about the damage myth and legend could do to important scientific progress and just listened to the waves.

'Do you have any idea what this area would be, without the visitors? The Highland economy is on its knees as it is. What do we have? The mountains, the glens, a couple of old castles and some battlegrounds. So we exploit what nature and history gave us – we sell it back to our foreign visitors in the form they want it. So we beef up our particular mythical beastie – who does it hurt?'

Mike flinched as a hand softly placed itself on his shoulder. He found himself turned slowly away from his contemplation of the loch's dark waters. Archie Campbell's face was close. Very close. A small smile played around those same lips which minutes earlier had been twisted into a scowl.

Mike stared, his cock curving and flexing against his stomach. Then Archie's other hand was on his waist and those lips were parting. And moving towards his. Mike moaned. The vow to Richard fluttered briefly in his brain. Mouth slack, every other muscle in his body rigid, he tilted his head and opened his lips to the kiss. What harm...?

The touch was brief. Briefer than brief. At his sides, Mike's fists clenched tighter than ever. Every sense was totally focused on that brush. He could feel the man, the soft fullness of his mouth. See him, eyelids half closed in the moonlight. Smell him, the slightly meaty odour of male sweat and a hint of fabric conditioner. Taste him – Mike moaned aloud, opening his mouth more as Archie Campbell's tongue slipped between his lips. Taste the sweet/sour spit.

Mike's nails dug into the palms of his hands. He let the man explore his mouth. He let Archie Campbell's fingers grip his shoulders, holding Mike steady as he slowly deepened the kiss and pushed his tongue further between his lips.

His own tongue lay passive. Motionless. Accepting. Somewhere at the back of Professor St. Clair's brain, a voice roared: What about Rick? But as the bristled skin of Archie's chin scraped against his cheek, the voice faded. It faded further when both Archie's hands moved to Mike's waist and he felt a thigh slide between his.

Just a kiss. Rick couldn't say anything about just a kiss. A kiss wasn't betrayal. A kiss was... just a kiss.

Mike's entire body was trembling. Now fully erect and straining just below the waistband of his jeans, his cock flexed violently against the other man's muscular leg.

Keep it in your pants had been Richard's instruction. And that was exactly what Mike intended to do. His balls tightened abruptly, clenching at the root of his prick. He groaned and began to grind himself against the hard thigh.

Archie Campbell's tongue was now moving more steadily in Mike's mouth. Parting his lips further, he sucked on it, nails almost drawing blood from now sweating palms.

They stood there, in the moonlight. Two men. One holding the other's waist and almost tongue-fucking his mouth. The other rigid but accepting, unable to fight the powerful messages from his own body.

Mike's prick was leaking arousal against the waistband of his jeans. Against his own hipbone, he was vaguely aware of Archie's cock, strong and solid and curving up against him. Mike moaned. He'd not come in his trousers since he was a teenager. It usually took much more than a kiss to get him anywhere near this stage. But there was something abut Archie Campbell. Maybe it was the hair – Mike had always liked redheads. Maybe it was the voice – that same baritone lilt he'd been attracted to in the stranded motorist. Or maybe it was five hours of foreplay, which had started the moment Archie had shaken Mike's hand back at the campsite, and continued on all through dinner at the Campbell Arms. The smiles, the glances, the touches. The attention.

Jack Dickson

Abruptly, the man broke the kiss and buried his face in Mike's neck. Professor St. Clair stood there, gasping and still feeling Archie's lips on his. That mouth was now sucking on his neck, while the hands which had previously held his waist were moving down to his arse.

Somewhere close by, an owl hooted twice. He barely heard it over the fizz of blood in his head and the sound of his own ragged breath. The hotelier's hands splayed over his arse-cheeks, gripping them tightly and using Mike's body as leverage to grind his own shaft against Professor St. Clair's hipbone. His lips tingled from the pressure of the kiss. Archie Campbell's saliva was cooling to a scum on the corners of his mouth. As the red-haired Highlander continued to kiss his neck, Mike's tongue traced the outline of his own mouth, tasting Archie all over again.

They were both grinding now. Mike gulped in air and dragged his aching cock up and down the man's thigh. He could feel Archie's mouth on his neck, feel the man's hardness against his hipbone – feel the pressure of at least seven thick inches of need so close –

Keep it in your pants!

– and yet so far. His bargain with Richard twisted and turned in his head. Mike moaned aloud. And an owl hooted back in mocking response. It wasn't even as though this was normal. He never got as many offers as he'd had in the past 24 hours. Maybe once a fortnight he'd go looking for it, maybe once a week. Sometimes he found it. Sometimes he just watched others, and wanked. Sometimes he came home and wanked.

Archie was biting his neck now, moving his hard-on in small circles against Mike's leg. Mike's balls clenched violently. Neck-biting did it every time. Rick used to bite his neck, just before he came. He squeezed his eyes shut, fighting orgasm – fighting the image of himself and Richard. Mike on all fours, on their bed. Rick inside him. Rick's pubes bristling and rough against his arse. Rick's mouth on his neck. Biting. Hurting.

The only time Mike had ever come without wanking was with his lover and partner's teeth gripping the skin on the back of his neck – some weird connection between that sharp pain and the way Rick's cock filled him inside. Something hardwired into his brain.

Fists clenched tightly by his sides, his lips hardened into a scowl. He stood there, another man against him. Another man's hands on his arse. Another man's cock grinding against his hipbone. And wanted Rick more than he'd ever wanted him.

'I saw it – I really saw it!'

'I know... now go to sleep. We'll talk about it in the morning.'

On the other side of the loch, in a tent, Dr Rodgers and Rajiv, minus his soaking trousers and barefooted, were attempting to put a now dry but still babbling Lionel to bed.

'Didn't you see it, Raji? It must have broken the surface. It moved right up past me and –'

'Shh... go to sleep, my friend.' Rajiv's voice was very soft, as if he was talking to child.

Rick watched Lionel's eyelids flutter in the dim camping light which hung from the roof of the tent. He pulled the sleeping bag up more tightly around the pale face then reached up to extinguish the lamp.

He waited for a few minutes, until Lionel's breathing became more even. When a gentle snore drifted up from the captain of the First Eleven, Dr Rodgers nodded to Rajiv and they both began to back towards the tent flap.

Outside, in the balmy night air, Richard rubbed his face and walked towards where the Volvo was parked. 'I hope he's okay. That water's icy cold – he could be in shock. We –'

'I'm sure he is fine, Dr Rodgers.'

Rajiv's ever-calm voice reassured him. Leaning against the car's bonnet, Richard lowered his hands and looked at the dark, solicitous face.

'It is you who got the fright, I think.' The Iraqi student continued. 'You who may be in shock. Sit down, Dr Rodgers.' Rajiv opened the passenger door and held it that way.

Richard smiled. 'No I'm fine.' But he moved to sit just inside the car anyway, his feet remaining on the grass. 'Want to tell me what happened? I mean, did you see anything?'

Rajiv sank to a crouch just in front of the open door and began to talk. Richard listened as he concisely recounted his colleague's great intake of beer during their meal and the drunken walk back which had culminated in Lionel's desire to take a moonlight dip:

'He was very drunk. I should have stopped him, I know – but he was out of his clothes and in the water before I could do anything.' Rajiv sighed. 'I presume he panicked and ran out of breath. He was down there for quite some time. I saw nothing, Dr Rodgers – nothing until he broke the surface, shouting and waving his arms. Which was when I waded in and dragged him out.'

Richard blinked, remembering the way Rajiv's mouth had been glued to Lionel's on his arrival at the scene. 'So he wasn't unconscious? I thought perhaps he'd bumped his head on something, under the water.'

Rajiv sighed. 'No, he was fine when he came out. But he did lose consciousness for a short while, on the shore, which is why I administered the lifesaving technique.' His eyes narrowed. 'What did you think I was doing, Dr Rodgers?'

Rick's eyes moved from the man's confused face to the outline of his brown, muscular legs which glinted in the light from the open car door. 'Um, nothing.' He laughed, suddenly self-conscious. 'I'm not sure.'

'I was not kissing him, if that's what you think.'

Richard felt his face start to flush up. He scowled. What was wrong with him?

'You must believe me, sir. I would not do that.'

A hand moved itself on to Richard's thigh. He flinched, skin on fire.

'Dr Rodgers. Sir. Lionel means nothing to me. He is barely a friend. We are colleagues, nothing more. Please believe me when I say –'

'I believe you!' Richard shot to his feet and pushed past the crouching man. His voice was tight, the words only just managing to emerge from his scowling lips. 'Now, you turn in, Rajiv. I'm going down to check the boat. I'll see you tomorrow, bright and early. Goodnight.'

And before the Iraqi student could say anything else, Richard strode off down the path which led to the small jetty.

His heart was thumping. He had the start of a definite erection. His head was all over the place. But one thing he knew for sure. If he'd allowed Rajiv Azad to continue his little declaration of infatuation, he would have been half way to fulfilling his side of the bargain he and Mike had made.

Richard quickened his pace. But he couldn't. Not like this. Not with a... student! Not that Rajiv wasn't attractive. He was: that hair, those big chocolate eyes, the long, muscular legs...

Reaching the jetty, his feet thundered over the decking as he made his way to where the motor launch was moored. If and when he ever did anything about keeping his side of the bargain, it would be his choice. When he wanted to. Diving down into the cabin, Dr Rodgers began to rifle through cupboards and drawers. He'd not smoked in – eight years? But now, for some reason, the craving was back. Rick scowled. Another disconcerting sign that this whole thing was getting out of hand. Another appetite, previously conquered, was pushing its way to the surface.

Deep in the back of a drawer of rope and oilskin gloves, he found a packet of cigarettes with one still in it. He hauled it from the pack and stuck it between tight lips while rummaging for matches. But there, he was out of luck.

Climbing back up on deck, Rick glanced shorewards, half expecting to see the lovelorn Rajiv standing mournfully on the jetty, like something out of a bad film. Thankfully, there was no sign of the student. However, in the silence, he could just detect the sound of approaching feet.

'Mike?' He called out, half-whispering.

The only response was the distant hoot of an owl. But the footsteps continued to approach.

Chapter Ten

It wasn't Mike. But it was smoking a cigarette.

Dr Rodgers sighed. 'Excuse me? Do you have a light?' He called out to the passing figure, cringing at the way his request had the tone of the clichéd come-on.

'Aye, that I do.' The voice was male.

Richard moved from the boat on to the jetty to meet the man half way. As he approached, he could see the guy had a pair of large binoculars slung around his neck, and was looking at the Harley Davidson.

'Thanks.' The cigarette still in his mouth, Richard stopped a few feet from the guy, who was now fumbling in the pocket of bulging cargo pants.

A flick. Then a flame flared in the darkness. Richard lowered his head to where the man's hands cupped around the lighter. Brushing the end of his cigarette into the yellow flicker, he inhaled deeply, moved back and coughed. The lighter flame vanished and they were once more in darkness. Richard coughed again, his eyes watering. The thing tasted foul – more foul than he remembered.

A low laugh. Then a hand was slapping his back. Dr Rodgers struggled for breath.

'Easy, easy!' The hand continued to slap. 'You okay?'

Rick ducked away and grabbed a tree for support. Eventually, his lungs returned to normal. He frowned, hating himself – the first smoke in eight years – and took another drag. He raised his eyes. 'Yes, I'm fine. Thanks.'

He looked at the man properly for the first time. The stranger with the binoculars smiled, nodded and glanced briefly again at Mike's bike. What on earth was the guy doing, wandering around here in the early hours of the morning? Then it dawned on him, and he smiled.

'Out for a bit of Nessie-spotting?'

The guy continued to stare at Mike's Harley.

'Eh?'

'Sorry – what?' The man with the sophisticated binoculars and the bulging cargo pants spun round.

Dr Rodgers laughed and repeated his question, nodding to the instrument which dangled around the guy's neck.

A responding chuckle. 'No, no – bird-watching.'

'Ah!' Richard remembered the owl and nodded. 'Infra-red, I take it?' He peered at the binoculars.

The guy seemed taken aback, but quickly recovered. 'Yes, they are in fact.'

Rick dragged on the cigarette, feeling the nicotine seep into his brain and spark that familiar light-headed relaxation. He smiled. 'Excuse my curiosity – and my rudeness.' He stuck out a hand. 'Richard – Richard Rodgers. I'm up here on a field trip from St. Aloysius College in Oxford. I wondered if you were a fellow scientist.'

'Kieran – Kieran McLeod.' A firm hand seized Richard's fingers. 'And no – I'm just here for a few days' break.' The hand moved away, waved vaguely up into the hills behind them. 'I'm up there. Better for the birds, you know.'

Richard didn't, but nodded anyway. He took another drag on the cigarette and scrutinised the man, who was once again peering at Mike's large motorcycle. Something about Kieran McLeod didn't quite ring true.

Maybe it was nicotine. Maybe it was in the wake of poor Rajiv's clumsy declaration. Maybe it was all in his imagination. The guy didn't look like a sneak-thief, but he was undoubtedly a bit shifty and there was something in the way McLeod was eyeing Mike's Harley that gave Richard the willies.

Unexpectedly, Kieran McLeod raised the high powered binoculars to his face and swung them over the loch. 'Fine clear sky for it.'

For what, exactly, Richard wasn't sure. 'So you're into... night hunters?' He watched the man watch something on the far side of the loch.

No response.

Richard pressed on. 'Owls?' He tried to think of more nocturnal predators but could come up with no other species. 'And that sort of thing.'

'Aye.' When the response finally came, it was casual and vague. 'That sort of thing.' Kieran's eyes remained hidden behind the powerful binoculars, his gaze still trained on the far side of the loch.

A sudden singeing around his knuckles told Rick he'd finished the cigarette. Flicking it away, he trod the end underfoot and prepared to make his excuses. Before he could:

'Does that bike belong to one of your party, Dr Rodgers?'

The fact that the man knew his professional title was less of a shock than the now overt reference to Mike's Harley. Richard blinked. 'Um – yes. It's Professor St. Clair's. Why do you ask?'

'Is this Professor St. Clair around?'

Richard frowned. He hated when people answered one question with another. 'Um – yes, he's around somewhere.' Especially when it was a question to which he could provide no satisfactory answer. 'Look, what's all this about?'

Eyes still hidden by powerful lenses, Kieran continued to stare at the east shore of Loch Ness. 'You and Professor St. Clair are here to carry out a study of the loch, is that right, Dr Rodgers?'

Rick bit back a splutter. 'How do you – ?'

'Take a bit of advice, sir. I see more than birds, on my wanderings at night. Watch what you're doing.'

He wondered where the 'sir' had come from. He wondered what on earth the guy was talking about.

As abruptly as he'd raised them, McLeod lowered the infra-red binoculars and looked at Richard. 'Have a pleasant evening, Dr Rodgers. Good night.'

Rick's eyes swivelled between the bird watcher and the direction in which he had been focused. But before he could utter any words of his own, the guy in the bulging cargo pants had sloped back off into the darkness.

He stood there, watching the night reabsorb the mysterious man who watched the night-hunters. Then Richard turned his head and stared out over the loch, every hair on his body standing on end.

'I'm sorry – I can't do this.' On the opposite shore, Mike moaned, his cock iron but still inside his jeans – despite Archie's Campbell's best efforts to unzip his flies.

'Come on!' He could feel the man's breath on his collarbone. One broad hand pushed up beneath his shirt. 'I know you want to. I saw the way you looked at me at dinner.'

Archie Campbell's left hand swept up through Mike's chest hair and cupped his pec. Professor St. Clair's cock flexed violently. 'Who are we hurting? If it's Morag you're worried about, don't.'

Back arching, Mike pushed himself into the man's hand.

'She knows the score. She has lovers herself.'

Mike clenched his teeth. The guy's wife was the least of his problems. As Archie's fingers tightened around his nipple, his other hand was back at the fly of Mike's jeans.

'Let me suck you, Mikey-boy. Let me taste your spunk. You know you want to.'

Professor St. Clair shuddered. It was what he wanted most in the world. Right here. Right now – if you didn't count wanting to feel this hot redhead's cock deep in his arse.

The fingers of one hand toyed with Mike's nipple while those of the other wrenched hard at the zip of his jeans. Archie bent his head, bringing his mouth to the other nipple.

Mike's balls spasmed. He fought orgasm for the third time, and finally managed to move one of his own arms, which had remained rigid, fists clenched, for the last hour. Eyes narrowed, heart pounding, he clamped his right hand over the fingers on his zip.

Keep it in your pants.

The other hand moved to the back of Archie's head. Teeth grazed his nipple. The redhead tried to move his fingers under Mike's. Keeping his palm steady, preventing any withdrawal, Mike began to grind against the hotelier's hand. He bent his knees, dipping down then rearing up. Inside his jeans, still within a layer of jersey underpants, the teeth of the open zip raked against his cock. A double layer of palm pressed back. Unable to remove his hand from the crotch of Mike's jeans, Archie stretched his fingers out then curled them down to the denimed V of Professor's St. Clair's thighs.

Mike moaned.

While the heel of his hand rubbed deliciously against Mike's shaft, the hotelier's middle and index fingers stroked his sac, still imprisoned by the fabric of his jeans.

Keep in it your pants.

The fingers of his other hand splayed over the back of the redhead's skull, groping for support. Mike moved his hips in small circles, pushing his length against Archie's hand. Another graze against his nipple. Another agonising brush of fingertip against bollocks. Blood pounded in Mike's brain. His hand hard and heavy on top of another man's, he dragged his cock along the length of Archie's palm. He dipped again, pushing the entire length up until the sensitive head impacted with the hotelier's forearm.

They stood there, in the middle of the night, in the middle of nowhere. They were the only two men in the world. Nothing else mattered. No one else mattered, except them and their need for release. Two sets of laboured breathing synched into one. Two bodies increased the speed of the grinding.

Mike clenched his teeth. He felt like a schoolboy again. Under his left hand, Archie's hair was soaked with sweat. Beneath his other hand, the man's knuckles were slick and rigid. And under all that, his cock was a thick length of aching iron against another man's palm.

Archie was biting his nipple now and Mike's shaft flexed violently. He inhaled sharply. At the root of his prick, a great numb heaviness clenched. Mike groaned. He'd postponed orgasm so often he doubted he'd ever manage to come again.

Then the hotelier's teeth almost met and Mike yelled. His knees gave way. He lunged forward, a sudden sharp clench in his balls focusing every nerve in his body between his legs. Into the hand against his cock.

Only Archie's solid footing prevented them both falling. Mike's hand tightened in the man's hair. He was vaguely aware that the hotelier was still humping his hipbone maniacally.

Seconds later, thighs cramping, his balls clenched again and he was yelling a second time, pumping warm spunk into his own underwear.

On the deck of the motor launch, the yell made Richard flinch. He leapt to his feet, grabbing his own binoculars from inside the wheel house before darting back out to peer into the darkness. He frowned. Nowhere near as powerful as McLeod's had been, and minus the nightsight facility, the instrument was worse than useless. He scanned, nonetheless, braced for another yell.

It didn't come. The only sound was the gentle slap of wave on hull as the motor launch bobbed peacefully under him. Rick lowered the binoculars, grabbed his torch and hurried from the boat. He had no real idea of the direction from which the sound had originated, but he knew he should check on the tents.

Drawing back the canvas flap, a quick glance told him everything was fine. Richard smiled at the two sleeping men: the tent was small and, although each sleeping bag had initially been laid out down the sloping sides of the structure, somehow Rajiv and Lionel had managed to roll together. Soft snores drifted up from the captain of the First Eleven's slightly parted lips. Curled on his side, his head resting on his colleague's chest, the Iraqi student's glossy black hair obliterated most of his face.

Richard sighed. Christ, the man was gorgeous. He'd never really thought about Rajiv sexually before. He never saw any of his students that way.

They were... students, after all. Okay, they were all well over the age of consent and fully grown men. Still, there was something about the teacher-pupil relationship which instinctively made Dr Rodgers hold back.

But now he stood there, shining the torch on the back of the tent, away from the sleeping faces and just looked at Rajiv Azad. For the first time, really.

The pact he and Mike had made hovered in his mind. Detached, anonymous sex. A quickie with a stranger. No strings, no emotional involvement. Just lust.

As he watched the rise and fall of the man's chest, Dr Rodgers became aware of a definite twitch in his groin. He frowned. It wouldn't be mere lust, with Rajiv. He knew the guy. He liked the guy. And that... complicated things. On top of which, he'd have to face him, next term, back in Oxford.

The beam of light wavered slightly, on the back of the tent. Richard switched off the torch and replaced it in his pocket with a shaking hand. Backing out of the flap, he wandered over to his and Mike's tent. Their empty tent.

Dr Rodgers sighed. His eyes flicked up to the illuminations he could just make out, further down the loch at Drumnadrochit. Lights were still on back in the Campbell Arms. Richard's stomach rumbled. He regretted he'd not gone with the rest of them and had a good meal – not to mention a drink. Falling to a crouch, he pushed the flap aside and crawled into the tent.

He knew all about lock-ins. Up here, miles from anywhere, Richard was aware the local constabulary would be few and far between and not averse themselves to an after-hours drink, courtesy of a friendly landlord.

Dr Rodgers fumbled for his rucksack, found it and unzipped a side compartment. Hauling out a packet of crisps and a banana, he shoved them in his pocket and made his way back down to the jetty. He could picture Mike now, ensconced in the Campbell Arms with half a dozen locals, knocking it back, laughing, chatting, the life and soul of the party the way he always was.

Richard peeled his banana and bit off a mouthful. He didn't feel resentful. Mike and he were two very different men. Finishing the banana, he placed the skin neatly to one side and started on the crisps. Maybe they would be better apart. What had once served to unite now only seemed to divide. He sat there, munching stale crisps and somehow knew Mike had been telling the truth, regarding his late arrival at the campsite. His partner was a bad liar. Rick could always tell when he'd been with another man and, despite the strong odour of musk which had risen from Mike's leather-clad body and his own irrational response to it, Rick instinctively knew it was Mike's own spunk he could smell.

Nothing wrong with a wank. Nothing at all. Like there was nothing wrong with enjoying an after-hours drink with the locals on what was going to be their only holiday, this year – and could well be their last vacation together.

He finished the crisps, looked back at the two small tents pitched a mere hundred yards away then beyond to the lighted windows of the Campbell Arms. Part of him wanted to take a wander up and join in. Another part knew they had work to do, and at least one of those in charge should get some sleep. Turning away from the hotel, Richard slid back the hatch and made his way downstairs to the small sleeping cabin. He undressed quickly, slipping his body between slightly musty-smelling sheets.

As soon as his head hit the pillow, the day's drive plus the stress of it all caught up with him. Minutes later, sleep pulled him from vague thoughts of the Campbell Arms and dragged him into unconsciousness.

On the beach on the other side of Loch Ness, Mike sighed as Archie Campbell's arms tightened around him. Beneath his legs, the sand was dry but cold. Inside his underpants, spunk crested his pubic hair and adhered it to his stomach.

'You okay?' The question brushed his ear, along with a half-kiss.

Mike moaned. Yes. His body was limp. Spent. His balls were loose and empty and, aside from the discomfort of the tug of receding cock against pubes, he felt wonderful.

... And no. He was a heel. A betraying, lying heel. Despite any amount of rationalising over the wording of it, Mike knew he'd broken his vow to Richard.

The knuckles of one broad hand rubbed his cheek. 'That was kind of interesting.' Archie chuckled.

Mike felt the soft laugher in the chest beneath his face. He wondered if the man had come. He wondered if he hadn't – and, if not, whether this in any way lessened the betrayal.

'Took me back to my youth, all that grinding.' Another chuckle.

Mike sighed. Whichever way you looked at it, he'd let Richard down. His partner was right: he couldn't keep it in his pants – not for a week. Not even for 24 hours.

Somewhere close by, an owl hooted. The sound pulled Mike from his self-reproach. Moving one arm from around Archie Campbell's waist he tried to sit up.

'Oh no you don't, pal!' The admonishment was soft. The grip which tightened around him was firm. 'You're gonna stay here till I decide I've had my fill of you.' Warm lips nuzzled his ear. One heavy thigh draped itself over his.

Mike inhaled sharply. His receding cock paused. And twitched.

'Ye like that, don't ya Mikey-boy?'

Professor St. Clair shuddered. The use of the semi-affectionate, semi-taunting name was doing things to his body. Or was it the tone? The unforced dominance in the low, Scottish voice? The note which said I'm in charge here, and I'll do with you whatever I want.

'Don't you?' The lips were moving to Mike's neck.

Blood fled from his brain, pumping downwards and swelling his cock again. Professor St. Clair's lips parted in a low groan. At any other time, in any other place, he would be putty in this man's hands. But not now. Not here.

'I think ye like to be held down, Mikey-boy. Held down and fucked.' The red-haired giant was moving now. Slowly but surely, he was slipping out from under Mike, still holding him but now more on top than beneath. His voice was still quiet. Still low. But the power was there. The assuredness. A confidence and natural sexual dominance which always turned Professor St. Clair's legs to jelly.

Instinctively, he reached up, his hands finding the man's shoulders. Mike curled his arms around Archie's neck.

'Fucked good and proper, eh son?'

His entire body trembled. No one had called him son in a very long time. Rough hands were moving too, travelling down over his sides... down to his arse. The mixture of arousal and a slight panic was a heady brew. Mike's feet were flat on the sand. He bore down, lifting his hips and feeling those broad hands slip under him.

The idea of being taken, here and now, by this virtual stranger in the middle of nowhere was doing things to his mind and his body. He was losing it. Seriously losing it.

Archie Campbell's mouth was at his throat now... then moving down the middle of Mike's chest, studiously avoiding his nipples despite Mike's best efforts to push them into his face.

The owl hooted again, closer this time, but Mike barely heard it over the pounding of blood in his brain. But he did hear it. And it went some way towards breaking the spell this man was casting over him. Marshalling every shred of strength, both physical and mental, Mike heaved himself free of his seducer and scrambled to his feet.

'I have to go.' He pushed his hard-on back behind the denim and winced, wrenching his zipper up over the thickening shaft. 'Sorry.'

'Hold on – I'll run you back.'

'It's okay – I'll walk.' Mike talked over the hotelier's offer, staggering back up the beach in what he hoped was the direction of the road.

'It's five miles – and it's dark.' Archie Campbell sounded most concerned.

'Honestly, it's fine... I like walking at night.' He just wanted out of there. Away from this man. Away from further temptation.

A distant, resigned sigh. 'Have it your own way. But remember to turn right not left, when you get back to the road. Otherwise you'll end up taking the long way back to the campsite.'

'Okay – thanks.' The man's instructions were distant. Mike was already grabbing the rock face, hauling himself up it at a speed no serious rock-climber would ever attempt.

Back on terra firma, he broke into a run, jogging up past Archie's Land Rover and on to the tarmac of the road surface. He paused. Right? Mike frowned. Every instinct told him to go left. But his brain was well fuddled. And the hotelier knew what he was talking about. Eyes acclimatising to the dark road, Mike turned to his right and began to trot along the grass verge.

Chapter Eleven

He was standing in a room somewhere... or maybe a cave. Indoors, anyway: he could hear the echo of his own lungs.

Richard blinked. Some hidden light source flooded the space, bathing what he could now see were stone walls in a rosy, almost molten glow. Everything was hazy, each sense sliding into another. He was vaguely aware of the sound of dripping water. The cold beneath his heels and toes was less vague. It told him his feet were bare. Richard glanced down at his body. And cringed. He was standing alone, totally naked. The beginnings of embarrassment tingled over his skin, then stopped abruptly. As he stared down at himself, it was like looking at someone else.

Two small but hard nipples poked through the thick mat of salt-and-pepper hair which covered his firm pecs and swept down over his stomach. Instinctively, Richard sucked in his gut – then noticed there was nothing to suck in. For some reason, the small paunch which usually made him grimace every time he caught a glimpse of himself in the bathroom mirror now looked not so pronounced. Richard narrowed his eyes. It was still there, but seemed to fit in with the rest of him a little better. Same for the grey in his pubes: in this light, it took on a silvery hue, glinting in the strange glow and looking more like the coat of a wolf than the sign of age Dr Rodgers usually interpreted it as.

It was easy to become obsessed with the minutiae of one's appearance. Youth was held up as ever-desirable, ever sought-after, ever to be chased – and ever, in Richard's case, remaining just out of reach.

The water dripped in the background, and seemed to be slowing. Richard continued to scrutinise his own body. At least he could still see his cock. He smiled at his own narcissism. Before he knew what he was doing, his hand was moving between his thighs to cup his bollocks. Lying on top of the soft hairy sac like some great sleeping snake, eight flaccid inches twitched against his fingers.

Dr Rodgers chuckled. Genetics had been kind to him. Okay, he didn't get much bigger hard, but his cock looked good soft, outlined in his jeans. As he stared at the thick length, his prick began to thicken further. Richard inhaled, feeling the member swell and flex against his knuckles. He grinned. Mike had always liked his cock – the usual size-queen tendencies aside. When they'd both been younger, Mike could spend hours after sex, lying between Richard's legs, his head on one thigh and just staring at it.

The grin slipped. He sighed at the memory. The memory of his fingers playing in Mike's hair. Mike's lips on his cock. Mike's tongue licking the spunk from around the glans under the heavy hood of foreskin. The way Mike's mouth felt, warm and wet on his cock, licking around his balls, then on Richard's lips as he hauled his lover up on top of him and kissed him. Tasting his own body in another man's mouth. Holding Mike against him... then fucking him all over again.

'Dr Rodgers? Sir?'

Rick's cock flexed, part in response to the reminiscence, part in surprise at the voice which drifted across the space. His eyes shot up from the self-admiration. And widened.

Ten yards away, Rajiv Azad was walking towards him. Also naked. Richard stared at the slender man's glossy skin. Rajiv was almost hairless. His smooth chest shone in the rosy light, large brown nipples gleaming in the ethereal glow. Dr Rodgers swallowed hard. He tried to speak, and couldn't. His mind tried to make sense of what he was seeing, and failed.

The hair on Rajiv's head was longer. It fell over his chiselled features in one great shining black veil and swayed, almost in slow motion, as Rajiv closed the distance between them. Richard watched the play of muscle across the man's taut stomach. He took in the ripple of sinew and tendon on his slender thighs as the guy moved, and the way Rajiv's small, circumcised cock bounced with each step.

Dr Rodgers's own prick was stiffening further. He could feel his balls fill, feel the heavy sac tighten and swell against his palm.

In one smooth movement, Rajiv turned. As he walked away, Richard's gaze narrowed on the man's firm, well-rounded buttocks. A sound fought its way from his tight throat. Dr Rodgers moaned, seeing light glance off twin, olive-coloured mounds. Deep dimples twinkled in Rajiv's arse-cheeks, deepening with each step he took. And between the man's thighs, surprisingly large bollocks were just visible.

'Hey, doc! All right?'

Richard's head swivelled at the Newcastle accent. He goggled. Also naked, his pale flesh glistening beneath a mass of brown hair, Lionel Banks winked across the space at him. Rick's cock bucked violently. Where Rajiv was slender and slight, his colleague was the opposite. Six foot three of stocky, well-bulked rugby-playing masculinity strode towards him, broad shoulders shimmering in the eerie light, the deltoids and biceps a great mass of moulded muscle. Lionel's skin was alabaster. Blue veins marbled the solid flesh on his upper arms, disappearing beneath the thick coat of hair which covered his forearms like the pelt of some animal.

Dr Rodgers's eyes were just about to move to Lionel's stomach and crotch when a third voice echoed across the vast space.

'Richard? It's been a while, old chap.'

His gaze dragged from a rear view of hairy arse-cheeks as Lionel swerved to stand beside the still-smiling Rajiv, Rick inhaled sharply and managed to speak. 'Gregory? Greg?'

His best friend from three decades ago – the boy on whom he'd had a seriously gut-wrenching crush for two years – grinned at him. 'Yeah, been a real while, old sport.'

Richard's stomach churned. The head of his cock brushed the inside of his thigh, now well on its way to full erection.

'You never did get around to telling me how you felt, did you?'

His stomach flipped over. 'You knew?'

'Course I knew.'

The man standing yards away was well into his 40s, but the roguish smile was the same. As was the voice. Despite the fact he'd last seen Gregory Blane when they were both 17, Richard would have recognised him anywhere.

'Question is, did you know how I felt?' Greg rubbed his hands together and strode over. 'What a pair, eh? You wanted me, I wanted you – hell, I used to wank about what it would feel like to touch your knob, old sport.'

Dr Rodgers's mouth was dry. The slick head of his cock tickled its way up the inside of his thigh towards his belly.

'But neither of us said anything. Too shy, too inhibited – too sure what we felt was wrong, eh? Wrong – and unreciprocated.'

Rick's balls clenched against the palm of his sweating hand. His other hand reached out across the distance. And the years. 'Greg, I –'

'And now it's too late, old man.'

'No!' His voice resounded in the large, rosy space. The years swept away and his body was responding to the same thing it had always yearned for in Greg Blane. 'It's not too late – it's never too late.'

'Ah, but it is, Ricky.'

Dr Rodgers tried to move forward. His feet were rooted to the spot. 'Richard?'

'Good to see you again, Mr Rodgers.'

'You can't park here I'm afraid, sir.'

As he continued to stare at Gregory Blane's naked body, Richard was vaguely aware of a variety of other figures entering the space. Everyone from a fellow lecturer he had half-fancied during his first teaching post to a traffic warden who had once made his balls sweat. All slowly joined Lionel and Rajiv.

All except Greg.

Something tight and hot burned at the back of Richard's eyes. He'd always remembered Greg: along with Jix Tyson, the guy had been the source of much torment during his teenage years. But now? Now, to have the chance of doing what he'd longed to do back then? To have Greg here, with him again?

Richard smiled. 'Come here, you daft bugger!' He released his balls and stretched both arms out towards the figure of his best friend. 'What have you been up to?' Now curving up away from his stomach, just under nine inches of swollen, aching need flexed in the rosy light. 'What are you doing, these days?' A second chance – a second chance to have the only man to turn him on as much as Mike had. 'I want to know it all – I want to hold you and fuck you and –'

'It's too late, Ricky old son.'

In seconds, the man had moved to just in front of Richard. He could almost touch him. And when Greg Blane did exactly that, his strong hand moving to Richard's shoulder, his cock shuddered. 'It's not – it's not too late.'

'Too late... too... late... too late...'

The words became a chant, soaring up from the assembly of men.

Tears prickled behind Richard's eyes. A newspaper cutting his mother had sent him, ten years back, suddenly sprang into his mind. She kept him up to date with any news of his old friends. But this particular cutting had saddened Rick. He'd half-intended to return to Scarborough for Greg's funeral. Bur something had come up: work, he supposed. And now he could feel the weight of Greg Blane's hand on his shoulder, feel his balls clench abruptly and...

His eyes shot open just as his arse left the bed. The force of the orgasm took the breath form his body. 'Greg!' Richard roared into the dawn light of the motor launch's small cabin. His cock shuddered against his curled fist a second time. Then warm, thick spunk was coating his own hand. He gasped, both aroused and appalled by the intensity of the dream.

His arse left the bed and he shot another load, his fingers slippery and sticky with the viscous fluid. He'd not had a wet dream for 20-odd years. He barely wanked, these days, and when he did it was a perfunctory chore.

Rick's head was full of men. And chances lost. Opportunities missed.

The Latin phrase *carpe diem* shimmered briefly in his mind. His balls clenched, working steadily to force another slitful of thick cum over his curled fist. And as his bollocks emptied and his fat cock soft-ened, his resolve hardened. Even as his body trembled with the waves of one orgasm, he wanted another.

He wanted a man. Any man. And he wanted him now.

Tearing back sweat-soaked covers, Richard leapt from the bed. His tweed trousers lay in a heap on the floor of the cabin. He grabbed them, struggled into the pants. The motor launch swayed violently. Dr Rodgers ignored it, pushing his still-dripping cock back behind the zip and thundering up the steps on to deck.

The sight which met his eyes as he emerged into dawn light was not what he expected. Floating free on pale pink water, a mirror of the brightening sky overhead, the vessel beneath his bare feet dipped and swayed again. Richard blinked, gripping the rail and staring back to-wards the jetty, which he could now only just make out in the dis-tance. His fingers tightened. What the – ?

A gentle swell moved beneath the now adrift motor launch. Richard frowned. He must have forgotten to secure the mooring ropes, the previous evening. Obviously, sometime during the hours of dark-ness the boat had moved away from the pier and was now drifting steadily towards... He turned his head. The looming, ominous outline of Boleskin was just visible, behind the tips of rosy-tinged trees.

Richard sighed. Idiot! What an idiot! He considered himself a semi-experienced sailor. And no sailor worth the title would fail to check his vessel's moorings before turning in for the night. Still berating him-self, Dr Rodgers glanced at his watch. Five-sixteen a.m.

Ducking into the wheel house, he pushed the starter button. There was still plenty of time to get back to the pier and pick up whoever was taking the first shift.

Nothing happened. Rick removed his finger and depressed the start a second time. Still nothing, not even a splutter. He glanced over the basic set of instruments: the needle was stuck at the bottom of the wedge of red at the extreme left hand side of the fuel gauge.

He was out of diesel.

Rick slumped back against the wheel house wall. So intent had he been on checking the echo-sounding equipment, he'd overlooked the most basic of requirements. Mike would rib him mercilessly about this. Pushing aside a cringe of embarrassment, Richard left the wheel house and went in search of the spare can of diesel.

On deck, a cool breeze ruffled the hair on his chest as he rifled in lockers. He found flares, lifejackets, endless lengths of rope, even what looked like a bullhorn, but not the one item he was looking for. Where the hell was it?

Straightening up in frustration, Richard stared back towards the jetty's distant outline. As he did so, his eyes fell to the beautiful, pink-tinged surface of the water – and another, less natural pinkness.

Between the motor launch's stern and the tip of the pier, an oily, telltale iridescence was just visible. Floating in the middle of the loch, no doubt having drifted on the same currents which had brought Richard to this spot, was an empty can of diesel.

Dr Rodgers swallowed hard.

And was it just his imagination, or did the launch seem to be sitting lower in the water than it should be?

He'd walked in the wrong direction. Legs aching, feet sore from endless hours tramping the road, Mike scowled. By the time he'd realised his mistake and turned back, he'd probably have been better keeping straight on.

Professor St. Clair trudged onwards. At least it was getting lighter. He'd passed Fort Augustus for the second time, two hours ago, had debated hammering on the door of the monastery and demanding someone give him a lift back to Drumnadrochit. But good manners had got the better of his irritation. After all, it was his own fault. He should have waited and allowed Archie to drive him to the campsite. Moreover, he should have listened to the man's shouted directions. But he'd been too worked up to hang around that beach, too worked up to listen to what the man had said. Still, he'd been pretty sure the hotelier had urged him to turn right, not left, when he reached the main road.

Mike listened to the sound of his boots on tarmac and trudged on. No cars had passed, during what had to be a five-hour trek. He glanced at his watch: twenty to six. Yeah, five hours.

Professor St. Clair stuck his hands into his pockets and picked up the pace. Ahead, he could just see the outline of Castle Urquhart, peeking round at him from beyond the next bend. His eyes moved to the water. No cars. No people.

And no sign of any bloody monster!

Mike sighed. It was beautiful, though. At this time of day, the loch was at its most attractive. The huge expanse of water glistened in the dawn light, stained the palest of reds by the rising sun. His frown softened into a slight smile. Maybe it had been worth it. Maybe that furtive session on the beach with Archie Campbell, his own panic and insistence on walking home had all been worthwhile just to see Loch Ness as few others ever saw it, still and vast and awe-inspiring.

Mike's eyes remained on the great body of water as he walked. His mind turned to Richard and he winced. He'd get hell for this. He'd be accused of all sorts. Inside his jeans, still scummy from the encounter on the beach, his cock betrayed him and stirred at the memory. But he hadn't meant for it to happen. And staying out all night had been the least of his intentions, when he'd accepted the red-haired hotelier's offer of a tour.

Something burst into the sky, just beyond a fringe of pine trees. Mike stopped and stared. Then it was gone – if indeed it had ever been there at all. Mike began to walk again. A trick of the light? The sun reflecting on the wings of an early seagull?

His mind turned to the forthcoming day, and the fact he'd had no sleep. Maybe Rick's postgrads could take the first shift sweeping the loch. Mike's stomach rumbled. Despite the previous evening's hearty meal at the Campbell Arms, he was hungry again. Probably all the fresh air, or the walk. He couldn't remember the last time he'd had so much exercise. Tiredness simmered just behind his eyelids. He just wanted to sleep. Eat first, maybe, then crawl into his tent and –

A sound like a gunshot pulled his eyes towards the loch, just in time to see the second rocket soar above the pine trees and explode into the sky. There was no mistaking it this time. Someone was on the water, some vessel. And that was undoubtedly a distress flare.

Jogging now, Mike veered off the road and plunged into the trees. He had no idea why any boat would be out this early. He had no real idea what help he could be. But there was always the chance the signal would attract attention from the village, and maybe he could scrounge a lift with whoever responded to the distress flare.

Clearing the trees, Mike scrambled down into a rocky cove and stared. Three hundred yards or so out from the shore, a small motor launch bobbed silently, buffeted by gentle waves. Mike listened for engine sounds, but heard none. He peered, shading his eyes from the rising sun. He didn't recognise the vessel itself. But there was no mistaking the bare-chested, bearded man who stood on the deck, waving his arms.

Another flare launched itself into the sky. Mike cupped his hands around his mouth. 'Rick!'

The name echoed around him. A flock of roosting birds soared into the air, from the trees behind.

Mike shouted again. 'Rick! What are you doing?' The beginnings of annoyance tightened his stomach. What on earth had possessed the man to start a sweep of the loch this early? Why the distress flares? And why was his partner half-naked? Staring at the drifting boat, Mike watched as the figure fell to a crouch, then stood up again:

'Mike?' Amplified by what seemed to be some sort of loudspeaker device, his name soared across the water to him. 'I'm out of diesel! I can't move her. And I think I'm sinking!'

Further startled, a doe and her fawn leapt from nearby bushes and fled along the shoreline mere feet in front of Professor St. Clair.

'Swim for it! Abandon ship!' Mike roared instructions at the man on the deck.

'I can't – I can't swim. You know that!' The answer was tinged with growing panic.

Without a second thought, Mike tore off his boots and socks. Jeans and shirt came next. Then he was wading into the loch, barely aware of the icy water which lapped around his knees, his thighs, and then splashed over his chest as he threw himself forward and began to swim out towards the slowly sinking vessel.

Chapter Twelve

Relief bathed Richard's body in a clammy sweat. Standing on the sloping deck of the motor launch, he watched Mike plough through the water towards him and ignited another flare.

Now with a lifejacket strapped to his chest, he barely heard the distress signal as it exploded overhead. Richard was still trying to work out what on earth had happened to the boat. First he'd apparently omitted to secure it properly. Then he'd somehow run out of diesel. And now he was sinking.

Less than 50 yards away now, Mike's strong arms scythed through the loch's still waters, closing the gap between them.

Rick shivered in the early morning air. He'd no idea what was causing the boat to list. He didn't even know where to start looking. Instinctively, his eyes moved to the dark outline of Boleskin, squatting behind the pine trees, a great, immovable presence.

He'd half hoped that whoever had been burning that light there the previous evening might have seen his distress flares. Maybe some passing motorist or early-morning hiker. The last person he'd expected to come to his rescue was Mike. Not that he wasn't grateful, but –

'I can see it!' A breathless cry of triumph interrupted Richard's thought processes. A pair of broad hands clenched the side of the boat. 'There's a gash here – just below the water line. Give me something to... stuff into it.'

Rick leant over, peering down at where Mike was now treading water and craning his head. 'What sort of something?' The very sight of the dark, heaving water made him straighten back up again swiftly.

'Christ, I don't know – anything, man!' Irritation tingled Mike's shivering voice. 'Your shirt'll do.'

'Okay – hold on.' Glad for an excuse not to look at the water, Rick raced downstairs, found his shirt and grabbed it.

Minutes later, Mike was pushing the sodden garment into the hole in the boat. 'Now get off her!' Minutes after that, eyes squeezed tightly shut, Richard jumped over the side into icy arms.

The shock of the sheer temperature of the loch pushed any fears of drowning from his mind: hypothermia was a far more probable cause of death. Limp and quivering, his head resting on Mike's chest, he allowed the stronger man to tow him to the shore. When his feet finally touched bottom, his legs gave way. Collapsing against his partner, Rick began to shake uncontrollably.

'What the hell were you doing out there?' Mike's arms tightened around him, but the voice was scolding. Richard could only shake in response. 'You might have been killed! You might have drowned! Why did you decide to sleep on the boat, instead of in the tent?' Rick's teeth chattered. He felt chilled to the bone – and not only by the water. 'At least we've stabilised her. But it was only luck I was around at all. I shudder to think what might have happened, had I not been.'

'What are you doing here anyway?' Jaw clenched, Rick spat out the words. He knew it was irrational. He knew thousands of pounds worth of equipment were, at the moment, perilously close to meeting a watery end on a sinking boat. He knew he would not have had the courage to swim to shore had Mike not been there. But the only possible explanation for his partner's presence still took precedence in his addled brain. It did seem an odd time to cruise, but he could think of no other reason for Mike to be here at six o'clock in the morning.

'Never mind that.' The arms tightened around him. The tone of voice changed. 'Are you okay, baby? When I think what might have…'

'I'm fine.' Richard hauled himself free of the embrace. His legs were still wobbly. Sinking down on to a nearby rock, he began to tear at the lifejacket with shaking hands. 'Was he good?'

'Was who good?'

'Whoever you were out here with.' His fingers wouldn't work. He tried to pull at the lifejacket's ties but with little success.

'I wasn't out here with anyone.'

'Ahoy there!'

They both turned to the loch.

A long white wake tailed back to Drumnadrochit. At its head, from behind the wheel of a snazzy-looking red speedboat, a tall red-haired figure waved to them. 'Do you need assistance?'

Mike cupped his hands around his mouth. 'Can you give us a tow, Archie?'

Rick frowned. Archie? He watched the speedboat slow, then curve round to draw up alongside the listing motor launch.

'No problem, Mike.'

Mike? Rick fought a scowl. He watched this brawny local switch off the speedboat's engine, grab a coil of rope and nimbly bound from his own vessel on to the listing motor launch. In seconds he had secured the rope and was leaping back aboard the speedboat.

'I'll have her back and beached in no time, Mike. What happened?'

'Not sure – think maybe Captain Ahab here drifted on to some rocks. There's a small gash, port side, just below the water line.'

A laugh from the speedboat.

Richard bristled – less at the joke at his expense than at the obvious intimacy between the two men.

'Okay, well I'll get Hamish and some of the lads to have a look at her, see if we can't patch the old girl up a bit. Is yer equipment okay?'

'Should be.'

'I'll make sure it gets loaded off first, eh?'

'Cheers, Archie.'

'And I'll send Morag round in the Land Rover to fetch the two of you back.'

Richard stood there, shivering and furious. He listened to the conversation continue around him, then watched as the roar of a powerful engine signalled the departure of two boats, one towed by the other, back across the loch.

'You'll catch cold.'

The voice was very close. Richard flinched as Mike, still only in soaking underpants himself, draped a thick plaid shirt around his shoulders. Pique and hurt made him shrug it off. 'I'm fine. I'll see you back at camp.' Tweed trousers hanging in heavy, water-soaked folds around his legs, barefoot and with the lifejacket still semi-strapped to his chest, Dr Rodgers set off in the vague direction of the road.

Half an hour later, Mike was sitting, wrapped in a tartan blanket, in the passenger seat of the Land Rover.

'Trouble in paradise, Professor?' At his side, Morag Campbell's semi-amused eyes brushed his body for the tenth time. Mike studiously ignored her. They'd passed Richard, stomping along the side of the road ten minutes ago. They'd stopped. Morag had offered him a lift, Richard had refused. Mike had pleaded with him, Rick had refused a second time. He'd begged; Rick had scowled. Finally losing patience, Mike had told him not to be an idiot and ordered Richard into the Land Rover. Richard had crossed to the other side of the road and stomped on.

Apart from leaping from the car and forcibly bundling the man into the back, Mike didn't see what else he could do.

'Next time my husband fucks you, I think I'd like to watch.'

Mike started. His head spun round to stare at the calm, unruffled source of the words.

Morag Campbell was smiling, her eyes still training on the road in front. 'Archie likes the open air for his nocturnal shags, but there's nothing wrong with our bedroom. More comfy for ye both. For all three of us.'

Mike's jaw dropped. The woman's bluntness was most unsettling.

'Unless ye have any objections to performing for me, Professor, of course.'

'No, no...' He finally managed to say something. Sitting there, less than a foot from this striking, blasé woman, wrapped in a blanket and dressed only in his underpants, Mike's body began to respond. He'd never considered himself bisexual. Not really – although he'd had the odd relationship with women, in the past. It had been years, though.

'Good.' Morag's Campbell's voice was still low, her tone unnervingly even.

Mike was appalled to find himself blushing. He liked strong women – always had. He admired the way they ran their lives. The academic environment was very competitive and tough for everyone. Women were no exception, and Mike was not unaware of a certain chauvinism – not to say misogyny – amongst many of his colleagues. He, on the other hand, had only the greatest respect for any female who managed to claw her way up the academic ladder. He'd even harboured the odd lustful feeling, from time to time, prompted by a mixture of respect and awe. But Morag Campbell was no steely, ambitious professional. She ran a hotel, for God's sake!

'Are ye a good fuck, Professor?'

The blush spread from his face, down over his throat under the tartan blanket. Mike's skin itched against the rough plaid as he tried desperately to phrase a response to the question.

Morag laughed softly. 'Archie will tell me everything, ye know.'

The idea of this striking couple, lying in bed discussing him was having a strange effect on Mike's chilled body. He was an object. Something to be talked about, not to.

Or maybe it was the way she continued to call him Professor, in that slightly mocking way. Or the fact her eyes remained trained on the road in front, despite the intimate topic of their conversation.

'So ye might as well tell me your side.'

Face scarlet, Mike stared at her handsome profile. Handsome was the best word for it. No way could Morag Campbell ever be considered pretty. Her features were strong, her hair was short, her skin roughened by working outdoors. Heightened colour just below her angular cheekbones gave her a fresh-faced, almost innocent look – despite the fact she had to be at least 40, and despite the far from naive words which fell from a large, generous mouth.

Mike swallowed hard. Morag Campbell was anything but mannish in appearance. The way her breasts pushed at the front of her plaid shirt told him that. But there was definitely something masculine in her attitude.

'Not shy, are we?'

Mike flinched. Perhaps dominant was a more accurate way to describe her...

Beneath the tartan blanket, his previously cold body was now glowing. His cock stretched, the sensitive head – sensitised further from the action of Archie's hand, seven hours earlier – thrusting upwards to graze the inside of the rough plaid.

And the dominant in this woman addressed the submissive in him. He answered it. His body responded to it.

'Professor St. Clair –'

Although the voice was still low, still calm, the slightest hint of a warning note sent shivers of arousal over Mike's sore balls. 'We didn't do much.' The words came fast, tumbling from his mouth in their urgency to placate this woman. 'I came, but I don't think Archie did.' His voice was tight: tighter than the knot of muscle which twisted in the pit of his stomach.

'Ah.' Morag sounded vaguely disappointed. 'Ye'd have liked it if Archie had come, eh Professor?'

Mike stifled a moan of consensus. His one regret – despite the fact that Richard seemed to know that something had gone on, last night – was that Archie hadn't achieved orgasm.

'There's something about a man's spunk.' Morag read his mind. 'I never feel like I've really had sex if my partner doesn't shoot his load.'

Mike tried to bite back another moan. And failed. She laughed softly. 'That moment of abandon. That brief loss of all control, when he is at one with his body. He has no mind. No thought. Totally focused.'

Mike squirmed, aware he was getting dangerously near the point of no return. The waistband of his underpants dug in across his swelling shaft.

'Maybe it's the act of coming. Or maybe the cum itself. The feel of it, in yer hand, after ye've wanked him off.'

Mike shuddered. Part of him wanted the journey to be over. He wanted to be back at the jetty when this woman's husband hauled the motor launch on to the beach. He wanted to check the damage and help with the repairs.

'There's something about a man inside you... the way ye can feel him there, for hours afterwards... feel his slime ooze out of you and grow cold and sticky on yer thighs.'

Another part of him was lost – unable to do anything but sit here and listen. Morag Campbell's hands never left the wheel. Her eyes remained trained on the road ahead. But Mike knew he was being seduced – as surely as if she'd reached into his damp underpants and hauled out his hard cock.

'But it's the taste I like best, I'd have to admit.'

Mike's shaft flexed. Heat from the blush now drenched his entire body. He gripped the edges of the tartan blanket in sweating fists, unable hardly to bear its touch against his skin but unable to let go either.

'The raw, salty flavour of it, when his cock shudders in yer mouth.'

A tiny tear of pre-cum wept from his slit. Just beyond Morag Campbell's semi-amused face, beyond the Land Rover, Mike was vaguely aware of a Post Office van overtaking them and speeding on round towards Drumnadrochit. But only vaguely. He licked his lips, running his tongue over the dry tight surface. He could almost taste salt there, but knew it had more to do with the briny waters of the loch than any man.

'Aye, there's nothing quite like it, eh Professor?'

A tiny whimper resounded deep in the back of Mike's throat. Beneath his thighs, vibrations from the car's engine trembled up into his balls. His mind was filled with Morag's low, teasing voice. And his cock was a solid rod of quivering need, bisected by the waistband of his sodden underpants.

'Take them off, Professor.'

Again, the woman read his mind. Mike didn't need to be told twice. In seconds, the tartan blanket was slipping from his broad shoulders and shaking hands were clawing at the wet fabric. He brushed his shaft in his haste to be rid of the soaking covering. As he did so, shivers of longing clenched his balls. This time the whimper escaped his mouth.

Leaning back, Mike arched his back and raised his arse from the passenger seat. The tartan blanket fell from around his chest. His knees came up as he dragged his underpants down over his thighs and kicked his feet free.

'Good boy.'

Mike's cock flexed. Not an object – a dog, an animal. Fit to do only the bidding of its master… He blinked rapidly, his eyes flicking between Morag Campbell's calm face and the mounds of her breasts… Or mistress. A dog whose sole purpose in life was to serve whoever owned it.

The tartan blanket had slipped down and now hung around his hips in folds. He could feel the head of his erect cock brush just below his navel. Between parted thighs, his balls were sweating. And his arsehole clenched and relaxed by turns as he ground down against the warm leather seat.

'Open the glove compartment, Professor.'

At one level, the instruction startled. On another, more profound plane Mike knew he was hers to command. With only the slightest of hesitations one shaking hand gripped the small handle opposite him and pulled.

'What do you see there, Professor?'

Mike moaned. His sphincter clenched violently. He saw the objects but had lost the power of speech.

'Professor?'

The warning tone in her voice, that slight hint of disapproval drenched his tired body in a clammy sweat. 'Um…' He cleared his throat. 'Condoms, a butt-plug, a… um, length of leather thonging, lube.' Even saying the words was an effort. Mike's voice was almost a whisper. This was the stuff of his darkest nightmares, things he'd never told anyone – not even Richard.

Mike had spent years dressing up his casual sexual encounters with rough trade as just that: casual, unimportant, meaningless. Whereas in reality, he knew they gave him the opportunity to indulge a part of himself which rarely got expression, either in his day-to-day professional existence or even his relationship with Rick.

'Take the thonging and tie it around the base of your prick, Professor.'

Heart hammering, mouth dry, Mike did as he was told. The slim length of leather was worn and supple with use. The sweat from his hands dampened it, causing it to stretch as he hurriedly bound the sliver of black hide around the root of his curving shaft. The action made his cock flex and jerk.

'Good boy.'

Morag's low words of praise made his balls twist in their hairy sac.

'Now loop it around yer prick – good and tight, mind.'

He did as he was told, criss-crossing the length of leather up his shaft. His face was scarlet. His entire body blushed. Mike cringed at the thought someone might see him. For only the second time he risked a glance beyond the Land Rover's windscreen and was surprised to see hills and greenery where before he'd seen the loch.

Where were they? Where the hell was she taking him?

'That's it, Professor.'

Mike flinched and looked away. He was well aware of the direction in which all this was leading, where Morag Campbell's low, measured instructions were guiding him.

And he couldn't have stopped if he'd wanted to.

'Now take the plug and the lube.'

She didn't use his name, this time. He had no name. He was nothing. A collection of body parts with needs, at best. But needs which concerned him little, now.

Mike reached forward. His fingers grasped the fat, wedge-shaped butt-plug then scrabbled for an old, almost flat tube of KY which had obviously seen better days. His entire being was focused on her voice, her commands. And pleasing her.

'Grease it.'

The plug slipped from his hand, coming to rest on the seat between Mike's parted thighs. He struggled with the top of the KY tube. A mixture of rust, congealed lube and other matter crusted the thread of the screw top. Add to that the fact his fingers were so slippy and sweaty he could have lubed himself up with them alone, and Mike

Jack Dickson

was faced with a task of Herculean proportions.

'Come on, come on.'

Although her voice was still ominously quiet, the slightest of irritated finger taps on the steering wheel jolted him into action. Mike wrenched the top off the rusty tube and grabbed the plug. In one surprisingly smooth movement he'd squeezed the near flat length of metal and coated the solid plastic wedge of the butt-plug thoroughly.

'Now get it up your hole.'

His heart thudded against his ribs. Sweat poured from his hairline, dripping down to gather in his thick brows before spilling into his eyes and making them sting painfully.

He was in the front seat of a car, for Christ's sake! There was no room. How on earth was he going to – ?

'Shall I draw into the side of the road and do it for you?'

The mere suggestion of her hands anywhere near his body drenched Mike's skin in a second clammy film and made his sphincter clench violently. His hand shook. Sweat stung his eyes. His cock was as hard with the wife as it had been with the husband. A different hardness – but hardness nonetheless.

Mike's trembling fingers tightened around the butt-plug. The lube slipped from his other hand. Easing forward, he braced one arm against the Land Rover's dashboard. With stinging eyes he glanced briefly beyond the windscreen. Apart from a few sheep, the road ahead was devoid of life. He kept his eyes there, as he leant forward further and raised his arse from the seat, because he couldn't look at her.

Couldn't look at this stranger. This woman who seemed to be able to read his mind. This woman who, without as much as glancing at him let alone touching him, had reached down into his very soul and found his deepest, darkest secrets.

Mike's knees contacted with the bottom of the dashboard. Legs bent, his body cramped and contorted, he guided the tip of the butt-plug to where she wanted it to be.

Because she was who mattered –

His sphincter tightened at the touch of rigid, slippery plastic.

140

– he was nothing –

Mike's lips parted. He breathed though his mouth, sucking shallow gulps of air into his heaving lungs.

– less than nothing.

Gripping the plug with quivering fingers, eyes narrowed and trained on the road ahead, he pushed.

His body resisted. His sphincter trembled, fighting the invasion. A mixture of nerves, over-tiredness, eagerness to please and intense arousal rendered every muscle in his body iron – including his cock, which Mike could feel hard and damp against his stomach.

As he hovered there, he became aware of the Land Rover slowing. Then a hand placed itself on his head and a low, calm voice drifted into his ears:

'Do it for me, Professor.'

His whole body seemed to give way under the encouragement. In one smooth, synchronised movement his arselips relaxed to accept the intruder and his balls knitted together.

A wild, feral noise tore loose from his throat. His cock flexed and, despite the leather thong around his cock, a shower of thick cum flew from his slit. Head lolling against his outstretched arm, Mike felt the warm spunk splatter his own face. His pushed against her hand, which returned the motion, thrusting Mike back on to the plug and burying it more deeply in his arse.

In the background, he was vaguely aware of the Land Rover slowing further. Then stopping completely. Then the hand left his head. Morag Campbell switched off the engine.

Head still reeling from the orgasm, Mike flinched as his own underpants hit his face:

'Put them on – and get out.' The voice was harsh. Unfeeling. 'Keep the plug there and the thonging in place until Archie tells you otherwise.'

Mike's body was ablaze with contradictory emotions. But he managed to struggle his way into the still-damp briefs, his arse muscles clenched tight around the plug. Head lowered, part in shame, part in awe, he felt her hands roughly arrange the tartan blanket once more around his shoulders. Cock still shuddering, his own spunk warm and wet on his right cheek, he grasped at the fabric, wanting to crawl into a hole.

'Now go and get cleaned up, Professor.'

Before he could make much sense of what he was feeling, a plaid-covered arm reached past him and opened the passenger door.

Mike was pushed from the vehicle. He landed on soft grass.

And found himself back at their campsite.

Chapter Thirteen

'Ye'll never repair that, son!' On the shore, Richard stood with Rajiv and Lionel, watching the ancient figure in the gum boots and oiled jersey who sat astride the motor launch's beached hull. 'Not in anything under a week. I don't have the equipment here. Not for a job this size.'

Around them, a variety of locals – including the striking, burly redhead who'd towed the launch back – hummed and nodded sagely.

Richard followed Hamish's gnarled finger to the long gash in the side of the vessel. For once the heavy insurance the university had to pay on these trips would come in handy – but it didn't solve their present problem. 'Can't you just patch her up a bit?' Five days left of a field trip, £10,000 of echo-sounding equipment and no boat.

'Can't do that, son.' The grey head shook slowly. 'And don't even think of trying to get her back into the water. As harbour master, it would be more than my job's worth to let you gentlemen go out in an unseaworthy vessel.' With surprising nimbleness, the near-80-year-old swung one leg over the hull and slid down from the boat, landing on the sand in front of them. 'Sorry.'

He wondered at the employment laws up here, which permitted anyone that old to hold any sort of formal post. 'Well,' Richard looked around at the assembled locals, 'can anyone rent me a boat? Five days – I'll pay the going rate, plus a bonus at the end.'

As one, the group of heads shook slowly. The red-haired one seemed to speak for them all: 'Any other time of the year that would

143

be no problem, Dr Rodgers.' Richard bit back a scowl for the man with whom he knew Mike had spent last night. 'But this is high season. All our vessels are contracted out to the tourists and the water sports enthusiasts.' As if on cue, what looked like a small fishing skip, packed to the gunnels with beaming tourists, sailed past. In the distance, the arc of a water-skier churned the dark loch waters white with spume.

Richard sighed.

'Sorry, Dr Rodgers. Looks like your field trip will have to be cancelled. And you came all this way, too.' The hotelier's face was sombre. Mumbles of commiseration trickled from the assembled locals. 'Tell you what, though.' Archie's deep voice brightened abruptly and his demeanour changed. He rubbed his hands together and beamed. 'Why don't you and your party move your stuff up to the Campbell Arms and spend the rest of your stay as our guests?'

No boats available, yet this man had rooms to spare, high season or no high season?

'Have a wee holiday. Enjoy some Highland hospitality.'

'Aye, do that son.' Old Hamish's voice joined in.

'Aye – get in a bit of fishing.'

'Drive up to Inverness, maybe.'

All of a sudden, the previously surly group of monosyllabic locals were all smiling and nodding encouragingly at him.

Richard narrowed his eyes. First he forgets to secure the mooring ropes. Then the motor launch runs out of petrol. The spare can mysteriously falls over the side. On top of it all, he somehow managed to hit something, when he was drifting on the loch. And now, what Rick was sure had only been minor damage when Mike had wadded up his shirt and shoved it into the hole was somehow beyond repair?

Something in all this was smelling a little fishy. He looked at Archie Campbell. 'Have you any idea what might have caused the damage?'

'Rocks, floating tree-trunks.' Old Hamish answered his question. 'Or, maybe' – the tone became slightly mocking – 'a swimming stag snagged your aft side with his horns, son.'

The locals chuckled. Dr Rodgers stared blankly. Whatever the joke was, it went over his head.

Archie Campbell moved forward. One broad hand laid itself on Richard's shoulder. 'What do you say we give you a hand with yer echo-sounding equipment, eh?' He nodded to the pie of tarpaulin-covered hi-tech apparatus which sat on the jetty. 'Ye can store it up at the hotel. Then we can move you gentlemen up there too.'

'Our field-survey will be going ahead, Mr Campbell.' Richard straightened his shoulders and glanced at his two companions, both of whom had remained silent during the exchange.

Rajiv Azad nodded solemnly. 'We will find a way, sir.'

Lionel Banks looked from the damaged motor launch to Richard then back again. 'I suppose we could do some of the research from the shore of the loch, rather than the water itself.'

Rick smiled, glad of the support. 'That's settled.' He glanced at the hotelier. 'Now, Mr Campbell, how much do I owe you for the tow?'

'Call me Archie, Dr Rodgers – and there's no charge.'

'I insist, Mr Campbell.' Richard's mouth hardened. Maybe Mike thought nothing of fraternising with the locals, but at least one member of their party was going to keep this on a professional footing. Plus there was still something vaguely disturbing about all that had happened the previous evening – the least of which was that most unsettling dream.

'Ye can buy us all a drink if ye like, son!' Old Hamish cackled. 'And now's as good a time as any.'

The locals laughed. Archie Campbell beamed.

Richard frowned. 'Later, then.' The night on the boat, not to mention his impromptu swim, necessitated a shower first. 'Can I leave you two in charge of the gear?' He struggled out of the lifejacket, then looked from Lionel and Rajiv to the tarpaulin-covered mound.

'Sure, doc!'

'Most certainly, sir.'

'Ach why don't ye come on up to the hotel and have a proper wash, Richard?'

Rick bristled at the man's over-familiarity. 'The campsite facilities will do me well enough, Mr Campbell. Now, if you'll excuse me.' And with that he strode through the semicircle of locals and made his way across to their tent.

Beneath the canvas, Mike's snores were punctuated by little whimpers. Rick ignored them and began to peel off his wet clothes. Sinking to a crouch, he grabbed his towel and his washing things from inside his rucksack, along with dry trousers, shirt and underwear. He wrapped the towel around his waist.

A tartan car-blanket lay in a heap just to the side of Mike's sleeping form. Richard glanced at it, remembering how Mike had swum out to the slowing sinking motor launch to rescue him. His eyes moved to his partner's restless features. Crouching there, he reached out a hand to stroke the man's still-damp hair.

The whimpers became mumbles. 'Morag... Morag... Morag...'

Richard stiffened. He wrenched his hand away and fought the temptation to slap the sleeping figure's face. So much for their deal! So much for a mere five days of celibacy! Frowning, he backed out of the tent, fingers tight around the towel. So much for his and Mike's future together!

The sound of running water greeted him as he entered the small, concrete structure. Richard sighed. Communal showers: he should have known. And occupied communal showers, at that. Dr Rodgers preferred privacy for his ablutions. But he could wait. Dumping his clothes on the slatted bench which ran the length of one wall, Richard stared at a back view of the two naked men who stood, washing and chatting beneath the same faucet. Two very different men.

The one on the right was blond and tall. His head was thrown back as the water coursed over his face, his shoulder length hair a dark mane against well-tanned skin.

Rick's eyes drifted down the lean, sunburnt back, pausing at the man's arse, which was rounded and firm. Between twin orbs, which were startlingly white in comparison the rest off him, the deep crack was slick with coarse hair.

Beneath the towel, Richard's cock twitched. He stared at the walls beyond the two, desperate for something else to focus on. The strong smell of carbolic soap and some sort of shampoo brought his eyes back to the blond's companion. Smaller and stockier, the guy was washing very short, cropped hair. Rick stared at the man's arms, watching the play of muscle along the biceps and triceps as he rubbed his scalp vigorously. His eyes drifted on, following the line of sinew downwards. Where the hair on the guy's head was barely a half centimetre in length, his armpits were dense with soft clumps of the stuff. Rick's cock twitched again. Still covered by the heavy foreskin, the head brushed the inside of his thigh.

The two men chatted easily, shouting a little over the drum of the water. Richard barely heard the conversation. His eyes had moved to the mat of hair which covered the stockier man's shoulders and back. More sparse across his deltoids, the hair thickened into a broad channel, spreading out over the man's back and curving round his sides.

Rick moaned, visualising the forest which had to adorn the man's pecs.

He thought about Mike. About lying with his head on his Mike's chest and feeling the soft covering warm against his face. He'd always adored Mike's body hair – the feel of it, the smell of that luxuriant covering, with just a hint of silver in its midst, even when Mike was in his 30s.

His cock was stretching thoroughly, the head pushing its way past the heavy foreskin to emerge sensitive and pulsing against the top of Richard's thigh. He stood there, staring at two naked men, his sponge bag clutched in his fist, and an unmistakable tenting in the front of his towel.

The blond was soaping the inside of his thighs, now. Richard watched as the man bent his knees and turned side on. Cropped-Hair continued to rub his scalp, digging strong fingers into dark bristles. He too turned side on – and as he did so, Richard caught a glimpse of his pecs. Heavily muscled and well-developed, the whole of the man's upper body was indeed coated with thick fur. And, as a bonus, one tiny silver ring winked at him from the left nipple.

Richard moaned and dropped his sponge bag. It clattered against the tiling and broke the spell. Pitching hurriedly to his knees, Dr

Rodgers was vaguely aware of a pair of legs turning, then a voice.

'Morning, mate!'

In his present, crouched over position, Richard scrabbled to gather his toiletries back into their bag. His hard-on bumped against his stomach and made him gasp. 'Um... morning.' He managed a mumbled greeting in return.

'Give us a couple of minutes then it's all yours.'

'No rush.' Rick scowled, cramming soap, shampoo and toothbrush back into their bag. He scrambled to his feet with what little dignity he could muster and turned to his two unwanted companions.

The sight that met his eyes made his balls clench. The taller man now had both hands on the other's waist. Strong fists frothy with shampoo, the stockier man was washing the blond's hair, massaging vigorously. He grinned at Rick. 'Long-haired buggers, eh?'

His head lolling forward, the blond chuckled.

Buggers.... Richard's stomach flipped over. These two could be friends. Or virtual strangers. Buggers... They could be colleagues. Work-mates up here on holiday, with a crowd of other men. Buggers....

Richard watched an activity which was at once both incredibly intimate yet totally innocent. But the ease with which the stockier man lathered and finger-combed the other's hair was belied by the tall blond's erection, which jutted out from his wet crotch to brush the air mere inches from his companion's thick rod.

Or they could be lovers. If they weren't, at the moment, they soon would be.

The stocky man grinned at the tenting in Richard's towel. Then winked. 'There's plenty of room for three, in here.'

The blond's hands moved, his fingers splaying out over his friend's waist. 'Yeah, in you come, mate!'

Richard's own hard-on flexed, part arousal, part envy. A cold knot of loneliness twisted in the pit of his stomach. 'No, it's okay – you take your time.' He wanted to join in. He wanted to share the nonchalance of the pair, to feel at ease with his own arousal at watching two men bathe together, but it only served to remind him of the unease and chill which characterised his relationship with Mike these days.

Holding his sponge bag, he turned and walked over to the slatted bench. Richard sat down and studiously stared at the concrete floor. Eventually, amidst a flurry of flicking towels and good-natured yells, the two bathers left.

Rick's hard-on stayed – stayed as he unwrapped his towel and padded over to the still-running faucet. Stayed as he stepped beneath it and surrendered to the pound of hot water. He sighed, lathering the soap and scrubbing vigorously under his arms, over his chest then down his belly to his crotch. That had been a very definite offer. Had he been able to summon the courage and accept the invitation, Richard had no doubt some sort of sexual encounter would have ensued.

He flinched, then gritted his teeth, cupping his balls in a soapy palm.

But he couldn't. Something stopped him, every time. Rick sighed. What was wrong with him? Turning his face up to the faucet, he let the water course down into his eyes and ran a lathered fist up the length of nine hard inches. He was aroused, he'd wanted to – so why hadn't he?

The thunder of water on tile filled his ears. Richard braced one arm against the back wall of the shower and lowered his head. Liquid warmth flowed on to his neck and over his shoulders. He stared down at his hard cock.

Barely held in check by the sliver of stretched foreskin, the large red head pushed up into the steamy air. Richard began to move his fist. Slippery with soap, his curled fingers glided up the length of his shaft. The water was running down his back now, trickling into his crack then spilling over the back of his legs. Richard moaned. Feet planted firmly on the tiled floor, knees bending slightly, he dragged his fist back down... then thrust again.

The room was filling with steam. As his cock pushed up against his palm, Richard raised his head and blinked. Swirls of cloudy air filled his eyes. Weaving their way between the wisps he saw the blond and the crop-haired guy. Kissing. Fucking.

He saw the taller man held against the wall by a broad palm. He saw the back of a cropped head, and shoulders slick with thick wet hair. Richard's fingers curled more tightly. He fucked his fist faster now. Alone with the thoughts of other men... mere thoughts.

He let his lids close. In his mind's eye, he saw the crop-haired man holding his own cock, guiding it between the blond guy's hard arse-cheeks. He saw the blond's arse-cheeks clench, hollowing at the sides at the touch. He saw Cropped-Hair's free hand grip the blond's hip-bone, bracing himself there as he stroked the guy's hole with the head of his cock. Richard's balls clenched.

The two men faded into the steam, to be replaced by another pair. Richard's jaw went slack. Every other muscle in his body was rigid. His cock flexed violently. Through wisps of water vapour, he watched Archie Campbell shove his thick, latex-covered cock, into Mike's arse.

On his knees, Mike pushed back, accepting the length, his knuckles clenched white on the floor in front of him, his features contorted with pleasure. Rick's emotions rebelled at the sight. Hurt and betrayal made his guts clench. But his prick throbbed on single-mindedly, quivering against his curled fingers. He fucked his fist furiously, part in anger, part in a desperate attempt to rid himself of the arousal. His eyes flew open.

And met a pair of huge, dilated pupils.

Richard roared, balls knitting together and the clench now deep in his body.

Rajiv Azad flinched, then turned and fled from the shower block, the camera around his neck clattering against the zip of his bright yellow jacket.

Eyes fixed on his watcher's departing shoulders, Richard's knees buckled as he pumped thick ropes of spunk on to the tiled floor.

On the jetty, Lionel watched the small Iraqi man appear abruptly from the concrete shower block. 'Aye, Jimmy – if you can get it down to us today, Doc Rodgers will make it worth your while.' He continued to talk into his mobile phone, thankful he'd remembered to pack it – and equally thankful he'd thought of Jimmy Moore, his left prop in the university rugby squad, who was up in Inverness for the summer with access to his father's motor cruiser.

'Aye, I'll be here. See you later, pal.' Lionel snapped the mobile shut and smiled at Rajiv, who was now less than ten yards away. 'Did you tell the doc?'

His question was answered by another. 'Would you care to go for a walk?'

Lionel slipped his phone back into his pocket and peered at the smaller man. If it was possible for dark-skinned men to blush, he'd say Rajiv was doing exactly that. He also seemed uncharacteristically flustered. 'Did you tell Doc Rodgers I've found us a replacement boat?'

Rajiv came to a halt at Lionel's side. 'Please – let's go for a walk. We can take the movement monitor.' He gestured vaguely towards the tarpaulin-covered pile of scientific apparatus with one hand, while huge pupils gazed beseechingly at Lionel.

Lionel groaned inside. The guy could pick his times! He'd give his body and soul to spend some time alone with Rajiv. But not now: someone had to stay here to guard the equipment and await Jimmy with his dad's motor cruiser. 'Um...'

Maybe the Prof would be up and around soon.

Lionel glanced at the tent into which Professor St. Clair had disappeared a couple of hours ago and from which there were still no signs of life.

He looked back at Raji. 'What's up, pal? You look like you've seen a –'

'Rajiv?'

Lionel's head swivelled, along with his companion's. They both stared to where Dr Rodgers was hurriedly pulling a shirt over still damp hair and making his way from the shower block.

'Can I have a word, please?'

'I've found us a replacement craft, Doc!' Lionel called over to where the older man was now tying his boot laces.

'That's good – now, please, Rajiv?'

The captain of the First Eleven frowned. He'd expected a bit of a thank you, at least. His eyes moved from Doc Rodgers to Rajiv and back again.

His frown deepened. There was something going on here, something important: he'd never known an instance when work hadn't
come first, as far as old Rodgers was concerned. 'You'd better go see
what he wants, pal.' Lionel lowered his voice. 'If you like, we can get
together later and –'

But Rajiv was already walking to where Doc Rodgers was waiting.
And he looked slightly flustered too. Lionel rolled his eyes and continued to watch as the two men joined up, then began to walk, side
by side, down towards the village.

Probably to do with Rajiv's grant, or something. But he had come
belting out of that shower block like a thing possessed. And he'd been
in there quite a while, for someone who was merely delivering what
Lionel had presumed would be good news.

As the two figures faded out of sight, Lionel sighed and sat down
on a bollard. Nothing else for it. He'd wait here, his curiosity killing
him, until someone had the good grace to put him in the picture.

Chapter Fourteen

Mike woke to the sound of laughing voices and a powerful engine. He blinked, moaned and rubbed his eyes. He had no idea how long he'd slept. He had no idea where Richard was. But he knew he should put in an appearance, and at least try to explain about the events of the previous hours – most of which now seemed like some bizarre dream.

Raising himself on one elbow, he began to ease himself out of the sleeping-bag. A sudden awareness of something hard and large in his arse sent shivers of panic through his body. Mike froze. This was no dream. This was solid. Real.

Tentatively, he moved one hand back inside the sleeping bag. His fingers inched downwards. Mike rolled on to his side, then froze again. His fingertips brushed something flat, circular and warm. The muscles in his arse clenched instinctively, and his cock twitched. Mike moaned and began to trace the outline of what protruded from between his arse-cheeks.

What had seemed like a dream came back to him in vivid waves. Morag Campbell. The Land Rover. And her last words to him. His fingers moved around the base of the butt-plug. As they did so, muscle clenched deep inside him. He was suddenly sweating. His pores opened, drenching his body in a warm, clammy film. Mike tried to estimate the plug's length, then decided it wasn't so much a length-thing. It was girth.

The sphincter between his arse-cheeks clenched at the thought. Far deeper inside his body, other muscles tightened in sync, aching to be stretched in parallel. A small whimper escaped his lips. Mike arched his back against the sensation. His nipples grazed quilted fabric. The whimper became a moan as shocks of pleasure vibrated over him. Two buds of flesh hardened further at the friction. His bollocks quivered, a thousand tiny invisible insects crawling over the delicate, hairy surface. Mike inhaled sharply, fighting the pleasure. Within the confines of the sleeping bag, he pulled his knees up and tried to curl into a ball.

Still criss-crossed by the length of thonging, his cock brushed one thigh. His arse-muscles clenched again. Mike bit his bottom lip. There was no way to escape it. Some invisible, erotic thread linked the plug in his arse with his cock, his balls – even his nipples. He couldn't move – couldn't move one muscle without delivering frissons of arousal to every part of his body.

Mike closed his eyes and stretched out on his back. He could always untie the thonging, take the plug out – but Morag Campbell's low, authoritative voice echoed in his ears.

No, that wasn't an option. Irrational though the feeling was, Mike knew he was incapable of withdrawing the thick plug from his arse.

'Professor? Um – Michael? You awake?'

A voice nearer to home blasted into his haze of arousal. Mike flinched, recognising Geordie tones. He debated feigning sleep. What little remained of his conscience wouldn't let him. 'Yeah – give me five minutes.'

'Okay, I'll see you down at the jetty. I think you'll be pleasantly surprised.'

Mike doubted, after the past 48 hours, that anything much could surprise him now, pleasantly or otherwise. 'Okay, see you there.'

But he knew he had to get up and get dressed. He had at least to attempt to function normally, regardless of how impossible that goal seemed, at the moment.

Five minutes turned into twenty.

Half an hour later, he was helping the stocky Tyneside postgraduate arrange the sensitive and expensive echo-sounding equipment in the wheel house of a pristine white motor cruiser.

Mike's entire body was alight. Wearing clothes was the worst torment he'd ever experienced. The mere touch of fabric on any area of his skin turned up the gas and aroused him further. Held within loops of leather thonging, his cock was rigid, flexing against his belly. His balls were a tight, swollen mass of need. His nipples chafed and rubbed themselves raw. And his mind was with Archie and Morag Campbell, and what they had in store for him.

'Jimmy said not to worry about paying him – just keep her tank full and his dad will collect her at the end of the week.'

Lionel kept up a barrage of cheerful conversation as they set up and tested each of the delicate pieces of apparatus. Mike could barely keep his mind on what he was doing, let alone what Lionel was saying.

'Fancy a test voyage, Prof? To make sure everything's functioning?' Mike managed a nod, wincing as he brushed against the door of the wheel house.

'Okay, you cast off – I've steered this baby before, so if you handle the echo-sounder I'll take care of the wheel.'

Mike stumbled out on to deck and limped over the side of the launch. Everything about his body seemed larger, more intense. And everything else around him shrank in proportion.

He stepped on to the jetty, tore the mooring ropes free and returned to the deck. Staring at the campsite, then back along to the small village, he saw people, trees, activity. None of it impacted on him. Overhead, seagulls circled, mocking his predicament. Beneath his feet, he felt the tremble of the engine, then movement as Lionel guided the motor cruiser away from the jetty and out on to the loch. The sun was shining, the water sparkled, wind ruffled his hair and a breeze stroked his hot, sweaty skin. None of it mattered. None of it made any difference. A deep, dark part of Professor Michael St. Clair had been grabbed and hauled to the surface. And he was helpless to turn his mind away from it.

Back inside the wheel house, Mike did his best to check the equipment while Lionel steered. To the accompaniment of a series of spaced electric beeps, Mike watched the graph paper feed out of the tracking machine. They were cruising down the east side of Loch Ness. Mike stared at the three needles, watching their progress and trying to concentrate on his work. Each indicator told a story: mass, density, speed. Each detected and logged an aspect of any object of significant mass moving beneath the loch's dark surface. Each monitored. Like the trio of arousal indicators into which his balls, cock and nipples had been transformed. A trio which was stimulated by the slightest movement of Mike's body.

He remained motionless, one hand gripping the side of the echosounder. Motionless, he felt less. A slight hum vibrated up through his fingers. It was almost soothing. He was light-headed, vaguely removed from his surroundings. His mind, at least: his body was a different matter. Even still, even standing here in a sort of stasis, his nipples tingled, his balls clenched and the head of his cock rubbed painfully against the waistband of his jeans.

'This thing's got cruise control, would you believe?' Lionel's ever-cheerful voice drifted into Mike's ears.

He couldn't remember the last time he'd been so aroused. If this continued much longer, he'd come without the touch of either his own or another's hand.

'Programme in a course, and it'll repeat it infinitum. Handy, eh?'

Or maybe because of the taut leather loops around his cock he'd remain like this, simmering just below the boil, hovering on the brink of an orgasm continually just beyond his reach.

'Leaves both crew members free to observe and monitor. No need for anyone to steer. Never used it, myself, but I'll give it a go, eh Prof?'

Observe and monitor... Observe and monitor... Mike managed a nod. Were they watching him? Was his progress being tracked remotely – somehow, from somewhere – by Morag and Archie Campbell? What did they expect of him? When would they come for him? What would they want of him? A shudder coursed over his body. Mike moaned as a change in the engine's hum mirrored a tensing of his sphincter.

'Okay, there we go, Prof – all set. The equipment's functioning fine?'

Mike raised his eyes from the tightly packed zigzags which decorated the graph paper and tried to tear his mind from his tightly packed arsehole. 'Fine.' The word came out as a croak. He cleared his dry throat and tried again. 'Yes, it seems to be.'

He was going to come. He had to come. He wanted to tear downstairs, throw himself into the cruiser's toilet, lock the door and wank himself silly.

'Anything showing up?'

Mike flinched, surprised to find the stocky captain of the First Eleven standing by his side. 'Um –' He had no idea what to say. He could smell the guy. The scent of fresh male sweat mixed with the vague odour of the loch's salty water filled his head and only served to add to his already over-stimulated state.

A low laugh. 'Couple of shoals of fish.' One stubby finger traced a dark, zigzag. 'And that looks like an underwater rock formation. It's stationary, so we can probably ignore it.' The finger swam before Mike's eyes. Lionel Banks talked on, pointing to this inked patch and that, interpreting and commenting. Mike's head was full of bees. His balls ached, his nipples burned, and his cock was a thick, inflamed, leather-looped rod.

'Michael? Can I... er... talk to you about something?'

The change in tone caught what was left of Mike's attention. His eyes regained some semblance of focus. He stared at the Tynesider's open, freckled face, and was surprised to see he was blushing.

Lionel bit back mortification and tried to form the words. Everyone on campus knew Prof St. Clair and the doc were poofs. Queers. Irons hooves. Mollies.

Lionel himself had shoved his cock into some pretty weird places, over the years, and he had no problem with where the two academics liked putting theirs. It was a guy thing: fucking was a guy thing. Along with some of his fellow students, after late night drinking sessions, Lionel had often mused as to who was the 'woman' in their lecturers' relationship – who took it up the arse – and they could never decide. Neither Doc Rodgers or Prof St. Clair seemed particularly feminine – if that was the way to look at it. And now, knowing the way he felt about Raji – and knowing what he wanted – Lionel desperately needed a way of looking at things. A new way. A new lens through which to frame his feelings. Hell, he just wanted to talk to another man who... had been with guys. Maybe he'd feel a bit less confused about things.

Lionel looked directly into Professor St. Clair's somewhat glassy eyes and bit the bullet. 'Man, what's it like?'

The glassy eyes blinked rapidly.

Lionel's face flushed up. 'I mean, what's it like... to get fucked?' He looked away, aware he was mumbling.

When the response came, it was low and slightly tremulous but clear. 'It's the best feeling in the world.'

The honesty only increased Lionel's embarrassment, but he could feel his erection, the start of which had been twitching inside his Levis for the last half hour, stretching into something more solid. Then he was talking. Or rather, babbling. And it all came out: The she-male magazines. How, more and more, when he was wanking, his fingers would edge into his own arsehole. The vague fantasies about wanting to be fucked by a woman. The firming up of those fantasies into a desire to be fucked by a man. One man in particular.

'Christ, I can't get him out of my head. I think about him all the time – what it would be like. Me and... Rajiv together.' His face was on fire. But as he talked, he calmed down a little. Which was more than could be said for his crotch.

Even the act of speaking his dreams aloud was a turn-on – more so than his thoughts. For the first time since he'd first become aware of himself sexually, Lionel was musing over what it was like to be the receptive partner. He'd shagged women for years, not really caring one way or the other if they came or not. It wasn't about them. It was about him. But not this time. This time, it was about Raji. And being a good fuck.

'Is it... um, is getting your arse shagged messy, Prof?' Lionel pressed onwards, unable to stop – scared to pause for breath in case his bottle went completely. 'I mean, should I... um, have an enema first or something? What if I... um, shit on him when he's in me?' He'd always prided himself on his Geordie bluntness, on his ability not to mince words and ask a direct question to get a direct answer. He was also aware that he should try to slow down – if only to allow Prof St. Clair the chance to answer even any of his questions. But he couldn't.

'Will it hurt? Do we use... um, lube? Christ, what if he's really hung? What if I tense up? What if he can't... penetrate me?' Lionel was appalled to find he was almost shouting now. He broke off abruptly, fighting both unexpected tears and a fierce erection.

Then he noticed for the first time that Prof St. Clair was smiling. A large broad hand moved to his shoulder. 'Its okay – it'll be okay, it's nothing to be scared or embarrassed about.'

'Fuck me, Michael.' Lionel's voice dropped an octave. 'Please. I need to know what to do – I need to know... what to expect so I don't... screw it up with Raji.' His eyes dropped and he stared at his feet.

In the background, the steady electronic bleep of the echo-sounder bleeped on – unlike Lionel's heart, which was hammering in his chest and threatening to break a rib.

He didn't receive an answer. At least, not a verbal one. But the hand on his shoulder pressed down. Then they were both moving away towards the hatch which led below deck to the cabin.

And neither of them saw the sudden increase in needle activity, on the graph paper, nor the broad pattern of inked zigzags as something huge passed just below the hull of the motor cruiser.

'I love you, sir.'

'No you don't.'

'I do. I know what I feel. I have loved you for many months, Dr Rodgers.'

Richard sighed and moved down on to the beach. 'I think you have a crush on me, Rajiv – it's very flattering, and I like you a lot, but –'

'Is it because I am not Christian, sir?'

Richard flinched. He spun round and gripped the slighter man by the shoulders. 'It is nothing to do with your religion.'

'The colour of my skin offends you?'

Richard scowled. This would be hilarious if it wasn't so damn stupid.

'This has nothing to do with you, Raji. Period.' If anyone had told him such a handsome, virile young man would be declaring intense feelings to him, Richard would have laughed aloud. 'I like you, I admire you – I respect you. And you are... very handsome.' He felt the slender, swimmer's muscles warm beneath his palms. 'But I am... not available.' He tried to believe what he was saying. And failed.

Abruptly, Rajiv wrenched himself free and stomped off along the sand. Richard sighed and hurried after him. Talking about this was doing no good whatsoever. For the best part of the last hour, all he'd done was try to reason with the obviously besotted Raji. And all Rajiv had done was make increasingly fevered declarations of his feelings. Time for a change of subject. Drawing parallel, Richard nodded to the camera slung around Rajiv's neck. 'Could you take some shots for me? For the record?'

In the middle of the still, blue waters a gleaming white cabin cruiser was making its way down from beyond Boleskin.

Certainly, Dr Rodgers.' Rajiv's tone was distant and studiously respectful. 'Any vista in particular?'

Richard cringed. Raj sounded so detached now, and slightly hurt. But it was better than the love-sick ravings of a moment ago. 'No, just some shots of the area, the loch... maybe the shoreline.'

Rajiv raised the expensive camera to his eye and trained it on the water. Both of them continued to walk. Richard noticed they had ended up a little along from where Mike had dragged him ashore that morning: they were almost parallel with Boleskin, now. The coastline was rockier here, but still passable on foot. As they strolled along the edge of the loch, the bank behind them sheered upwards. After ten minutes or so, the road – which had been in sight since they'd left Drumnadrochit a good few hours back – disappeared behind tall trees, replaced by a series of unexpected caves. Wet moss covered the rocks beneath Richard's feet. To the accompaniment of the whirring of the camera's shutter, they strode on.

Every large body of water was tidal, to some degree. But from the dampness around his feet, and the trailing line of debris, he knew Loch Ness must be tidal in a more dramatic sense. Maybe it was the underground tunnels, rumoured to connect it with other lochs, as well as the North Sea itself, which made it act more like ocean than lake.

'Raji? Could you take some shots of this.' Richard indicated the caves and the surrounding line of flotsam left behind as the water ebbed. He was sure he'd have seen the caverns earlier: they must only be visible at very low tide.

'Certainly, sir.' Rajiv swung the camera away from the loch and began to photograph the areas concerned.

Dr Rodgers sighed. The guy veered between extremes, but if he had to chose between passionate declarations of undying love and icy reserve, Rick knew which was easier to work with. As Rajiv continued to photograph, Richard's eyes drifted back out on to the body of water.

It was a clear, warm afternoon. The sky above blazed blue, turning the normally dark waters into a sparkling sheet of azure. A gentle wash of waves brushed the shoreline. There was little traffic on the loch, at the moment: on the far side, the pleasure cruiser hauled its cargo of sightseers back towards the lock. In the centre, the white cabin cruiser was now repeating its trawl of the deeper water.

Richard fought a frown. He thought about the damaged boat. He thought about wasted money – a wasted trip. Yet another attempt to examine the loch doomed before it had even got off the ground.

'Dr Rodgers?'

Rajiv's voice tore his attention from futile contemplation. His eyes swivelled back to where the small Iraqi student was now standing, camera lowered. Richard followed one outstretched arm to a bank of thick sea-grass.

Just visible from within the tall fronds was a black, contrastingly non-indigenous curve. The side of an inflatable dinghy, all but hidden by the thick sea grass.

Richard took a step forward. Before his mind had time to make sense of their discovery, a sudden whoosh of surf crashed on to the rocks behind them. Both he and Rajiv turned as one. Two sets of eyes scanned for the vessel. Two pairs of ears strained for the engine of whatever was responsible for this amount of wash.

Nothing. The pleasure cruiser was just visible in the distance, approaching the lock to the canal which would carry the tourists back to Inverness. The white cabin cruiser was making its way back down towards the south end of the loch.

Richard frowned. Then they both leapt back as something large and black broke the surface about a hundred yards off shore. 'The camera... the camera...' His voice was a whisper.

At his side, Rajiv raised the instrument to his face. A series of rapid shutter clicks filled his ears.

It remained visible for the briefest of seconds, then dived. And Richard was moving, scrabbling along the rocky coast. His eyes remained trained on the outline of whatever he had just seen, as it made its way towards the promontory beyond Boleskin. The rapid shutter clicks accompanied him as Rajiv ran beside then overtook him.

Dr Rodgers had no idea what they'd just seen. But whatever it was, they now had it on film.

Chapter Fifteen

He couldn't believe his luck. In the small but luxuriously appointed bedroom, below deck in the cabin cruiser, Professor Michael St. Clair stared at Lionel's bare arse. The guy had kept his shirt and jacket on – even his socks – and for some reason, that made it all the more arousing.

'Okay.' The stocky Tynesider threw himself across the bed. 'Let's get on with it!'

Despite the comradely tone of the guy's voice and the fact he wasn't feeling in quite the mood to fuck, Mike's already inflamed body was reaching new heights of torment.

Lionel had a great arse. Your classic bubble-butt. It stuck up in two glorious, bristle-covered mounds, the top of the crack just hidden by the tail of his plaid shirt.

'What do I do? Is this position okay? You got a condom?'

Mike swallowed hard. The earlier embarrassment had vanished. The guy was very matter of fact about it all, now – something which made Mike's cock throb more than ever. 'Um – how are you on... blow-jobs?'

Lionel's crew-cut head turned. He looked at Mike curiously, then sighed. 'Fuck – yeah, he might want me to suck his knob. I hadn't thought of that.' The blunt face creased. 'Christ, I don't even know how to do that.'

Mike's balls clenched. It was heaven and hell all rolled into one. A young guy, a virgin – at least as far as the delights of male-to-male sex

Jack Dickson

were concerned – here, offering himself to Mike to do with as he wished.

At any other time in his life, Professor St. Clair would have needed no encouragement. But now? Two thoughts filled his mind: his promise to Richard, and Morag Campbell's words. Each reinforced each other, and jarred with the situation he now found himself in.

Lionel continued to frown thoughtfully.

Mike sat down on the edge of the bed before his legs gave way completely. He moaned as the plug in his arse was pushed more firmly back into place.

'I'm game if you are, Mike.' The frown vanished and Lionel sat up and turned round.

Mike stared at the guy's cock. Lionel crawled across the bed on his hands and knees. Mike watched the way the Tynesider's thick, curving shaft swayed as he moved. At its base, a pair of heavy balls swung slightly. Mike moaned again. Inside his shirt, his nipples tingled. In his arse, muscle clamped tight around the wedge-shaped plug.

Lionel chuckled. 'I've had enough of them, so a decent blow-job shouldn't be beyond me.' Stopping a few inches away, the postgraduate student stretched out a hand for Mike's fly.

Professor St. Clair flinched. 'Um... let me.' His own hand reached down both to cover and restraint Lionel's. He hesitated for the briefest of seconds.

'Ah, okay – Rajiv might want to unzip himself, right?'

Mike's heart pounded. He couldn't give a toss what Rajiv might want to do. All he knew was he wanted his cock in this guy's mouth. He wanted to come hard, because maybe if he did he could bear the rest of the torment of Morag Campbell's instructions. He leaned forward, one arm braced between himself and the half-naked man, the other hand moving towards his zip. As he shifted position, so did the base of the butt-plug. The angle of the wedge-shaped bung altered abruptly and Mike moaned aloud. He sat down hard.

'You okay?' Lionel's words were solicitous.

As the plug reinserted itself, the tip pushed against Mike's prostate. He was suddenly drenched in a new film of sweat. His body was being pushed towards new heights of arousal. Wrenching down his zip, he hauled his leather-looped cock free and grabbed the back of Lionel's neck.

The Tynesider stiffened. 'What's that wrapped around your cock?'

'Ignore it.' Mike felt the strength of the man's instinctive resistance. But he wasn't about to explain why his cock was trussed up like a turkey, even if he'd known where to start. Keeping his hand there, he managed to focus on Lionel's face. 'For Raji, eh?'

Something seemed to melt in the man's eyes. Then Mike was shuddering as an eager mouth clamped itself around his raging hard-on and began to slide downwards.

The captain of the First Eleven gripped Mike's waist with one hand. The other wrapped itself around the base of his cock. His lips tightened. Professor St. Clair shuddered as the leather thonging dug in and dragged. Lionel was moving too fast, in his eagerness. Mike's balls shimmered. His jaw clenched. If the blow-job continued at this speed, he'd shoot his load in seconds. 'Easy, easy...' He tightened his grip on the bristly skin at the back of the man's neck, easing up on to his knees.

Lionel ignored him. Mike closed his eyes. He threw back his head, his free hand moving down the man's back, searching for skin.

The fist around the base of his cock squeezed. Mike inhaled sharply. His glans bumped off the roof of Lionel's mouth. More blood pumped into his shaft, tightening the leather criss-crosses until they dug into the engorged flesh. Instinctively, his hips bucked forward. A choking sound drifted up from somewhere beneath his hand. Waves of pleasure broke over Mike's body as an efficient gag-reflex kicked in and spasms of muscle rippled over the sensitive head of his cock.

He drove more of himself into Lionel's mouth. His free hand pushed itself between them. Mike roughly uncurled the man's fingers, hauling his fist away from the root of his cock and thrusting the entire length of himself between Lionel's increasingly tight lips.

The captain of the rugby team was panicking. Mike felt the struggles and increased his grip on the back of the man's neck. There was no doubt Lionel was the stronger of the two, but Mike had the advantage when it came to physical position – and need. And now that he was breaking his promise to Richard in no uncertain terms, he was determined to make it worth his while.

Lionel could barely breathe. He could barely see. Almost bent double, his arse in the air and both hands now holding on to the Prof's waist like his life depended on it, all he knew was the smell of the man's crotch, the taste of what he now recognised as leather, and the feel of another guy's cock in his mouth. Adrenalin spangled through his veins. His heart was beating furiously. He, Lionel Banks – who prided himself on his fitness, on his bulk and sheer muscle power – couldn't find the strength to pull away, even though instinct was telling him he should.

Blood buzzed in his head. A sea of black dots floated before his eyes. His lungs were bursting. He tried to suck air in through his nose, he tried to stop swallowing, he fought the urge to throw up. And he fought to take more of the man's leather-trussed knob, loving the way it filled his mouth.

Michael was fucking his face furiously now. Lionel moaned as the man's balls smashed his chin. He remained motionless. It took every shred of effort his helpless body possessed just to keep still – not that he needed to move. Tilting his head up a bit, Lionel prayed for his gag to relax. He wanted it deeper. He wanted to feel the head of Michael's knob bump off the back of his throat.

Contradictory emotions and urges he'd never before experienced crashed into each other. He was something to be used by a man, the way he'd used women for years. And he was the most important person in the world. He felt like dirt. And he felt more valued than ever before. He shivered. Sweat poured from his body. Fear gripped his guts and twisted hard. A stronger hand on the back of his neck reassured him. He hated it. And he loved it.

Then something warm and firm touched his bare arse. Lionel would have cried out, was it not for the cock in his mouth. It took a fraction of a second for him to identify the presence as the Prof's free hand. Two seconds later it was moving. Lionel struggled harder than ever as an alien finger moved down the crevice between his clenched arse-cheeks. His throat closed up. The grip on his neck tightened further. The flight or flight response struggled deep within his brain. Then the digit was stroking his arsehole.

Despite the wanks, despite the way he'd often finger-fucked himself, Lionel rebelled. Everything he'd ever been taught since he was old enough to learn swam to this surface and told him this was wrong. Arses were for the evacuation of shit. This wasn't right. Stuff came out. Stuff didn't go in.

The cock in his mouth paused. The grip on his neck relaxed a little. Lionel knew he was going to pass out. He couldn't breathe. He couldn't think straight. Somewhere, on the fringe of consciousness, he was aware of a tensing in the body which covered his face. Then the finger was pushing past his clenched arsehole and his throat was opening and Mike's cock was impacting with the hard cartilage at the top of his windpipe and cutting off the airway.

Lionel's eyes watered. His fingers dug in hard, gripping tightly on to Professor St. Clair's hard waist. He coughed around the thick length of the man, vaguely aware of a sudden spasm in his own crotch. Abruptly, the thick length shuddered. The hand on the back of his neck clamped hard and hauled Lionel's head down further. He tried to breathe through his nose but his nostrils were full of pubes.

Then the bed was moving beneath them as, below that, a wave of wash from something very large hit the motor launch. Michael's body jerked forward, knocking the Tynesider on to his back. The leather-trussed cock slipped from his lips and slapped against his cheek.

As he lay there, another man straddling his face and with a cock flexing hard against the side of his head, all Lionel knew was an overwhelming sense of coming home.

Before he had the chance to savour much of the moment, the body on top of his was pulling away and the Prof's voice was cutting through the receding waves of pleasure:

'Christ, what was that?'

Lionel blinked through a daze, watching the man hurriedly zip up and head for the stairs. Seconds later, the stocky Tynesider was tucking his own still-hard cock back into his jeans and bounding after him.

What he'd just done with one of Richard's postgrads vanished in the face of what he now saw. In the wheel house, Mike stared at the echo-sounder's printout. All three needles were zigzagging frantically, covering the graph paper with dense, black readings.

'Man oh man – what the hell?'

Mike dragged his eyes from the printout and looked at the half-dressed Lionel. 'Get us back to the jetty.' He nodded to the controls then bounded out on to deck.

The loch was smooth as a millpond again.

Shading his eyes form the sun as the motor launch turned and headed back to shore, Mike peered over the water, looking for any large vessel which could have been responsible for the violent wash which had rocked the boat. Both his rational mind and the evidence from the echo-sounder told him the disturbance had been below the surface of water.

A hundred yards away, someone was waterskiing. The double masts of a small ketch were just visible, further on, as it sailed its way down towards Fort Augustus. And on the opposite shore, Mike could just make out two figures, one in Rajiv's distinctive bright yellow waterproof jacket, who were now running towards the small huddle of buildings that made up Drumnadrochit.

Richard pushed open the door of Campbell's Chemist and General Store and elbowed his way through the crowd of customers. Breathlessly, he grabbed the camera from around Rajiv's neck and hurriedly removed the already rewound spool.

'Good morning, gents!' Archie Campbell beamed at them from behind a display of postcards, flu remedies and tacky souvenirs. Assorted locals and tourists parted as Richard and his companion reached the counter.

'And what can I do for you?'

'You can develop this, please.' Having practically run all the way from their encounter near Boleskin, Rick carefully placed the rewound spool on the counter and nodded to the Kodak sign above the tall red-haired man's head. 'In an hour?' He kept his hand over the roll of film.

'No problem, Dr Rodgers – holiday snaps, is it?' The hotelier-cum-campsite-owner-cum-shop-keeper-cum-just-about-everything-else reached out to take the spool.

Richard was just about to lie when Rajiv piped up.

'We saw it! We saw the monster!'

An audible gasp echoed around the small shop.

Dr Rodgers cringed. He would have preferred to keep this quiet until they'd had a chance to examine the developed film in detail. The last thing he wanted was exactly what ensued.

'What did you see?'

'Where?'

'How big was it?'

'Did you get many photographs?'

At least twenty people of various nationalities were now shouting, pushing forward and demanding answers.

Unexpectedly, Richard felt Archie Campbell's hand tighten over his. Then a whisper cut through the racket as the broad redhead leant over the counter. 'Go through to the back. I'll join you when I get rid of this lot.'

Richard looked to the small door behind the counter. He managed a nod.

'Sorry, my friends – closing early for lunch. Come back at half past two.'

As Archie Campbell moved to herd his disappointed customers towards the way out, Richard grabbed the film and hauled Rajiv past racks of postcards and confectionery towards the small back shop.

Ten minutes later, the three of them stood beside a large automated developing machine.

'So you saw Nessie, gents?'

'Well, we saw something.' Richard shot Rajiv a warning glance in anticipation of any other wild claims. 'It could have been nothing.' He knew he was playing down what both he and Rajiv and seen with their own eyes. He had to. He had to detach. He was a scientist, a theorist not an empiricist. The senses could lie. The evidence of his own eyes would never be enough – especially in terms of convincing the sceptical world of marine palaeontology. He needed proof. Richard watched Archie slip the spool into a compartment at the bottom of the developing machine. He needed what was on that roll of film.

'Ach, this is great news – I'm pleased for you, Dr Rodgers.' Archie pressed a switch and a low hum filled the room. 'We can always do with more pictures of Nessie.'

Richard flinched. He didn't like the way this was all going. Something about this man – over and above whatever was going on between him and Mike – made his hackles rise. What had caught his attention just before he and Rajiv had seen whatever they'd seen pushed its way back into his mind. Rick seized on the opportunity to change the subject. 'Do you own a dinghy, Mr Campbell?'

'Call me Archie, please.' Facing away from Richard, the hotelier continued to keep watch on the developing machine. 'A dinghy?'

Dr Rodgers stared at the back of the man's head. 'Yes, a dinghy – we came across one, hidden in bushes over by Castle Urquhart. Not far from where our boat hit... whatever it hit.' The implication of his own words suddenly started to sink in. 'I wondered if it might belong to you.'

'Kids, most likely, Richard.'

Rick flinched at the uninvited familiarity.

'Summer holidays, you know what it's like. I warn them all abut going out on to the water in small craft, but what can you do? They probably ripped the bottom out of it of rocks, then abandoned it there.'

'This dinghy wasn't abandoned. Hidden, more like – concealed intentionally in bushes. And it didn't look like something kids would be messing about in.' Richard found himself bristling.

'Yes, it more resembled a craft designed for night work.' Rajiv piped up again. 'It was black. It had oars. And looked most seaworthy, if I may say so. Like something out of a James Bond film – you know?'

Archie Campbell spun round. The former geniality had vanished. In its place, the generous mouth was a hard line and the brown eyes narrowed. 'I do not own any such vessel. Nor does anyone I know. It must belong to a tourist or one of the students who are camping on the other side of the loch.'

Irrationally, Richard shivered. He took a step back, shocked by the gruffness of the previously friendly voice. 'Um – okay. Fine. I just wondered.'

Archie Campbell continued to fix them with a steely stare.

'Er – an hour, you said?' Richard nodded to the developing machine, suddenly eager for an excuse to get away from here. 'For the film to be ready?'

The redhead dipped curtly. 'Make it an hour and a half – I'll bring the prints over to your base.'

Richard glanced at Raji, who was looking equally startled at the change in the man's attitude. 'Um – okay.' His hand moved to the wallet in the pocket of his shirt. 'Shall I pay you in – ?'

'No need, Dr Rodgers!' The man laughed heartily, all traces of defensiveness vanishing as suddenly as they had appeared. 'You go back and have your lunch and I'll bring your prints over the moment they are ready.'

Richard could only nod. Then he and Rajiv were making their way back into the front shop and off the premises, both confused as to exactly what had taken place in front of Archie Campbell's developing machine.

No sooner had they arrived back at the camp site than Richard saw the shiny white motor launch moored at the jetty. A figure was disembarking, running towards them.

'Lionel, where did that come from?'

The stocky Tynesider ignored his question, grabbed Rajiv by the arm and walked swiftly towards their tent. Richard goggled after them. What on earth was going on? Turning his attention back to the unfamiliar vessel, he knew there was only one way to find out.

He strolled down to the jetty, taking in more of the pristine cabin cruiser. It had to be worth a hundred grand, at least. And who had moved their equipment from where he'd last see it? Stepping on board, he glanced around. 'Anyone here?'

No answer.

He wandered along the deck, then ducked into the wheel house.

Richard recognised the hunched, somewhat dishevelled form bending over what looked oddly like the university's echo-sounding apparatus. 'Mike? What's going on? Whose boat is this? What's been – ?'

'A shoal of fish.' His partner straightened up, and turned.

Richard glanced at the ashen face, then looked down at where Mike's slightly trembling index finger was pointing to a section of printout.

'It has to be.' Mike talked on, his voice hoarse. 'Okay, it's a little more dense than one would expect from fish, but what other explanation can there be?'

Rick's eyes darted to the time, which was documented down the side of the graph paper. At 1104 precisely, the equipment had picked up something large and slow-moving, some 50 feet below the loch's surface towards the western bank.

In his mind's eye, he clearly saw the glinting face of Rajiv Azad's expensive digital chronometer, as the man had raised the camera to his eye.

11.06.

'We saw it.' His voice was low, almost tentative. 'We saw what gave that reading. And we got photographs.'

Mike's eyes narrowed.

Dr Richard Rodgers, for years the laughing stock of the marine palaeontology world, smiled with pride. 'And it was no shoal of fish.'

Chapter Sixteen

The last man in the world Mike wanted to face right now stood inches away, saying the last thing in the world, academically, he needed to hear: 'It was an animal – some sort of creature.' But it was better than having to explain what he'd just done with one of the postgrads.

'Rubbish!' Mike stabbed at the printout paper with a still-shaking finger. 'It could be anything.'

'We saw it.' Richard's voice was very calm. 'Rajiv and I saw whatever it was, from the other side of the loch.'

Too calm. Mike wanted to look his partner square in the face but dared not, in case the man saw his guilt there. He took a step back, sudden aware he must stink of sex.

'And we got photographs.' Dr Rodgers's voice remained low, almost serene in its detachment. Mike frowned. He knew he should be relieved that Rick was too obsessed with whatever floating log he and Rajiv had seen to pick up on any telltale sign of sexual activity. But for some reason, it irritated him. No wonder he went looking elsewhere. No wonder he felt ignored, taken for granted. It was always the same: once Rick got the scent of even the most slender of threads supporting his preposterous theories, nothing else mattered. Mike risked a look at his partner.

'This could be it. This really could be what I've waited a lifetime to find.' Eyes trained on the graph paper, Richard's face was alight. 'Photographic evidence, combined with these readings – combined with my hypothesis, will provide irrefutable evidence that, despite the contradiction in logic, despite every mainstream theory of marine palaeontology, somehow some form of pre–Ice Age life has survived and still exists in the loch.'

The frown slid into a scowl. Mike's lips tightened into a hard line. It never changed. Nothing else mattered. Not him, not their life together, nor any future they may or may not have.

'This'll show them, the stuffed shirts!'

Michael stopped listening to his partner's babble. He continued to stare at the animated, glowing face. The muscles in his arse clamped around the plug. His flaccid cock, still scummy from Lionel's spit and crusted with drying spunk, twitched against the inside of his thigh. Mike bit back a moan. 'Rick?' The word was hoarse. 'I let that... student suck my cock.' And the admission was out before he could stop it.

Richard's head jerked up from his study of the printout. 'Don't you see what this means?'

Something stung behind Mike's eyes. The end of them? The end of their relationship? He tried to nod. And failed.

Something blazed behind Richard's. 'I'll be taken seriously. For the first time, my theories will have the empirical back-up to force them all to take notice.'

Mike's mouth fell open. 'Did you hear what I said?'

'Yes, yes – we'll talk about all that later.' Dr Rodgers glanced at his wristwatch. 'That guy with the red hair said he'd bring the photos over in – an hour.'

Sparkling eyes linked with Mike's.

'I wonder if there's a fax around here? I'll want to get these registered as quickly as possible, before the copies appear.' A brief shadow crossed the ecstatic face. 'You know, I'm wary of that fellow – what's his name? Campbell? He seems to own everything around here. If there was anywhere else to get the photos developed I would have gone there.'

'I got myself off against Archie's thigh.' Mike tossed the comment in, mid sentence.

'And we found some sort of dinghy, hidden in the bushes.' Richard charged on regardless, oblivious to whatever Mike said. 'Very close to where I had my mysterious accident with the boat.' The shadow lingered. 'I don't trust that Campbell character.'

'His wife made me put a butt plug up my arse and told me to keep it there until she gave me permission to remove it.' Mike's face was scarlet – half embarrassed at the admission, half furious at the way Rick was ignoring everything he said.

'Hmmm...' Richard looked at Mike.

Mike's sphincter tightened around the plug. Had it finally penetrated? Were his words at last making an impression?

A thoughtful expression crossed Dr Rodgers's face. 'I hate to consider it as a possibility, but I wouldn't put sabotage past Campbell. Although why he'd not want us to find a monster, I have no idea. I mean, after all, concrete proof of activity in the loch would only increase tourist potential.'

Professor St. Clair turned and walked away. He couldn't listen to any more of it.

'Mike?'

He ducked, leaving the wheel house and making his way out on to deck.

'What's wrong? What is it?'

He continued to walk, the soles of his boots heavy on the weathered wood. But not as heavy as his heart.

'Where are you off to? Don't you want to wait and see the photographs?'

His eyes stung. He could show Richard shots of him and every man from here to John O'Groats and still the guy would only see his precious bloody monster. He stepped quickly on to the jetty and turned left, up towards the hills.

'Mike!'

A note of irritation had entered Dr Rodgers' voice. It only served to increase Mike's feeling that he didn't matter. None of it mattered. Despite all his partner's claims, Mike knew one thing for certain, now. He could never overtake Richard's work, as far as priorities were concerned. He would always come second.

But there were those with whom he came first. With his partner's shouts still echoing behind him, Mike quickened his pace and strode up into the hills. He had no idea where he was going. And, at that exact moment in time, he didn't care.

He walked for hours, and as he walked the sun slowly lowered in the sky. Drumnadrochit became a tiny cluster of buildings somewhere far below him. The loch shrank from a huge body of water to a smaller pool. The western sky blazed red, turning the heather a vivid purple and the surface of Loch Ness to a sheet of shimmering red glass. Mike walked on, pushing past bracken bushes and vaulting streams. The tears dried on his cheeks. Sweat from the exertion of the hike cooled on his face then grew warm again. A breeze ruffled his hair as he climbed higher.

The butt-plug chafed the lips of his arse, keeping him open. Keeping him ready. Ready and aching.

Slowly, the hurt left his mind, taking the reason for their trip with it. He no longer cared about any of it. The sun on his head meant nothing. The stiffening breeze had an equally minor effect on him.

His cock was still hard – thanks to the thonging – his balls full and heavy due to the constant movement of the plug in his arse caused by every step he took.

By the time he'd reached the summit of whatever hill he'd ended up climbing, the sun was sinking in the distance. Twilight descended around him. The sound of the birds slowly faded. Mike's feet veered off moorland and hit the tarmac of a narrow road. He tramped on, unaware of the car which had been following him at a distance for the last five miles.

He'd passed no one, encountered no other human being in the course of his hike. Blood pounded in his head, drowning out the sound of the wind over the heather. He didn't hear the Land Rover's engine as the vehicle increased its speed and closed the distance between them. But he noticed its lights on the road ahead. And when he turned and saw the open passenger door, Mike didn't hesitate.

'Sorry, Dr Rodgers. These things happen.'

On the quay side, just in front of Campbell's Chemist, Richard flicked through the sheaf of overexposed photographs a second time, in the vain hope one had got through.

'Light must have got into that bloody machine – we had the service engineer out twice last week.' Archie Campbell sounded genuinely apologetic. 'Of course, there will be no charge, since your snaps are ruined. I shall write a strong letter of complaint to the rental company and perhaps we can get you some compensation.'

'It doesn't matter.' What could in any way compensate for the fact their shots of the creature were now a series of blinding, glossy rectangles? Richard stuffed them back in their envelope and bit back frustration.

At least they still had the echo-sounder's printout. That section of graph paper was now dated and locked in his briefcase, buried under a heap of clothes in his tent.

'I'm really sorry, Dr Rodgers. I feel bad about this.'

A broad hand settled on his shoulder and rubbed. Rick flinched.

'What do you say to dinner on me, up at the hotel?'

Richard frowned. First their boat sank, now their photographs failed to develop. He was just about to tell Archie Campbell what he could do with his dinner, his chemist shop and his hotel when the sound of laughter and shouts drifted up from further down the quay.

They both turned towards the commotion. The red-haired hotelier began to chuckle, his hand still resting on Rick's shoulder. Richard could only stare. Beyond a growing crowd of tourists and locals, something large and black and rubbery-looking was being towed on to the shore by a group of grinning fishermen.

'Ach, see these students? They'll be the death of me!' Archie's chuckles increased.

Rick scowled. As the object got closer, he could see more detail. It was large, black and semi-inflated, with several large inner tubes somehow attached to its back, to give the effect of humps. At the front, a long neck reared up out of the shallow water. On the tip was painted a bright yellow smiley face.

'Every year it's the same.' The red-haired hotelier talked on through laughter. 'Always some prank or another.'

The rear portion of the inflatable monster was listing somewhat, but even at the distance it was remarkably convincing.

'They get caught in nets, snagged in the propellers of boats – sometimes even some unsuspecting visitor catches a glimpse of one and thinks he's seen the real thing.' Archie slapped Dr Rodgers on the shoulder for emphasis and sniggered.

Richard suddenly felt very stupid. As the fisherman dragged the object from the water and on to the beach, it listed further then collapsed completely. Only an idiot could see it for anything other than the collection of inner tubes it was. Only an idiot, who only saw what he wanted to see, could have been fooled by it in the first place.

'It's actually quite a clever feat of engineering, this time.'

Richard found himself moving, eased forward through the swelling crowd which had gathered around the shore by Archie Campbell's strong hand. As they approached the beached effigy, he could see a small, outboard motor attached to its underside.

'Usually, they just throw them in and let them drift. This one, it seems, is remote controlled. And all the more realistic for it.'

As if on cue, a trio of youngsters in denim cut-offs and baseball caps appeared through the falling dusk. One held a small control console from which protruded a short aerial. As he pressed a button, the exposed propeller on the inflatable's underside whirred feebly then died. Everyone laughed. Richard's heart sank.

'Was that what we saw, sir?' A whisper by his side.

Rick turned his head and looked at Rajiv Azad's disappointed expression. He could only nod.

'Bloody clever contraption, though.' Lionel Banks's grinning face appeared over the smaller Iraqi man's shoulder. 'That would fool me – and I bet it's what we picked up on the echo-sounder, this afternoon.'

There was no doubt in Dr Rodgers's mind. He'd been conned – well and truly conned.

'Do not blame yourself, sir.' Rajiv's voice was soothing and full of empathy. 'It is very convincing.'

No photos. No echo-sounding printout that couldn't now be

explained away. It was probably just as well the photographs hadn't come out. How Mike would have laughed. How the entire marine palaeontology world would have had a good old chuckle at his expense. Again.

'Now what about a drink, Dr Rodgers, along with the meal? Up at the Campbell Arms, on the house?'

Richard sighed. Archie Campbell's bonhomie only served to heighten his disappointment and embarrassment.

'Yes, sir – please join us.'

Unexpectedly, Rajiv touched his arm. Richard tensed and drew back. 'Um – no thanks.' He needed to be away from here. 'Have any of you seen Professor St. Clair?' He shrugged off the red-haired hotel's hand, his eyes scanning three faces.

Rajiv and Lionel both shook their heads.

Richard blinked and focused on the third.

'No, sorry – not seen Mike for hours.' The reply was even in tone. Richard blinked rapidly. Did a flash of guilt fleetingly cross Archie Campbell's bluff features? Or was it more of the same overactive imagination which was making him see monsters everywhere?

'Maybe he's at the hotel.' The redhead grinned. 'Let's go up there and see.'

'I'll catch up with you later.' Richard managed a mumble of explanation as he turned away. Pushing through the crowd and the gathering dusk, he began to walk in the direction of the western shore before he embarrassed himself completely.

Morag Campbell neither spoke to him nor glanced in his direction. Mike clutched the edges of the passenger seat, staring at the side of her handsome, angular face as the Land Rover picked up speed. Doing at least 60 on the narrow twisting road, she expertly steered the vehicle round bends and over hills. He had no idea where she was taking him. He only knew he couldn't turn back now. Whatever this strange, complex woman had in store for him, Mike knew he had to go through with it.

'Take off your shirt.' After 15 minutes, something other than the

Jack Dickson

hammer of his heart and the roar of the engine broke the silence between them. Wrenching white-knuckled hands from the sides of the seat, Mike began to fumble with buttons then gave up and hauled the plaid shirt over his head.

'Boots and socks.'

He didn't need to be told twice. As he leaned forward to obey, his arse titled up and the base of the plug brushed the back of the seat. Mike moaned. A different moan. Far from being uncomfortable or awkward, the plug inside him was now almost soothing.

His fingers slipped and slid over the laces of his boots. His brain could only think about the hard thickness in his arse. How long had it been there, now – four hours? Six? He hauled off his boots and tore at his socks. His cock jutted up, the sensitive head rubbing against the inside of his shorts. Now exposed to the night air, which was flowing into the Land Rover from the open windows, his nipples hardened further.

It was as if it had always been there. The plug in his arse was now part of him, put there by someone who knew his body better than he knew it himself. Mike raised his head, leant back in the passenger seat and stared at that someone.

'Now your shorts and underpants, Professor.' Again Morag Campbell's eyes remained trained on the road ahead. And she'd used his name – albeit in that same mocking tone. But at least she'd used it. His eyes never leaving her face, Mike's fingers stumbled with his belt then his fly. Part of him wanted all her attention. Part of him wanted to feel her mocking eyes on his body as he undressed. And part of him was glad, as he clumsily dragged his trussed cock and bare arse free of underwear and shorts, that no one – not even this intriguing woman who controlled his body as skilfully as she steered the Land Rover – was witness to his debasement.

Finally he sat there, naked. Still looped by the leather thonging, his cock stuck almost straight up from his groin. Drawn up tight and full against the root of his shaft, his balls quivered with the engine vibrations. Waves of sensation tingled in his nipples. His face was scarlet. His entire body was alight with anticipation and need. He'd never been so exposed, so vulnerable, so completely and utterly helpless. Or so hard.

Morag Campbell had taken everything away from him. His dignity. His self-respect. His sense of worth. There was nothing more she could take. He was hers completely, to do with as she pleased.

The note of the engine climbed higher. The Land Rover slowed, the gears changing down in sync. As she drew the vehicle to a smooth halt a little way off the road, Morag finally turned to look at him.

'Now take it out.' Long, masculine fingers casually switched off the ignition. Mike stared at her in bemusement. His cock flexed under her gaze.

'Take out the plug.' Her voice was as casual as the way she tossed the car keys into the air and caught them again.

An icy fist clutched at his guts. 'Please...' He stared into her detached, amused eyes. Tears were now flowing freely from his own. Every muscle in his body rebelled against the prospect.

'Professor.' A warning note entered her voice. Mike didn't care. He didn't care if she gave him the worst tongue-lashing of his life. He didn't care if she hit him. She could do anything else she wanted with him – his body was no longer his own. But that plug stayed.

Mike sniffed, throat burning. His eyes stung. He sat there, naked, gripping the sides of the passenger seat and cringing under her gaze.

'I won't ask a second time.'

His arse ground down against the sweaty upholstery. The movement pushed the solid wedge more deeply into him. His nipples tingled. His cock flexed in the air between them. Then her glacial gaze pinned him with a new ferocity. Mike's stomach flipped over. His balls churned. Deep in his arse, muscle clenched. He tried to look away. Couldn't. His fists tightened, fingers digging into the leather of the passenger seat. He tried to close his eyes. They refused to obey him.

Something in her gaze was penetrating him more than any butt plug ever could. Something about the woman was reaching deep into his mind, touching a part of him no one had ever touched – and making it hers.

Blood pounded in his ears. Salty tears ran down his face and slicked dry lips. Then his arms were moving and Mike was leaning forward. One hand braced against the dashboard, he raised his arse from damp leather while the fingers of his other hand gripped the circular base of the butt plug.

His eyes never left hers. Her eyes never left his. Cock shuddering and so close to coming, Mike wrenched the plug out of his arse.

Chapter Seventeen

He could smell his own body. The rank stench of his terror, the hot odour of his humiliation and arousal. And the base, visceral stink of shit, sweat and precum.

The plug slipped from Mike's shaking fingers. He was vaguely aware of stumbling sideways, of grabbing the door handle, turning it and falling from the Land Rover on to dew-dampened grass. Then he started to crawl. He had to get away – from this, from her and the way it all made him feel.

The dew was cold beneath his palms. On his hands and knees, face burning and head lowered in abject embarrassment, Mike made his way around to the front of the Land Rover. He bumped into a wheel, veered left away from it and continued to crawl. He didn't care that he was stark bollock naked. He didn't care that his clothes were somewhere back in the car and he would have to slink back down the mountainside in the dark. He'd do whatever he had to: whatever it took to get away from this aching need.

Then his knees gave way. Mike slumped forward. Everything was wet and dark around his clammy body. The ground felt cool against his burning face. But it didn't help. He slipped sideways, curling into a ball. That didn't help either.

His sphincter spasmed wildly. His entire anal canal was a shimmering tunnel of longing. His mind was full of the memory of it. The way it had stretched him. Filled him. Made him complete. In the deepest recesses of his brain he could still feel the plug wedging him open, keeping him ready, waiting... available. Mike's chest and shoulders heaved. He was sobbing now. Because its loss was greater than any memory. He wanted it back. He needed it back.

He lay there in the darkness, curled into a foetal ball and listening to the vague sounds of a door opening and feet hitting the ground. Then lights blazed against his tightly closed eyelids, boots sounded on the grass. Two sets of boots.

'Professor?'

He sniffed, fighting the sobs which continued to wrack his body. Morag Campbell's voice was a beacon cutting through his torment. A flame to his moth. Another stick to beat his sorry body with. He squeezed his eyelids more tightly shut against the glare of what he now knew were the Land Rover's headlights.

'Mike?'

His entire body shuddered at the second voice.

'Oh Mike...'

The gentleness in Archie Campbell's voice sent more tears streaming down his face. He raised his head and opened his eyes. Morag was nowhere to be seen. Mike stared at the backlit turn-up of a man's jeans. Slowly, tentatively, he raised his head more, his eyes tracking up strong legs to the illuminated bulge in Archie's crotch.

'I wanted you the other night.'

Mike whimpered and backed away on his hands and knees. His neck hurt, but he continued to move his gaze upwards.

'I wanted you so badly.'

Archie Campbell's form was backlit by the headlights. Mike couldn't see his face. He didn't know if it even was Archie Campbell. But he knew the voice.

And he knew what his cock was telling him. His balls shuddered in the cool evening air. 'Fuck me.'

Tiny insects hovered in the beams of the headlights, drawn to the beacons in the same way that Mike was drawn to whoever stood before him. He waited for an answer. The vague rustle of the wind in the grass was the only response.

Tears ran down his face. He blinked them from his eyes, pleading with the backlit form. 'Fuck me – please?' His pulsing shaft quivered, six inches of solid need fucking the air between his legs. And his arse-hole clenched, longing to be filled again. By anyone. With anything.

Then his head was lolling between his shoulders and he was crawling forward. In one frantic lunge he reared up and threw his arms around the legs of whoever stood in front of him. 'Fuck me... oh please, just fuck me!' Mike was sobbing again, his cock throbbing against his stomach.

He almost didn't hear the sound of more footsteps on grass. Mike gripped the legs more tightly, his wet face sliding down denim until it reached the tops of laced leather boots. Before he knew what he was doing he was kissing the worn hide, his mouth opened, his lips parting in half moan, half adoration. Still on his knees, he lowered the rest of his body, prostrating himself in helplessness, and began to lick the leather. His arse stuck up into the air, naked and vulnerable. His hole spasmed, aching to be filled.

The familiar sound of foil packaging being ripped drifted into his ears, followed by a groan. Then something warm and rounded and latex-covered was pressing against his sphincter while rough hands grabbed his hipbones.

Mike groaned and pushed back hard. Despite his need to be fucked, the tight muscle at the entrance to his body instinctively fought the invader. Despite the pre-lubricated condom, the cock slipped. Despite hours of arousal, his hole was dry and unlubed.

The head of the cock dragged against already-chafed and sore skin. Unseen fingers clutched his hipbones more tightly, hauling him back. Mike winced with pain and turned his face side-on to the leather boots. Keeping it there, his cheeks wet with tears and his own spit, he tried to relax the muscle and bear down on the cock he wanted so much.

A growl from behind. 'Fucking take it, ya cunt!'

Mike's shock at the realisation this was no voice he knew was brushed aside by the tone of the exhortation. And the words.

He gasped, and with that gasp his sphincter relaxed just enough to let the faceless stranger push in. Then someone was screaming and the someone was him and the pain in this arse was almost unbearable and he felt something rip and his heavy balls were knitting together and the force of the man's thrust pushed him forward on to the other man's boots and his cock was flexing violently inside the leather criss-crosses and his own spunk was splattering hot and slimy on his own face as the stranger's cock forced itself into him.

The unseen man fucked Mike through his own orgasm, grunting with pleasure as Mike's spasming anal muscles gripped and caressed his shaft. Mike only knew two things: the way the cock in his arse was filling him and tearing him, and the fact he'd waited all his life to be used like this.

And he wanted more. Grabbing the legs of the man who stood in front of him more frantically than ever, Mike licked a smear of his own spunk from his upper lip and surrendered to the fucking.

His cock was still flexing, his balls still pumping the last dregs of an orgasm postponed for hours up into his shaft and out through his gaping slit. His rectum was on fire, chafed almost raw with the force of the fuck. The guy's hairy balls slapped off his cheeks with each solid thrust. Mike's arse-lips were stretched paper thin, painfully sensitive to every drag of the guy's cock. His ears were full of the sounds of his own laboured breathing, and his mind throbbed with another man's need.

It seemed to last for hours, and was over in minutes. Mike's cock was already reviving when the fingers gripping his hipbones dug in agonisingly. The man inside him grunted release.

He moaned, mouth open on the toes of the leather boots. The thick root of the cock in his arse trembled. Mike flinched deep inside, eliciting another grunt from his fucker as a response well beyond Mike's control massaged and caressed the spasming, latex-covered cock.

Then it was retreating and Mike was howling into the night. 'Put it back – oh, please put it back!'

The man ignored him, slipping from his body in one shuddering movement. Something wet and warm hit his arse and Mike knew the guy had thrown the used condom at him.

His stomach flipped over. His chest tightened and tears sprang to his eyes once more. Mike's very soul seemed to go with the departing prick. Without a cock in his arse he was nothing. His knees were shaking, his legs had turned to rubber. He could feel the man's spunk start to ooze out of the condom making the puffy lips of his arse sting as it dribbled over his balls and down the insides of his thighs. Mike pushed back, tilting his arse upwards in the direction of his departing fucker. 'No, no, no!' His own cock was now half hard again, but he barely noticed.

This wasn't about him. This wasn't about his cock or his pleasure. This was about others. Using him. Fucking him. Seeing and recognising him for the fuck hole he was.

He didn't have to wait long. Face pressed against the toes of the leather boots, Mike gasped as a second man grabbed his waist. The gasp melted into a low animal moan as another condomed cock pushed its way into him.

Then Mike was panting. He was a bitch in heat – a thing with no urge other than the need to be fucked. Mike gripped the calves of the guy who stood before him and clung on for dear life as the unseen stranger in his arse began to thrust.

This cock was different: shorter but thicker. Mike whimpered. His swollen and chafed arse-lips were dragged almost inside out by the girth of the guy's shaft. His own cock bounced with each fierce stroke. His balls were filling up again as the man behind him changed the angle of the fuck.

An arm encircled his waist and hauled him up off the boots. Mike screamed as the head of the guy's cock bumped against his prostate gland and an alien mouth clamped itself on to the back of his neck. Then a hand gripped his chin, taking advantage of his open mouth – and another cock was forcing its way between his lips. A naked cock.

Instinct took over – some deep, primal reaction made Mike sheathe his teeth. He threw back his head, opening his throat and suppressing his gag. Tightening his lips around the shaft, his hands made contact with the guy's waist. He took it. He took it all.

The head of the guy's cock pushed past his soft palate. Mike fought suffocation as the thick prick threatened to cut off his airway. He tried to breathe through his nose and only succeeded in inhaling wiry pubes. Panic rose in waves. Mike's fingers dug into the guy's calves.

The cock in his mouth thrust in, the swollen glans impacting with the cartilage at the back of Mike's throat, which immediately closed up, spasming around it. Then the cock in his mouth slowly withdrew. Mike moaned. The prick in his arse thrust ever upwards. The moan sank to a low, animal utterance. Mike pushed back, meeting the thrust and taking the guy deeper than ever. And slowly, a rhythm was established.

His naked body was bathed in sweat, both from the exertion and the headlights which he could feel burning into his skin. Along with eyes. At least six pairs, maybe more.

The two strangers in his body worked Mike in tandem. The guy in his mouth pushed him back on to the thick prick in his arse. The guy who filled his rectum jolted him forward, burying Mike's face in the other's pubes until tight balls ground against his chin and his mouth was slimy with precum.

Friction was rubbing his knees raw. Mike spread his legs wider, tightening his arse muscles around the stubby cock. He clutched the other guy's legs like his life depended on it, letting him fuck his mouth deeper and more thoroughly.

The guy in his arse came first, biting the back of Mike's neck hard as he did so. Mike's lips and teeth tightened around the cock in his mouth, pushing the other over the edge so that his throat was slick with spunk seconds following the orgasm in his arse. He had no idea if he himself came or not. And he didn't care, because as soon as they'd spent their seed, the two were pulling out to be replaced by another pair.

And Mike was taking them too, taking everything they had to give. He knelt there, his fists now gripping handfuls of scrub-grass, knees bleeding as pair after pair used him and came in him.

He'd never felt so alive. So free.

Halfway through the fourth couple, his mind seemed to separate itself from the rest of him. Looking down from somewhere above, he saw the Land Rover. He saw the grass around it littered with discarded condoms. He saw Morag Campbell standing with Archie, smoking a cigarette. He saw other men whose faces he didn't know, but whose cocks he knew had been in him. Some were standing alone, still stuffing their scummy pricks back into jeans or track-pants. Others were passing a bottle of whisky around, grinning and whispering to each other. But all were watching. Every eye on that deserted hill top was focused on the triumvirate.

The guy in front was young, around 19, long black hair falling over narrow shoulders clad in an Adidas T shirt. The boy was gripping Mike's face, the hands on his cheeks, holding the head steady as he bucked his hips and pumped methodically between the parted lips.

The man at the rear was older – Mike's age or more. Bearded and with salt and pepper hair, his jeans bagged around his knees. His arms were bare, ropey with muscle and drenched in a thick covering of greyish hair. His hands held Mike by the hips. And naked between them, on hands and knees, Mike was caught in the Land Rover's headlights – barely recognisable as the Head of St. Aloysius College's marine palaeontology department. Barely recognisable as a man.

Mike's cock flexed. His arse ached from the fucking. His stomach churned from the volume of spunk he'd swallowed. He stared down at himself, watching the way his body was completely controlled by the men at either end of it. His two holes, his arse and his mouth, used in turn by each of those present – as he was made to be used. He'd been waiting his entire life for a moment like this.

Mike had no idea how much time had passed. An hour? Two? It was almost dark. Through the dazzle of the headlights he could see a thin red line in the distance, all that remained of the day's sun. And it didn't matter. Nothing mattered except what was happening right here, right now.

A tightening grip on his head brought Mike's mind back to his body. For the first time, he raised his head and looked up at the man who was fucking his face. The boy's eyes were squeezed shut in passion, his lips parted in arousal as his slender hips bucked one last time. Mike was vaguely aware of the guy in his arse roaring his release, then the boy was coming and Mike's own cock flexed and jerked and he fell forward on to the boy's cock, propelled in part by the man in his rectum and part by the force of his own orgasm.

Someone was sobbing. Someone's arsehole was sore with the fucking from half a dozen men. Someone's throat muscles were spasming convulsively around the head of a jerking cock.

And as he hovered there, on the brink of unconsciousness, someone knew he'd found what he'd been looking for.

In the gathering twilight, Richard trudged along the deserted road. A few cars had passed him further back, a few hikers returning to camp or one of the bed and breakfast establishments in Drumnadrochit. But that had been hours ago. For the last few miles, it had just been Richard – and his thoughts.

He was an idiot. A total idiot. There was no monster. There never had been. Oh, perhaps once, at the turn of the last century, some drunken local had seen a particularly large pike or sturgeon, maybe even a conger eel which had somehow got into the loch from the North Sea. The creature would not have survived long, given the sparse food sources available in Loch Ness. It would have either died or found its way back to the sea. But the legend had started then, the flames of a one-off sighting fanned by commercialism and perhaps the need to believe that there was more on heaven and earth than could be explained away by science. Richard sighed and walked on.

And he had fallen for it, hook, line and sinker. He of all people! Logical, rational, down-to-earth Dr Richard Rodgers. His entire academic career had been based on myth. He'd spent 25 years of his life in pursuit of something which did not exist outside the mind. A creature of imagination. And he had no idea where he was going to go from here. The field trip was a sham. All that money – all that energy and effort. And for what?

Richard frowned. There was nothing to find, nothing to prove one way or the other. Mike had been right: Mike and the entire marine palaeontology community. And he had to face them, sooner or later. Starting with Lionel and Raji, the two postgraduate students he'd dragged up here on this wild goose chase.

Richard turned, intending to make his way back round to their campsite.

'A good evening to ye, Dr Rodgers!'

Richard froze.

'I didn't expect to find you away out here.' A hoarse laugh. 'Or maybe I did.'

Turning slowly, Richard found himself a few feet from a gnarled, grey-haired face. He recognised the old man as the harbour master, one of those who had helped drag their boat on to the beach. 'Um – er, good evening, um –' Hamish Something. Richard had no idea about the elderly gentleman's second name.

'Down for a look at Boleksin, eh?' Old Hamish moved closer.

Richard blinked. Initially confused, he glanced over the ancient fig- ure's shoulder, and again found himself staring at the high towers of Boleskin House. What was it about the place that seemed to draw him again and again? 'Er... um, I –' He was still goggling at the dark sil- houette of the building when the old man spoke again.

'I hear yer photographs of Nessie didn't turn out very well, Dr Rodgers.' Old Hamish chuckled and slapped his thighs. Richard re- turned his attention to the shadowy figure and fought the beginnings of a scowl. He was a laughing stock already, and even with those who didn't know his academic lineage.

'Aye, well there's all kinds of monsters, son.' As abruptly as he'd chuckled, the old man suddenly sobered. 'Some of them don't quite take the form ye'd expect them to.'

Richard peered at the gnarled face. What was the guy implying?

'Mr Crowley knew that – Mr Jix knows that too.' In the dying light the old man's eyes took on a strange, otherworldly cast. 'And I think you know that too, Dr Rodgers.' The man's voice was a hoarse, almost reverential whisper. 'You know what's in the loch, what's always been in the loch.' He took a step closer. 'You have an open mind, son. You have eyes to see and ears to hear, where others do not.'

A blast of whisky-breath made Richard eyes water. He sighed, want- ing to believe the old fellow, but also aware that it was probably the drink talking – on top of the fact that this man's livelihood depended on the continuation of the Nessie myth. His mind was suddenly read.

'I'm not drunk, son.' The leathery, weather-beaten face was very close. 'And don't take my word for it.' One arm shot out, a wrinkled hand pointing down on to the shoreline. 'Go and see.' The other hand patted Richard's shoulder. 'Go and see for yourself.'

Rick's eyes swivelled in the direction indicated. Through the gloom, he could make out several landmarks which told him this was the same area where, earlier, he and Rajiv had found the rubber dinghy and the semi-accessible caves. The tide was lower now, but it was dark. A shudder of apprehension coursed through his body at the thought of investigating those caverns on his own. 'Hamish, would you – ?' As Richard turned back to his companion, he found himself staring into an empty space.

The ancient harbour master had disappeared. Richard scanned the road in both direction and listened. There was no sign of the fellow, no sign he'd every been there at all.

Adrenalin ran through Rich's veins. But beyond that, a deep-seated curiosity combined with his characteristic thirst for knowledge. He had to know. He had to know once and for all. Taking his courage in both hands, and with night steadily falling around him, Richard slowly made his way down on to the rocky beach.

Chapter Eighteen

Mike woke up shivering, his body soaked in an icy sweat. Raising his head from the ground, Mike risked a look around himself. The Land Rover was gone. Everyone was gone. Beyond the discarded condoms which littered the grass, his eyes fell on a shadowed pile. Recognising his clothes, Mike eased himself on to his knees and began to move forward.

After two seconds he had to stop. His entire body was shaking. His balls hung loose and sore, between quivering thighs. His arsehole felt puffy and swollen, the lips raw. Although they were all gone, he could still feel them.

Mike licked dry lips, dragging his tongue over the scum which crusted the edges of his mouth. He swallowed, then coughed. He could taste their pricks. He was aware of bruising at the back of his throat, a vague rasping soreness which he knew would hurt badly in the morning. The smallest smile of satisfaction crept on to his lips.

But most of all, he felt fucked – well and truly fucked. Grabbing his clothes, Mike began to dress. He had no idea how many he'd taken. How many had used him, stuffing their cocks into his arse and mouth and fucking him until they came. He had no idea what time it was either. Hauling his torn shirt over his head, Mike glanced around and saw the moon was already high in the sky. What little light there was came from that full, shining globe. He pulled on his jeans then sat down gingerly, easing on to one cheek as he grabbed socks and boots.

The smile broadened, then changed to a gasp as his arse made contact with the hard ground. Mike winced, shifting his weight as he tied the laces of his boots.

Something had happened. He had no idea whose idea the whole thing had been – Archie's? Morag's? Of all the things that could have transpired on this field trip – of all the wild fantasies Professor Michael St. Clair had ever entertained in the darkest recesses of his mind – he had not expected this.

Part of him felt dirty. Violated. Abused. Another, greater part felt whole for the first time.

How had they known? Why had they been so sure he wouldn't have run a mile or fought back? Maybe the signals had come from himself? Mike grabbed his jacket and eased himself to his feet. His legs still a little wobbly from the earlier exertions, he staggered slightly.

Maybe all it took was eyes to see.

Limping more than a little, and with every muscle in his body glowing, Mike wandered off in what he hoped was the direction of the road. As he made his way through the heather, his mind filled with odd thoughts.

Richard had never fucked him like that. But there had been times – a few occasions, years back, when a combination of circumstances and moods had brought Mike very close to where the Campbells plus their numerous friends had taken him. Inside his jeans, his sore cock twitched. Mike moaned.

Richard could be rough. He was a strong man and, despite the quiet, mild-mannered demeanour, a ruthlessly detached academic. Still waters ran deep.

On several occasions, back when they still had a sex life, Mike had caught glimpses, in bed, of what Richard might be capable of. When Rick wanted sex, he wanted it badly. Mike had woken up in the night, quite a few times, to find Rick inside him, his own cock hard and flexing. Afterwards, his lover was always very penitent and extra tender, almost as though he regretted what he'd done. Mike never had the guts to tell him that those had been some of the best times.

Abruptly, his feet hit tarmac. He was now walking along a narrow road, with the moon high above him and his brain alive with thoughts. Okay, he'd well and truly broken the pact he'd made with Rick. He'd gone after Archie Campbell and Morag, as well as more than willingly submitting to what had happened on the moor, less than an hour ago. But maybe something good would come out of it. Maybe it would help him find the courage to put into words and explain to Rick exactly why Mike needed sex – and the specific type of sex he needed.

As he wandered along the road, smiling to himself, he eventually became aware of footsteps parallel to his. Mike froze. Listened. Nothing.

Mike walked on – and heard them again. Not on tarmac, not that distinct, but the solid, rhythmic pad of boots on heather told him he had company. His stomach churned. Flashes of recent memory thrust themselves back into his mind. He spun round. Peering through the darkness, Mike stared at a broad outline ten yards away, holding binoculars and walking across the hilltop towards him.

'What are you still doing up here?' The tone was formal, with a hint of surprise. Still?

As the man got closer, Mike recognised the goatee and freckles of the stranded motorist he'd rescued three days ago. The precise words of Kieran McLeod's greeting circled in Mike's head. Had this guy been watching him? Had this guy been part of it all?

Seconds later, Mike was staring into Kieran McLeod's green, narrowed eyes. His cock twitched again, as he remembered the feeling of them both on the bike, the freckled man's hands tight around Mike's waist, his half-hard cock pressing against the back of Mike's leathers.

Mike blinked. He never thought he'd be in a position to turn down more sex. But at the moment, he only cared about getting back to camp and finding Richard. In desperation, he groped for some casual response. Mike eyed the man's binoculars. 'Bird watching?'

'Listen, Mike – Professor St. Clair, rather.' McLeod ignored the remark. 'I've talked to your colleague – Dr Rodgers, is it?'

Mike shivered, but nodded.

McLeod raised the binoculars and turned towards the distant loch, miles below them. 'There's... matters afoot here, which I think you

Jack Dickson

and your party may have inadvertently been caught up in.'

Mike blinked, for the first time noticing the two-way radio which hung from the man's belt. 'What do you, um, mean?'

As if on cue, the device crackled. McLeod grabbed it and raised it to his lips. 'All clear so far, sarge – over and out.'

Mike could only stare. Sarge?

Kieran sighed and returned the two-way radio to his belt. 'Okay, I suppose you have a right to know.' He eyed Mike. 'But not here.' He turned and strode off into the darkness. Mike, thoroughly confused, followed.

After a 15-minute tramp through the hills, they reached a small tent beside a Ford Fiesta. McLeod unlocked the driver's door and a light illuminated the interior. Mike leant against the side of the vehicle as the bogus bird-watcher opened the glove compartment and rummaged in it. He had no idea what was coming, but after the past few days, he was prepared for anything.

Withdrawing a small leather wallet, the man thrust it into Mike's face. 'DC Kieran McLeod. Grampian Police – seconded to HM Customs and Excise, Professor St. Clair.'

Mike was glad the man had read it for him, because his eyes were refusing to focus.

'We've had this whole area under surveillance for the past two weeks.' Mike raised bemused eyes to the guy's face. 'So you'll understand why I couldn't... say anything to either you or your colleague, sir.'

Mike could only nod.

'We're after a cartel of hoteliers and publicans, who are in receipt of alcohol and cigarettes from the continent, on which no duty or tax has been paid.'

Mike's throat was dry. 'Smuggling?'

Kieran laughed wryly. 'Well, I suppose in the old-fashioned sense, that's exactly what's going on.' Then he sobered. 'There is, however, a lot more than a few kegs of rum at stake, so get rid of any romantic notions, sir.'

'But we're landlocked here. The coast is miles away.' Mike was confused. 'Except for the canal – which I presume is easily patrolled.'

Kieran sighed. 'I would have thought you, of all people, Professor, would be aware of the underwater channels which lead directly from Loch Ness both to surrounding, smaller lochs and out to the North Sea.'

Mike stared. 'But that's never been proved.'

Kieran pinned him with an icy green gaze. 'Doesn't mean they don't exist, does it? Like their bloody monster – but a damned sight more probable.' The undercover police officer slipped his warrant card into his back pocket and ran a hand over his short cropped hair. 'Okay, I'll spell it out for you, sir.'

This was all a bit much for Mike, who edged into the Fiesta's driver seat and sat down, wincing slightly as his chafed arse-lips came into contact with the leather.

'We know for certain that Archibald Campbell, Morag Campbell, Ewan McGrath – he owns the pleasure cruiser used for the tourist trips – and his brother Jimmy are involved. We know the contraband is coming in through an underwater channel, on the east side of the loch, carried in a small, probably remotely controlled submarine. We know they are using the myth of Nessie to explain away any possible sightings of this underwater vessel.'

Something began to make sense in Mike's addled mind.

'We know there's a big shipment coming in any time now. And we also know the last thing Campbell and his crew need at the moment is a team of academics sweeping the loch with echo-sounding equipment.'

Mike shivered.

'They are ruthless, sir – ruthless criminals. There are large sums of money at stake here, and they will stop at nothing.' McLeod frowned. 'So your boat was sabotaged. Dr Rodgers' photographs of whatever he and Rajiv Azad saw yesterday morning conveniently came out overexposed.' An uncharacteristic blush tingled the freckled face. 'Attempts have been made to... um, distract you from the object of your trip.'

Heat spread over Mike's own face. The guy had been watching though those damned binoculars! Worse still, Mike had been well and truly set up. He had been used in more ways than the mere physical.

'As I said, Professor, Campbell and co will stop at nothing.'

Mike stared at his feet in total mortification. McLeod cleared his throat. 'Anyway, after the contraband enters the loch, it is unloaded and carried up into these hills, via a series of subterranean passages dug by Jacobite rebels in the 18th century. Again, we know these tunnels exist – these hills are like rabbit warrens, but we have yet to locate the precise route the contraband is taking. And after that? Into a waiting van and an hour's drive to Inverness where it supplies half the pubs and off-licences in the city.'

Mike raised his head; McLeod avoided his eyes. 'Perhaps I should have alerted you and your party earlier, Professor. But it's more than my job's worth to compromise the integrity of an operation which has been months in the planning.'

Mike would not have traded his time over the past 48 hours for all the kudos in academia. 'I understand.'

'But just so you know, my superiors believe tonight's the night. Campbell and his bunch of rogues think they have you safely... um, trussed up. And, from what I've seen, your two postgraduate students have eyes only for each other.' The police officer chuckled, then sobered. 'But Dr Rodgers is their main worry. He's a bit of a loose cannon, in that respect, what with his complete determination to prove the existence of a monster. Do you have any idea of his whereabouts at the moment, sir?'

A small moan escaped Mike's dry lips. He had no clue – no clue at all. So absorbed had he been by the attentions of Morag and Archie Campbell that the most important person in his world had been elbowed aside. 'I'll find him.' Mike sprang up from the seat. 'Wherever he is, I'll find him.'

'Just one word of warning, sir.' McLeod grabbed Mike's arm. 'The signal that contraband is entering the loch is given in the form of an owl hoot. Should you hear this, at any point, please back off.'

Mike was no longer listening. With a renewed spurt of energy, he was bounding off towards the road, aware of only one thing: Richard could be in danger. He had to find Richard.

Beyond the mouth of the cave, the low, eerie call of the night hunter echoed a second time.

Richard ignored it and pressed on. The cavern in which he found himself was dark and damp. He could smell the sea. His boot soles scrunched on still-wet sand as he moved forward, walking in the direction of a blast of air which told him there was an outlet in here other than the one through which he'd entered.

Behind, the hoot of the owl was faint. The sound of dripping water filled his ears. Richard cursed himself for not bringing a torch. The cave was vast. The initially wide entrance soon narrowed as he made his way through tunnel after tunnel, ducking his head to do so. He could spend hours wandering around in here, was it not for his instinct to follow the draught of air. Each time he came to a junction, the source of the breeze made his choice for him.

Sometimes, the narrow passageways dipped steeply and Richard had to grip on to the walls to stop himself falling forwards. At other times, he was walking upwards, the muscles in his thighs starting to ache and burn with the effort of the climb. He had no idea where he was going, where this would all lead, but something spurred him on. Old Hamish's cryptic comments about Jix Tyson and Aleister Crowley refused to leave his mind. Dr Rodgers no longer cared about monsters. Only one thing preoccupied him. One night, when he was 15. One night in a hotel room in Hammersmith, watching two men fuck. One night which had changed his life. And about which he still had questions. One night, and an unfulfilled dream.

As he walked on, stumbling against rocks, he became aware of a change in the air around him. The dampness was easing off. This part of the labyrinth was drier. Richard tried to estimate how far he'd walked, or in which direction. At first, he'd thought the caves would lead up into the hills. Then he'd sworn he could hear rushing water close by, which led him to believe the tunnels had somehow twisted back on themselves and he was now moving somewhere beneath the floor of the loch.

But no: he was climbing now, the rock and shale under his feet turning into rough steps – worn with age, but steps nonetheless. His heart pounded in his chest. Anticipation dried his mouth. Sweat formed in the pits of his arms and slowly trickled down his sides leaving cold trails. And then there was light.

Richard blinked and rubbed his eyes. Yes, definitely light. A vague glow from some hidden source ahead was flooding the passage around him. Richard's eyes darted left and right. The walls glistened with rock quartz and the fool's gold of iron pyrites, carved with oddly familiar but unidentifiable symbols. His head tilted upwards as he continued to mount the ancient stairs. Neck craning, Rick saw the rock above his head had been carved with the same alien-yet-familiar symbols.

His eyes were still entranced by the cabalistic inscriptions when his feet hit something smoother and more recently manufactured. Lowering his gaze, Richard paused and stared at the black and white tiles beneath his sandy boots. He took a deep breath before raising his head to see exactly where he was. And as he did so, his lungs filled with a smell which joined the strange carved symbols and swept away the years – the heady, cloying odour of burning white sage and other herbs.

The memory of what smouldered in an abalone shell, on the bedside table in a hotel in Hammersmith. Only one thing was missing: the tape recorder and the crackly voice.

Standing there, in what was undoubtedly the basement of Boleskin, Richard blinked rapidly, his eyes acclimatising to the dimly lit room. Vaguely circular in shape, the area swam in a haze of wispy smoke. Candles burned in sconces dotted along the walls. Their waxy fragrance joined the smouldering incense and caught in the back of Richard's throat. The flickering flames cast ominous shadows, both hiding and illuminating the room's content.

Richard took a step forward. Then he heard it, and the memory was complete. The words were low and unintelligible – more syllables than words, really... or maybe even vowels. He paused, scanning the smoke-screened area for the source of the incantation. Because this time, the voice wasn't crackly or pre-recorded. It wasn't some ancient tape. The low baritone which drifted into his ears was almost un-recognisable from an output of albums which spanned the entire decade of the 1970s – but Richard would know Jix Tyson's voice any-where. The voice he'd wanked to for months. A voice which could still make him hard.

Shaking but undeniably aroused, Richard moved across the floor to the source of the incantation. Towards his nemesis.

As he approached the midway point, the smoke seemed to clear and he could see more. Cock stretching, palms sweating, his brain both fuddled and more clarified than ever by whatever he was inhal-ing, Richard paused. Less than two yards away, a figure sat cross-legged on a raised platform. Long-fingered hands cradled the abalone shell, from which great puffs of white smoke billowed.

Jix Tyson was naked from the waist up. His chest had lost none of the fine muscle tone which had given the 15-year-old Richard wet dreams for over a year. The man's abs were pale cubes of flesh, his arms still wiry and roped with sinew. Shoulder-length blond hair – no plat-inum spikes any more – hung tied in a loose thong at the back of a bent neck. A white sarong fell in folds over his thighs. At the end of pale legs, bare feet were just visible, tucked beneath the chanting man's slender arse-cheeks.

Something about the syllables which tumbled from Jix Tyson's lips both demanded a response and insisted on silence. Richard's throat was dry. He wanted to speak but the words wouldn't come.

He stood there, letting the sounds and the sights and the smells fill his head. Richard marvelled at how little the guy had changed in – what, 25 years? He would have recognised Jix Tyson anywhere. Then the lowered head slowly raised itself and clear blue eyes gazed at Richard from within a ravaged face.

Chapter Nineteen

As he met and held that clear gaze, Richard knew rationally he was an intruder in this man's home as well as a virtual stranger, unless you counted one brief meeting in an alley which led to lost hours in the Earls Court Hilton. Part of his mind groped for explanations and excuses, some justification for his presence here on private property and in the middle of what was obviously a personal act of meditation.

The eye lock continued. The incantation continued. Wisps of white smoke drifted up between them. Time passed strangely, as it had done that night, 25 years ago. It could have been minutes... or days.

Richard's legs gave way. He found himself on his knees, in front of the raised platform. He and Jix were now on the same level. Eye contact had not been broken. Kneeling in front of the platform, Richard didn't question the fact that the man could see him. More than see him, in fact – those clear blue irises seemed to penetrate his very soul. Richard moaned, his half-hard cock jerking abruptly as a sudden rush of blood fled his brain to swell the thick member.

I'm glad you came.

Richard could only nod, aware the voice was in his head and that the strange disjointed syllables continued to flow from Jix Tyson's lips.

I knew you would come.

Clouds of smoke billowed around them. Richard inhaled great lungfuls of it and let it fill his chest.

I have waited for you, Ricky.

His balls tightened.

I have waited so long.

Richard's arms were moving by themselves, his hands extending to cup the long elegant fingers which held the abalone shell.

Since that night.

Their hands made contact.

A jolt of static shuddered up Richard's arms. He gasped. The hair on the back of his neck stood on end. His stomach flipped over. Inside his trousers his thick cock flexed, the swollen head pushing past the last millimetres of foreskin to rub against the fly.

I need you, Ricky. I need you to finish this.

Alien sounds poured from the man's lips.

At first I thought it was Dick. Dick Dawson. Then I thought I could find it in the far corners of the world.

The word resounded in Richard's head.

Then I retraced my steps, back to that night. I thought me and Dick were alone, in that hotel room. I was wrong.

A sudden frisson of guilt, a shiver of embarrassment shuddered down Rick's spine.

I was so wrong.

Then Jix's lips stopped moving. The chant carried on, joining the wisps of smoke from the smouldering white sage.

Richard's fingers tingled. He slipped them between the other man's, fanning out the long slender digits until they were both cradling the abalone shell.

The electricity was stronger now. The shell seemed to be the source and they were both mere conduits. A sudden wind blew through the circular room. Candles flickered, and a new smell joined the scent of the incense. From within the clasped bowl, light shone, whether reflected from the candles Richard couldn't tell for sure. All he knew was that Jix's face seemed to glow with iridescence, bathed in colour, blues, greens and pinks from the mother-of-pearl shell flickering over his ravaged features.

Rick's body quivered. And he could feel those hues. Smell them. Hear them. Something was happening to his sensory appreciation. Wires were crossing in his brain. Messages sent to his eyes were intercepted and redirected to his ears, his mouth, his fingers.

Richard moaned, tasting the warm rosy pink at the back of his throat while his tongue twined around a spicy blue. The room was spinning. But Richard felt more solid than he'd ever felt before. His mind was slipping away from him. He no longer had any use for it anyway. Information was seeping through his skin, communicated wordlessly by means which were simultaneously beyond his comprehension and something he'd always known was possible. He'd known it that day in the record shop when he'd first clapped eyes on Jix Tyson's image. He'd known it when he listened to the music. He'd known it strongest of all that night in the Earls Court Hilton as he watched two men explore each other's bodies to the backdrop of what he now realised was a recording of Aleister Crowley's voice.

A recording which, until minutes ago, had been pouring from between Jix Tyson's full lips.

Then they were both on their feet, their hands still clasped together around the abalone shell. Jix Tyson's sarong slid from his skinny hips.

Somehow Richard knew he too was naked. The colours from the shell's mother-of-pearl interior bathed them both in an unearthly light. Then the shell was moving by itself. Guided by some invisible hand, it was floating upwards away from them. Richard flinched as it smashed against a wall, somewhere to his left. But he knew it didn't matter.

Knew it didn't matter that Crowley's incantation was continuing on somewhere either in his head or in the room, intoned by unseen voices.

He and Jix Tyson stood less than a yard apart, fingers linked. Richard stared at the man's wiry body, his eyes drifting down from the piercing blue eyes to jutting collarbones. He took in the large, swollen nipples which tipped smooth, gleaming pecs before his gaze came to rest on the slim, engorged cock which curved up from a totally shaved groin.

Drawn up tight at the root, Jix's balls seemed huge in their hairlessness, framed by sinewy thighs. And at the base of his cock, a broad metal ring twinkled in the candle light. Simultaneously strong and ethereal, the man stood before him, waiting.

With his beard, moustache and thick covering of dark body hair, Richard felt like a beast come face to face with an angel. A predator with his prey. His eyes returned to Jix's. Then their hands were moving apart and Jix was unclipping the ring from his balls and holding it out.

Somehow, Rick knew what to do with it. He clamped it shut around the base of his own cock. The metal was warm against the chilly skin of his bollocks. Then the slender man was turning, sinking to his knees on the raised platform.

Richard stared at his idol's arse. A skinny arse. Muscle dimpled, shadowing deep hollows each side of clenched buttocks. Richard's cock flexed, jolting in the smoky air in front of him. The part of his rational mind which still remained was swept away by a wave of sheer lust. He grabbed his shaft, barely aware of the touch of his own hand as he fell to a crouch behind the blond angel. His other fingers dived between the clenching arse-cheeks, moving down the shaved crack to the heart of the man.

The delicate pink skin around Jix's arsehole resisted his touch, shivering instinctively. Richard's balls clenched. Roughly, he pushed index and middle fingers into the man's body. The responding gasp of discomfort made his cock flex again. Richard pushed on, his other hand gripping the pale waist.

The walls of Jix's arse were tight and rippling. They fought the invasion all the way and only increased Richard's arousal. When the man tried to twist away, Rick moved his hand to the back of the guy's neck. Under the loosely tied ponytail of pale hair, his hand spanned warm flesh. Richard held Jix Tyson firmly, and began to withdraw his fingers. Curling the digits, he dragged his hand back further while the head of his cock oozed a fine string of precum on to the base of the guy's spine.

Part of him knew he was stretching the man, opening his arse for what was to come. Another more primal part revelled in the force, in the unnecessary violence with which he both gripped the guy's neck and shoved two fingers back into Jix's hole. The more roughly he fucked the tight muscle, the more the man fought him – and the harder Richard's cock became.

Gradually, the finger-fuck became a little easier. Sweat drenched both their bodies, their stink joining with the musky fragrance of the white sage and the candle wax. His idol – his victim – was ready. He was aware of Jix Tyson struggling in his grip. He was aware of a sudden cruelty, joining with the lust.

And he was aware of a third presence in the room.

Scattered around the floor, among strewn herbs, odd swatches of coloured cloth, incense and ashes, Rick saw the shining squares of foil packets striking an incongruously modern note among the gothic trappings of the scene. Jix had left nothing to chance. The thought of him planning this bizarre self-sacrifice, right down to the details of the strategically placed condoms, made Richard smile.

But there was little time for reflection; Jix's arse was about to swallow his cock. Richard kicked a condom towards himself, bit the packet open with his teeth and had just time to roll it down the length of his cock and do the same with a sachet of lube before Jix was backing into him. Positioning the head of his cock against the entrance to the man's body, Richard braced his free hand against Jix's left hip and thrust savagely into his arse.

Nine thick inches of torment tore into Jix Tyson, impaling the man, dominating him, making Jix his bitch. Then both Rick's hands were on the man's shoulders. He bucked with his hips, jolting the last inch of himself into the wiry body and feeling the shudder as his balls impacted with Jix's arse-cheeks.

His chest hair sparkled, drenched in perspiration. Inches below, the skin on the other man's back sheened in the flickering light of the candles. Richard rested there, fighting the pounding blood in both his head and his cock. Fighting some dark part of him, some long-suppressed urge he'd always tried to ignore. And losing.

His fingers leaving deep red bruises on the man's shoulders, Rick hauled his cock halfway out of Jix and then pounded into him again. Jix was half off the floor as Richard controlled his movements. He pulled him back on to his cock, thrusting ever deeper into the man, then pushed him away as he withdrew.

The sound of their fucking filled his ears. The smell of their bodies was all he knew – that, and the low moaning cries from the man beneath him. Richard increased the speed of the fuck and shortened his strokes. Over the pound of the blood in his head, another sound seeped in. Jix's formless moans were solidifying into syllables.

Ae – thyr, Ae-thyr, Ae-thyr, Ae-thyr...

The word or words jolted from the man's lips, synchronised with the fucking, in rhythm with the slap of Richard's groin against his skinny arse.

Then his own mouth was moving and his voice was joining the incantation. 'Ae-thyr, Ae-thyr...' Somewhere, around the front of Jix Tyson's sweat-sheened body, Richard know the man's fist was moving furiously up and down the length of his hard-on. He moved one hand to the man's ponytail, grabbing the damp hair and hauling the man's head up and back.

He saw four bruises left by his fingers but was beyond caring. As they fucked, as they both chanted and both fucked their way closer to climax, the third presence in the room seemed to grow. He could feel it behind him. In front of him. All around... in his head. In his very soul.

Richard was tearing into the man's arse in a way he'd never dared do with anyone else. Something about the man – something about all of it – had unleashed a darker part of himself, a part he'd always been reluctant to acknowledge. A part which scared him, and which also made his cock harder than it had ever been. Loth as he was to admit it, Richard knew whatever had happened that night in a room in the Earls Court Hilton had stayed with him.

'Chornozan, Third Aeythr of the Elder Gods –'

Abruptly, Jix Tyson's chant expanded into words. Richard's balls spasmed against the broad metal band which dug in at the root of his cock.

'I bid you return to whence you came.'

The words were tight and jerky, uttered from between clenched teeth. But they filled the space, amplifying and drifting up to the ceiling.

The candles flickered violently and went out, plunging the room into darkness. The stench of the slaughterhouse increased. Then Richard was coming, his body propelled forward deeper than ever into Jix Tyson's hot arse. His balls knitted together. His cock shuddered violently. A sea of red hovered before his eyes. The ring at the base of his cock was preventing the spunk leaving his balls, but he was coming anyway – his whole body felt the dry orgasm – and as the man's arse-muscle clenched around his shaft, Richard knew Jix was coming too.

'Go back, Chornozan! I bid you, go back!' The words were half screamed as the body beneath his tensed.

'Go back!' His mind blank, the force of his orgasm jerking him forwards and on to Jix, Richard roared his release into the shadowed, stinking air. The man's arse muscles were quivering uncontrollably. Held in the vice-like grip of two sphincters, one at the root, the other like cheese wire around the head, Richard's cock seemed to explode into the shimmering tunnel.

Jix's knees gave way. He slumped forward on to his own fist, shooting spunk over his fingers and chest. Richard twisted the ponytail around his fingers. His body collapsed on to Jix's, his free arm curling around the man's neck. The darkness was pressing in on them. Richard tried to close his eyes. Couldn't. The room was spinning. The smell was everywhere. Even as he came, even as the guy's quivering body jerked around him, part of Richard knew there was still tension. In him. In Jix. Swirling around them both, unseen but heavy in the dark.

Then, as suddenly as they'd been extinguished, the candles flickered back into life and the air was full of the salty sweaty smell of orgasm. Richard moaned, burying his tear-streaked face in the back of Jix's neck. He was vaguely aware that the man beneath him was sobbing now. His own chest was tight while the rest of him felt spent and drained, even though no ejaculate had left his balls. Slowly, his cock still hard inside Jix, Richard eased himself sideways until they were both lying on the raised platform, his body wet and clammy and curled around Jix's.

He had no idea how long they stayed like that. Richard could feel the hammer of his own heart, added to the way Jix's was still beating rapidly against his forearm. Slowly, his mind seemed to return from wherever it had gone. Vague questions as to what had happened tingled on the fringes of his brain.

Richard moved his face, gently kissing the closely shaved skin of the man's jaw line. 'It's gone, isn't it?' He moved his still-stiff cock gently inside Jix's battered arse.

Jix moaned and nodded. 'I don't know what we summoned, 25 years ago, that night in London. But I know it killed Dick.'

Richard shuddered, remembering a newspaper report of Dick Dawson's suicide a few months after the band had broken up.

'It nearly killed me too – sent me wandering all over the planet in search of some solution.' A wry laugh shook his body. 'I knew I had to send it back. And slowly it dawned on me I couldn't do it alone – I had to have the help of someone who had been present when Chornozan, one of the Third Aethyrs was summoned. Mistakenly, I thought buying the house of someone else who had summoned an Aethyr would be the solution.'

Richard found himself blushing.

Jix's hand reached back to stroke Richard's sweat-soaked hair. 'Christ, how old were you, when you watched us?'

'Fifteen.' He rubbed his head against the still-shaking hand.

'We thought you were sleeping – we thought that door was locked, between the rooms. I wasn't sure what to do with the kid who'd fainted, round the back of Hammersmith Odeon. I was going to wait till you woke up, then call you a taxi.' The man's voice steadied out. 'But what Dick and I unleashed last night sort of... took over. I forgot I'd even brought you back, let alone that you might have been... part of it.'

Richard's mind reeled. 'What did you unleash?'

'Chornozan. An Aethyr – one of the Elder Gods, if you believe Aleister Crowley's writings.' Jix wriggled round, turning in the arms that held him and leaning his blond head on Richard's shoulder. 'I was into all that heavily, back then: LSD, altered states of consciousness, etcetera etcetera.' He sighed. 'A seeker after the truth – that's how I saw myself.'

'And now?' Richard tightened his arms around the naked man. His cock slipped out of the loosening sphincter and pressed between sweaty thighs.

'Now?' Jix paused thoughtfully. 'Maybe I was just a washed-up 70s has-been, clutching at whatever straw of excuse I could to justify falling record sales. Maybe all that acid fucked my brain more than I knew.'

'You broke up the band at the height of your career.' Richard nuzzled the blond head. 'You threw it all away.'

'Maybe.' The blond head nodded thoughtfully. But I know something for sure.'

'What?'

'It feels different, now.'

Jix Tyson raised his face and looked at Richard.

Rick looked back, shocked to see that the man's face was now almost line-free. Twenty five years had taken its toll, but in a natural way. The ravaged look had vanished. 'Yes, it does feel different. It's gone.' Whatever it had been.

Jix laughed. 'Maybe it's all been in my mind – maybe I was just waiting for my 15-year-old number one fan to grow up and come back to me.'

They both smiled.

Richard stroked the side of the man's face. 'Um... I'm sort of involved, you know.'

Jix nodded. 'The big guy with the Harley?'

Richard's turn to laugh. 'You've seen him?'

Jix nodded. 'Hot-looking bastard.' Abruptly, the ex-rock star reached up and took Rick's face between his palms. 'Are you happy?'

Richard stared into clear blue eyes. 'Um – well, yes, I think so.' It suddenly dawned on him he had finally fulfilled his part of the bargain. He was lying here, naked, with another man. He had fucked another man. And it felt... right.

Then they were both laughing. The sound echoed around the circular room, banishing any lingering shreds of whatever had possessed Boleskin.

'Oh man!' Jix leapt to his feet. 'You have no idea how good it feels to have my soul back!'

Richard grinned, propping his head up with one hand as Jix Tyson grabbed the discarded sarong and wiped his wet face with it.

'Listen.' He turned, his face alight. 'I want to give you something.' Jix wrapped the length of cloth back round his skinny hips.

Richard shook his head. 'You've already done more for me – me and Mike both – than you'll ever know.'

'No, I wanna do this.' He stuck out a hand, grabbed one of Richard's hands and hauled the man to his feet. 'I want to give you this, because I know it's important to you.'

Jolted upright, Richard stared, his brow creasing in curiosity.

'You've got to promise me one thing, though.' Jix tossed Richard's clothes to him and talked on while he dressed. 'You must promise you'll keep the secret.'

His balls ached against the ring. If the guy thought he could even begin to make sense of what they'd just done in his own mind, let alone communicate it to anyone else, he was very wrong. As Richard dragged on his tweed trousers, the metal band still in place at the root of his cock, he saw from Jix's expression that he was referring to something else. 'Um – which secret?'

Jix laughed, and grabbed a lighted candle from one of the wall sconces. 'You'll see – but promise?'

He solemnly placed his hand on his heart. 'Okay, I promise. But what is it?'

The man's face was that of an excited child. 'Oh, just something I stumbled upon, up here, trying to exorcise Crowley's bloody Aethyr.' Jix slung a skinny arm around Richard's shoulder and began to steer him towards a door on the far side of the circular room. 'But it will interest you, Ricky... it really will.'

Chapter Twenty

Two miles away, half way up Ben Mhor, Professor St. Clair was completely lost. It was dark now, and with only the moon to guide him he had the distinct feeling he was walking in circles.

His mind reeled with what Detective Kieran McLeod had told him. Thoughts of smugglers, secret passages and remote-controlled submarines full of contraband swayed around in his head.

One thought dominated: Richard, and the danger he might be in.

Mike staggered on, cursing himself for not insisting the police officer give him a lift back down to the village. He didn't have a clue where he was. There were few landmarks to guide him. Everything looked the same – what little there was to see – and he couldn't even tell anymore which direction he was walking in.

Then the moon disappeared. The ground beneath his feet gave way, and he was falling. Panic jolted through his tired body. He made a grab for a nearby clump of heather, bu it was ripped from his fingers by the weight of his own plummeting body.

The smells changed to earthier tones. Fibrous roots swept past his face. He got a mouthful of dirt as he scrabbled for purchase on the sides of what seemed to be some deep pit. He fell, unable to stop himself. He squeezed his eyes shut. A scream echoed in his ears. He realised it was his own.

Then abruptly his feet hit something solid. Mike gasped, rolling instinctively. Arms wrapped around his head, knees drawn up, he went with the momentum. Seconds later, spitting earth from his mouth, he came to rest. The back of his neck impacting with something angular, Mike flinched and lay there, waiting for his body to return to normal, waiting for his mind to make sense of what had happened, waiting for the terror and shock to recede.

Finally, his heartbeat slowing to some semblance of normality, Mike began to uncurl. His eyes remained closed, though. And the first thing he became aware of was light beyond his eyelids.

Mike lowered his arms from around his head and blinked. He was in some sort of room – if you could call a space hollowed out of the ground and with roots and vegetable matter still protruding from the walls a room. A room lit by electricity, at that.

He edged on to his knees, staring up at the safety lights which hung from a loose wire high on the banks of excavated earth around him. The space was small and roughly oval. Mike raised his eyes, staring up at the ceiling and the darkness through which he had just tumbled. He sat there, plucking twigs and severed roots and fragments of dirt from his face and hair. Then he leant back and the angular shape dug in between his shoulder blades.

Whiplash tingled down his spine as his head jerked round. Mike stared at the large, rectangular shape concealed beneath a blue tarpaulin. Things started to make sense. Remembering Kieran McLeod's theory about tunnels and passages dug by Jacobite rebels at the end of the 18th century, Mike scrambled to his feet and grabbed the edge of the tarpaulin. Flipping the heavy covering back, he stared at a stack of cardboard boxes.

Stamped on the sides of some, the Johnny Walker Red Label. Smirnoff emblazoned others. Mike took a step back. There had to be at least a dozen of each, all containing roughly twelve or so bottles of whisky and vodka on which no duty or import taxes had been paid.

Mike dragged his eyes from the piled boxes and turned. Three similarly covered mounds stood against the other wall. Mike blinked. He'd found it! He'd found what the massed undercover forces of Grampian Police had failed to find. There had to be at least £20,000 worth of booze here, at UK prices, waiting to be moved on by the Campbells and their partners in crime. But how did they get it out on to the road? He glanced briefly up at the hole through which he'd fallen. No – too awkward, too visible a way of hauling the contraband out of here. His eyes moved along the string of safety lights. Wiping dirt and earth from his clothes, Mike started towards the far end of the space, to where the wall lights continued then disappeared.

A vague glow emanated from just beyond his line of vision. Mike's eyes darted back to the way he'd entered the chamber. He sighed. Maybe if he piled all the boxes on top of each other, he could manage to scramble up and back out. But he had no real idea how far underground he was. And he had no desire to be caught here by Archie Campbell and his cronies.

His need to escape and his curiosity were both leading him in the same direction. Taking a deep breath, Mike flipped the tarpaulin back over the boxes of booze and set off down the narrow aisle which led from the room.

Fifteen minutes later, Mike glanced at his wrist watch and sighed. He was no closer to finding a way out than he'd ever been. The place was a maze. Tunnels intersected with other tunnels, some seeming to lead back up in the direction in which he'd just come. Mike took the downward fork every time: there had to be an entrance somewhere near the loch, if that was where the contraband was coming in. He sighed and trudged on. The sound of his own footsteps was, so far, his only companion. Gradually, as he walked, the earth around him solidified into rock. It started with the curved ceiling above his head and spread down the walls. The sound of his boots on the floor changed: soon he was walking on bare rock. And the smell was changing too: still musty, still earthy, but now tinged with the scent of the sea.

He passed more tarpaulins, these covering plywood cartons containing thousands of cigarettes, which could be bought wholesale on the continent for less than a pound a packet and sold on, in Inverness, for a whacking 400% mark-up.

Mike walked on, following the labyrinth as it twisted and turned. He had to be somewhere near the village by this time. Glancing at his watch, he saw that nearly an hour had passed. His mind returned to DC Kieran McLeod's words. If there was another shipment coming in tonight, Campbell and co would have to move it on fast. Their little store rooms were close to full already.

Unexpectedly, the tunnel along which he was walking began to slope steeply. Mike gripped the walls for support, and felt wetness beneath his hands. The tramp of his boots on stone was joined by a new sound. A distant drumming echoed around him – a steady rumble which seemed to be coming from the other side of the walls. Mike kept walking, the surface beneath his feet now slippery with moss.

The drumming increased, pounding through the stone and into the palms of his hands. One of the wall lights was flickering now, blinking on and off against the glistening surface. Its buzz joined the constant drumming and helped Mike to place its source.

He'd somehow missed Drumnadrochit: he was now walking under the loch itself. The realisation both gave him hope and sent another shiver of panic through his body. Where the hell was he going? And what was waiting for him, at the end of his journey?

Richard craned his neck, gazing up in awe at the large limestone stalactites which clung to the roof above his head. 'Where are we?' His sense of direction was gone. Jix had led him down another steeply sloping tunnel to emerge in this large, natural cavern.

'Below the loch – half a mile below it.' Jix laughed softly. 'Awesome, eh?'

The sound of gently lapping water dragged Rick's eyes from the rock formations. He blinked and found himself staring at a wide body of water, which took up half the floor space in the cave.

'Something to do with air pressure, or something – don't ask me, I was always rotten at physics.' Taking Rick's hand, Jix led him over to the edge of the pool.

Light from the candles the man held in his other hand bathed the cave in a sepia glow. Flickering flame reflected on the dark water, cresting the rippling waves which played across the surface.

'This is where it is strongest.' Jix's voice was solemn, almost reverential. He paused, at the edge of the pool.

'Where what is strongest?' Richard stared at the flickering water.

'The spirit of the loch.'

Rick's eyes slowly raised themselves to look at his companion. Jix Tyson's face was alight. His blue eyes glinted out from skin bathed in golden light from the candles. A small smile stretched those narrow lips. The smile of a small, enchanted boy.

Richard blinked. 'Sorry, you've lost me.'

The man laughed again. 'The beastie... Nessie... the Loch Ness monster – whatever you want to call her.'

Richard could only stare.

Jix squeezed his hand. 'I am her keeper, now – I watch over her, the way Aleister Crowley did. The way someone always has, for the last five millennia.' He chuckled. 'I bought this damn house, hoping to rid myself of one unearthly force and find I have taken on another.'

Richard's eyes narrowed. He began to wonder just how much Jix's mind had been damaged by his years of dabbling in the Dark Arts.

'But she's no bother – no bother at all, really. I come down here to talk to her quite a lot, actually.' The man babbled on.

Dr Rodgers was starting to doubt the guy's sanity. Hot sex was one thing: but this?

'She... um, tells me things.' He smiled. 'She told me you were coming to help me.'

Richard sighed. Either the Crowley stuff or years of doing acid had seriously addled the guy's brain.

'She told me the time was right to reissue my old recordings. And she was spot on!' Jix laughed. 'I'm making more money now than I ever did.' Then he sobered. Setting the candles down on a nearby rock, the man took both of Richard's hands in his. 'But it's not about the money, really.'

Rick winced under the intensity of the blue gaze.

'It's about peace of mind. About the kind of tranquillity and ease of soul I've never found anywhere else. Even with that Aethyr dogging my steps, I could feel it.'

Dr Rodgers wondered whether to run now or humour the guy. He settled on the latter and nodded.

'It's stronger now – stronger than it's ever been. Which is why I need to ask you this.'

They stood there, holding hands, one dressed in tweeds, the other wearing a light sarong. The light from the candles cast their shadows huge and curving on the walls of the cave. Richard squeezed the man's fingers.

Jix smiled. 'Stay with me, man. Don't go back... we can be together for ever.'

Despite his certainty that Jix had well and truly lost his mind, Rick was tempted. He felt drawn into the gaze, completely absorbed by the blue of the man's eyes and the memory of what they'd done, back in the circular room. What was there to lose? His academic career was in ruins. What was there for him in Oxford after this fiasco of a field trip? He stared into the surprisingly youthful face.

'How long have I waited – 20, 25 years?' Raising one of their linked hands, Jix ran the side of a finger down Richard's face. 'How long have you waited, my friend – for someone who really appreciates you?'

Rick winced. Suddenly, despite the truth in the man's words, his mind was full of Mike. Was it just habit that made them stay together? Was it only fear of being alone which made him overlook all his partner's little indiscretions over the years? Was it insecurity that made him accept Mike's professorship when he knew it should be him, Richard Rodgers, who was receiving the academic accolades?

Slowly, Jix drew their linked hands towards his face. He kissed Rick's knuckles. 'We can have a future, you and I.'

A shudder shook his body. There was a definite chemistry here, he couldn't deny that. Adolescent adoration aside, Rick felt a bond with the man who stood before him. Something about Jix Tyson tugged at him. Something he couldn't ignore.

Somewhere along the trek, the wall lights had come to an end. Mike staggered on in darkness, focusing on a vague glow just ahead – a different light, more like the glow of candles than the fluorescent lights strung along the passage walls.

Then he heard the voices. Male. The first he didn't recognise at all, the other was all too familiar.

Mike began to run, his feet slipping and sliding on the smooth wet rock towards Richard's voice. Abruptly, the passageway widened out, and he found himself standing in the mouth of a great cave. And the sight which met his eyes took the breath from his lungs.

In the middle of the cave, beside some sort of pool, two men. Richard and some skinny, half-naked blond with a towel around his waist. Holding hands. And the blond was kissing Rick's fingers!

Mike groped for the wall beside him, grabbing the rock to steady himself. Richard's voice drifted over to him:

'Thanks – thanks for earlier.' Dr Rodgers drew the blond man closer, breaking the finger link but settling one hand on the man's towelled arse.

Mike watched in disbelief. His stomach churned.

Richard lowered the blond's hand from his lips and moved those same lips closer to the man's face. Something like motion-sickness swept over Mike's body. His head spun. Sweat poured from his skin, cooling rapidly in the damp air.

'You have no idea what you did.' Rick's mouth was very close to the blond's. 'What it means to me.'

The guy in the towel smiled. 'Man, you fucked me good and proper.'

Mike moaned again. Tears sprang at the back of his eyes. He wanted to close them – along with his ears – in an attempt to stop the over-whelming hurt which had just exploded in his mind. But it was too late. His head was full of them – Rick and this... blond. Naked. Fucking. Rick deep inside the guy the way Mike longed for his partner to be deep inside him. Then their mouths were moving towards one another. Two very different faces – one bearded and moustached, the other smooth and very boyish – met.

Mike watched his lover's lips open on the blond's in a long slow kiss. He watched the air around them shimmer as the blond tilted his head to take more of the kiss. He could almost feel Rick's tongue slip between the guy's lips. He could almost taste Rick's spit. His heart hammered against his ribs. The aching jealousy was immense.

When had this happened? Who was the blond? Where had Rick

Jack Dickson

and he met? Dogging the tail of each question was the painful realisation that Richard was only complying with his side of their bargain.
Mike himself was responsible for what was taking place before his very
eyes. He'd nagged Rick, bullied him into trying casual sex in a self-serv-
ing attempt to justify his own sluttish ways – and what had happened?

Blinking back tears, Mike faced the truth. Whatever Rick had found
with this blond, it wasn't casual. It wasn't some blow-job in a lorry
park, a quick fuck in some cottage. Mere physical need could not ac-
count for the passion of that kiss. He slumped against the wall of the
cave, hurting more than he'd thought it ever possible to hurt.

Was this how Richard had felt? Was this what his idle dalliances
had done to the man who mattered most to him in the world?

Mike sighed. He knew he was a hypocrite. Mere hours earlier, he'd
let Christ knows how many men fuck his arse and mouth – and even
then, despite coming more than once, he'd felt oddly empty because it
hadn't been Rick. Because if it wasn't Rick, it would always leave him
wanting. The knowledge made him feel more vulnerable than any
gang-bang ever could.

And now, he'd lost him completely.

As he watched, unable to tear his eyes from the source of his torment, Richard eased out of the kiss:

'I am flattered – so very flattered, by your offer.' Richard's hands
moved to the man's waist. 'And not a little tempted. But, like I said, I
have someone.' Mike saw the disappointment on the blond's face. A
vague flicker of recognition ignited at the back of his jealous mind.
Richard smiled and talked on.

'And anyway – from what I hear of your recent record sales, you'll
be back in the limelight very soon and moving down to London.'

Mike continued to peer at the skinny blond. No – it couldn't be!

The man didn't smile. His hands on Rick's shoulders, he sighed instead. 'I don't need money – I don't need fame and recognition any
more. Even if I did, what I need is no longer important. As Guardian
of the Loch-Spirit, I have duties and obligations.'

He could make no sense of the man's words. As Richard drew
the blond against his body and wrapped his arms around him,

Mike's stomach tightened.

'She will survive, Jix – she's survived millennia.'

Jix Tyson! The blond suddenly placed himself. Mike scowled. He thought that old 70s acid casualty had kicked the bucket a decade ago.

'But I can't stay with you. Okay, Mike and I have our problems, but we'll work them through.'

Jix Tyson laid his head on Rick's shoulder, turning his face to where Mike stood, raw and hurt in the shadows.

Professor St. Clair flinched. Although his rational mind told him there was no way the man could see him, at this distance and in this light, Mike felt Jix Tyson's electric blue eyes lock with his, for the briefest of seconds.

Then the guy was turning back, raising his head from Rick's shoulders and moving away. 'Good luck, then – and thanks for earlier. Thanks for everything.'

Richard shook his head. 'Nothing to thank me for – I wouldn't have missed that for the world.' He reached out his hand and ruffled the now-loosened blond hair. 'Good luck, Jix.'

The intimacy between the two men sent a shiver of fear through Mike's body. He watched the blond figure stroll over towards yet another tunnel in the far side of the cave.

Then he made his own move.

Chapter Twenty One

'I see you found someone.'

Dr Rodgers was still smiling, still feeling Jix Tyson's lips on his when another voice made him turn.

'And I see you enjoyed yourself.'

Richard stared to where a somewhat dishevelled Mike was making his way towards him from the shadows. 'Mike!' The smile broadened. 'Oh, I've got so much to tell you!'

'Was he good?' Mike's mouth was a hard, unsmiling line.

Richard cocked his head. Then laughed. 'Mike, that –'

'Was he better than me?' His partner stopped, two feet away.

Richard saw the pain in the guy's face. The words stuck in his throat. All he could manage was another smile.

Mike's mouth hardened further. 'I see you're not denying it. You did fuck that... old has-been.' He spat the accusation.

Richard flinched. The hurt in Mike's blazing eyes made his stomach flip over. But the irony of the situation was not lost on him. Unable to stop himself, Dr Rodgers began to laugh. 'You told me to! The bargain, remember?' The words were interspersed with deep chuckles. 'I was only doing what you wanted me to, baby. Casual sex – a no-strings, unemotional shag.'

It was his partner's turn to flinch. Mike's brow furrowed. 'Unemotional? No strings? I saw the way you two looked at each other. He as good as asked you to move in with him!' Mike's voice rose to a shout, echoing in the high-roofed cavern. 'That's no one's idea of... casual!'

Richard continued to laugh. 'You idiot! Don't you see?' He stretched out a hand to his partner's shoulder.

Mike leapt back. 'I see very well. I ask you to get yourself a quickie and you end up doing God knows what with... Jix Tyson! Could you not have found someone more... ordinary?'

Richard beamed. 'Oh, Jix and I go way back – we had unfinished business to settle.'

'I don't want to hear it!' Clamping both hands over his ears, Mike turned on his heel and started to walk away.

Richard sobered. He grabbed one arm, hauling the man who meant most to him in the world around to face him. He grabbed the other, pinning both arms by his partner's side and holding him there. 'Shut up and listen!' He stared into Mike's furious, wounded eyes and tried to calm down. Rick lowered his voice. 'Don't you see? This is how I feel, when you... play around. Doesn't matter how casual it is – doesn't matter how much I know, deep down, we're more than a fuck, it still hurts to think of you with other men.'

Mike's arms were rigid in his grip.

Rick sighed. 'But, for the first time, I can sympathise with what you get from others.' He smiled at the memory of a mere hour earlier. 'It's intense – very intense. For that one moment, it's all that matters. Your cock is all that matters – or his cock. Or his arse. Or your arse.'

Mike visibly shuddered. He stared at his feet, unable to look his partner in the eye.

Richard gritted his teeth and said what needed to be said to the top of Mike's head. 'And it is just one moment. Out of thousands – hundreds of thousands of moments. I understand that now. And you know what?'

Silence, then Mike managed a muttered 'what?' from between clenched jaws.

'It was hot. And I'm glad I did it. Because it makes me want you even more.'

A snort from the man in front of him.

Rick sighed. 'I never stopped wanting you. But other matters got in the way. Our work – professional envy. Then stupid irrational jealousy, when I knew you were getting it elsewhere. That made me think you didn't want me. And the whole thing just turned back on itself.'

'I've never stopped wanting you.' The words were low but clear. 'I thought you'd gone off me.'

Still tacky from Jix Tyson's arse, his cock twitched. Rick loosened his grip on Mike's arms and slid his hands down to the man's wrists. 'Never.' Thumb and forefinger ringed the broad span. The very feel of Mike's skin against his was arousing him all over again. Somewhere at the back of his mind, he wondered vaguely if the man had adhered to his part of their bargain. Thoughts of the red-haired hotelier flitted on the periphery of his brain. Then his cock was twitching against the inside of his thigh as he imagined what they'd got up to.

Behind that damned metal band, his bollocks were aching and full. On top of his session with Jix Tyson and the dry orgasm, his mind filled with bodies and cocks and sweat and the sound of fucking. Rick's grip tightened further on Michael's wrists. 'Mike?'

Professor St. Clair's head remained lowered.

'Look at me, Mike.' Richard's voice was quiet.

His partner moaned, but obeyed. Slowly, he raised his eyes.

Brown irises stared into hazel. Maintaining the eye lock, Dr Rodgers eased Mike's wrists behind his strong waist. He held him there, seeing the arousal in his ex-lover's face – and knowing that prefix was about to go.

Then his mouth was on Mike's and they were kissing like teenagers. No time for finesse – no time for recriminations or regrets. In the middle of an underground cave, far beneath Loch Ness, Richard ground against Mike's mouth, opening it further and thrusting his tongue between dry lips. Mike moaned. Richard gripped the wrists one-handed, applying pressure and bringing his partner's body hard against his. With his free hand, he cupped the back of Mike's neck, angling his head and deepening the kiss.

Mike's back arched. Rick felt the man return the passion. He felt Mike suck his tongue further into his mouth. His cock still fully erect and thick, Richard groaned. His hips were moving by themselves, grinding his length against Mike's thigh and he was aware of the other man's shaft hard and urgent somewhere to his left.

It had been years – literally – since they'd kissed like this. Richard ran his tongue around the inside of Mike's mouth, exploring, caressing, reacquainting himself with the most intimate part of the man. Arses were easy. Getting sucked off or sucking was easy. But kissing was different.

Their tongues twined together. Mike's beard rasped against his. Rick hardened his lips, forcing Mike's further apart. He nipped the skin of the man's bottom lip and heard him wince. And he felt Mike's tongue push back between his teeth. He sucked it further into his own mouth, tasting the man's saliva, recognising the flavour of the one who could still turn him on more than anyone else.

His balls were full and sore. His cock flexed. Suddenly he needed to feel skin against his skin, Mike's body hard and aching under his. Thoughts and needs totally synchronised, Rick released the man's wrists. Still kissing, still lost in each other's mouths, both men were soon tearing at their own clothes in the urgency to be free of them.

Now naked, Richard broke the kiss, Mike's spit wet and warm on his lips. Sweaty fingers fumbled for the ring at the base of his cock. He wrenched it open, gasping as he nearly came then and there. Then Rick grabbed Mike's shoulders, lowering him to the floor of the cave.

Mike slipped to his knees, his hands holding Rick's waist and his mouth open and moaning against Richard's groin.

Dr Rodgers inhaled sharply. Staring down, his hands resting on the mounds of Mike's deltoids, he watched as the man nuzzled the thick length of it. He watched him cover the shaft with kisses, Mike's head dipping down as he caressed the hairy root with his lips, then lick back up Richard's fat knob to drag his tongue around the rim of the meaty glans. Richard moaned and bucked with his hips, smashing his length against Michael's face.

But now it was Mike's turn to set the pace. Richard inhaled again, the breath filling his lungs as Mike's fingers dug into his waist, holding him there as he licked and nuzzled and kissed every inch of the flexing, curving cock while studiously refusing to take it into his mouth. His tongue moved languidly, snaking down and following one of the raised blue veins which pumped more and more blood into the swollen nine-inch cock.

Richard's bollocks clenched. Mike took the signal, trailing his tongue down further to lap around and over the heavy sac. A shudder racked his body. Richard exhaled loudly. The cave filled with the sound of his need as Mike nuzzled each ball in turn then sucked the left into his mouth.

Rick's hands moved. He clutched the sides of Mike's slick face, wanting to fuck it like he'd never wanted to fuck anything in his life, wanting this to last for ever. Then Mike was sucking on his right ball. Richard's back arched in pleasure. He tried to slam himself against Mike's face but was again held firm in those strong hands.

Michael spat the hairy puckered skin from his mouth and rubbed his beard against the sensitive inside of Richard's thighs. The sensation was almost unbearable. Throwing back his head, Rick howled up at the stalactites which hung from the roof of the cave.

Mike rubbed again, dragging the soft bristle over the delicate skin. Rick moved his feet, finding his stance on the cold rock and fucking the air in front of himself. Then the mouth was back, trailing kisses between his legs. The action dragged Rick's attention downwards. On the head of his thick, curving prick, a tiny droplet of precum oozed from his slit and glistened on top of the painfully swollen glans.

Mike was biting now, nipping the skin on Richard's thighs then licking where he'd nipped. Muscle thrummed in his legs. His calves were tight, hamstrings rigid and quads tensed and straining with postponement. Every fibre was focusing on his cock.

Despite the lavish attention, despite the way Mike was nipping and licking and kissing and nuzzling, Richard knew what he wanted – what they both wanted.

Gripping the back of Michael's neck, Rick hauled his face up. He stared at skin slick with his precum and Mike's own sweat. The man's eyes burned into him, pupils swollen until the iris was a thin ring of hazel around a huge black centre. Mike's mouth hung open, the lips wet with spit, the tongue half out in invitation. Richard needed no further bidding; still clutching Mike's neck, he forced his nine inches into the waiting mouth in one swift movement. As the tight ring of flesh descended over his shaft, Richard's bollocks, now free of the restraining ring, spasmed violently. He gritted his teeth and fought orgasm.

This wasn't over.

This wasn't over till he said it was over.

Angling Mike's head back and opening the man's throat, Richard pushed further in. On his waist, Michael's fingers were digging in painfully, adding to the torture. The head of his cock bumped against the roof of Mike's mouth. His balls clenched a second time and the muscles in his stomach knotted. Tight lips descended over the rest of his shaft, massaging and gripping the flexing length of flesh.

Richard forced more of himself into Mike's mouth. Abruptly, the man's gag reflex kicked in. Spasming muscle massaged the upper half of Richard's cock in violent, rhythmic waves, while Mike's lips tightened down towards the root. Rick moaned and fought a clenching in his balls for a second time.

Somewhere beyond his cock, Richard was vaguely away of choking sounds from deep in his lover's throat. He scowled with need, shoving the last inch of himself into Mike's mouth and rubbing his heavy balls against the man's beard.

He looked down, staring into Michael's red-rimmed eyes. His gaze broadened out to take in the flushed skin, the creased forehead and contorted lips, tight around his thick shaft. Richard's stomach flipped over. His hands holding the man's head, Mike's hands gripping his waist, the guy had never looked better. More desirable – or more fuckable.

He paused there, the head of his cock now flexing against the hard cartilage at the back of Mike's throat. Jolts of pleasure shuddered down the length of him. His balls knitted together, every sinew in his body totally focused and totally alive. And with Mike.

Slowly, he began to withdraw. Mike's fingers dug in sharply, fighting the movement. Rick winced and continued to ease himself from the man's lips. He watched his shaft, now slick with spit, edge from Michael's mouth. The choking sounds subsided; Mike was whimpering now.

Richard felt the reluctance, the man's overwhelming desire to keep his cock there. A tinge of the same selfish cruelty he'd experienced with Jix shimmered on the edges of his mind. The corners of his lips curled upwards into a parody of a smile. He continued the withdrawal, savouring both the anguish in Mike's eyes and the pressure of ever-tightening lips around the departing shaft. Only three inches remained when Richard groaned and drove himself back into the welcoming hole.

The motion knocked Mike back on to the floor of the cave. In seconds, Rick was straddling the man's face, knees in Mike's armpits, pumping his aching prick in and out between those bruising lips. He seized the man's wrists, pinning Mike's arms against the rocky floor of the cavern and holding him there as he fucked his face ruthlessly and selfishly.

Michael's eyes rolled back in his head. Richard slammed his balls against the man's chin, grinding the swollen sac against soft beard each time he pushed in then dragging it away each time he pulled out. He wanted to come now. He wanted to come in Mike's mouth and choke him with his spunk.

And he wanted more. As the dank cavern filled with the sounds of their passion, Richard ripped his cock from between Mike's shocked lips and deftly flipped him over on to his stomach.

Before Mike had the chance to even gasp, Richard was behind him, nudging Mike's hairy legs apart with one knee. He grabbed his own cock with one hand, his shaft sticky with precum, sweat and Mike's saliva. Kneeling there, Mike on all fours in front of him, the fingers of his other hand fumbled between softly haired arse-cheeks.

Mike roared as Rick stroked the entrance to his body. He pushed back, trying to sink on to Rick's hand. Richard pulled his hand away, his palm resettling on one clenched arse cheek while he deployed another of the condoms so thoughtfully scattered around the floor. With a smart slap on Mike's upturned arse, Richard lubed up and guided his cock to where it wanted to be. Leaning the engorged, purple head against Mike's quivering arsehole, the muscle in his thighs were iron.

His cock was rigid, the shaft jerking at the touch of Mike's arse-lips.

Then he was moaning, leaning forward and using the weight of his body to drive himself into the other man's arse. Now the whimpers subsided into a long, low primal moan. Mike bore back and on to Richard's cock. Rick inhaled sharply, gripped Mike's shoulders and pushed on in.

Nine inches. Nine thick inches. Mike's breath was short and shallow as he fought to accommodate that length and girth. His lungs hurt from a breath he couldn't exhale. Richard winced, the friction making his fingers clench and his balls shudder. Mike's rectum was as tight as ever. He felt the skin was being torn from his shaft as rings of muscle held him in a vice-like grip and seemed to pull him in further. Then his heavy balls were impacting against the back of Mike's thighs and the breath gushed from his lungs.

Before either of them had the chance to get used to the feeling, Rick's body was moving. The muscles in his thighs trembled. His back arched and he was withdrawing, almost to the head then pushing back in. Mike mirrored the movements, fucking the cock in his arse as much as his lover used it to fuck him.

Rick moaned, lowering his face as he pushed back in, his lips open and dry on the neck of the man beneath him each time their bodies met, slapped together then moved apart again.

Different from Rick and Jix. Different even from what Rick could remember of the way he and Mike had fucked, back in the old days. Slower and – despite the need they both felt – easier. He knew the body which trembled beneath his better than he knew his own. Through the scowl of passion, a small smile twitched Richard's lips. Releasing Mike's shoulders, he slid his hands down to the man's hipbones as he withdrew and changed the angle of the fuck. Rick winced as the head of his cock bumped against the rounded gland half way up Mike's anal canal.

A howl blasted from the lungs of the man under him. Mike's entire form shook. His arse muscles clamped abruptly. Richard roared, feeling the start of orgasm tremble deep in his balls.

Then they were screwing faster. The easy, languid lovemaking was replaced by a hard, violent fuck. Rick knew Mike's knees would be scraped raw – and he didn't care. Mike was bearing down on to his cock more furiously than ever. The cave was filled with the slick, wet sounds of two animals fucking, each chasing its own goal and joined by the other's part in that goal.

Seconds later, Rick felt as if the top of his head was about to blow off. He slammed into Mike, balls knitting together and feeling his entire body peak as his cock shuddered violently. Pumping spunk into Mike's arse, he roared a second time as the ring clenched abruptly around him and he knew Mike had come too – without wanking, without moving his hands from where they gripped the rocky floor, white knuckled.

The pressure around his cock tore another slitful of hot spunk from him. Rick's hips were bucking wildly, his body responding mid-orgasm to the body beneath his.

The cave filled with their release. Mike's tensed arse-cheeks curled and sweating against his groin, Richard slipped his arms beneath Mike's and hauled the man's body up against his. As he buried his face in his lover's neck, he caught a glimpse of Michael's cock, stiff and jerking, shooting thick ropes of milky spunk on to the floor of the cave.

They stayed like that until Rick's cock softened and slipped out of Mike's arse to nestle, limp and sore, between the man's thighs. A second spent condom joined the other among the debris on the floor – only this one contained what looked like half a pint of long-withheld spunk. Mike's hand reached around to cup the back of Richard's neck. Rick covered the side of Mike's face with exhausted kisses.

No need for words. No need to say anything. Richard had no urge to move from where he was.

Slowly, the buzz of blood left his brain. His arms tight around Mike's chest, his face buried in his lover's neck, he felt the outside world begin to edge in on them. Distantly at first, like a low rumble. Then more audibly. Rick stiffened and felt Mike do likewise. They both looked towards the tunnel at the far side of the cavern, through which Mike had arrived.

Footsteps: unmistakably footsteps. Lots of them. And they were running in their direction.

Springing apart, both Mike and Richard grabbed their clothes and fled towards the mouth of a similar passage on the opposite side of the dank cave.

Chapter Twenty Two

He'd never moved so fast in his life. One minute Rick's arms were tight and reassuring around his chest, the next they were both dashing across towards the shadows of another passageway. In the seclusion of the tunnel, Mike's legs were rubber. The part of his mind which still functioned told him what was about to explode into the cave.

They dressed hurriedly, the thunder of footsteps drawing ever closer. Mike's arse felt like he'd had a locomotive train up it. But he hauled on underpants and jeans, constantly glancing over his shoulder towards the approaching furore.

'Oh Christ... oh Jesus Christ – it's the Third Aethyr!'

Richard's panicked hiss brushed his ear. Mike looked up. 'It's the what?'

Hurriedly, his lover babbled something unintelligible about raised Elder Gods and Aleister Crowley. Despite his own anticipation, Michael laughed. He was just about to bring Richard up to date with his conversation with DC Kieran McLeod when a great commotion over the other side of the cavern took both their attentions.

Archie Campbell, Morag, Old Hamish and a variety of other men Mike recognised from around Drumnadrochit flooded into the room. They were sprinting. They were shouting.

Archie yelled something Mike didn't catch to his companions and headed for the pool. Mike blinked, following Campbell with his eyes. Then his jaw dropped as what he'd presumed was part of the water's dark surface moved. And the head and shoulders of another man appeared from what Mike could now see was the hatch of a small submarine.

The man shouted to Archie. Archie shouted something back, waving his arms wildly at the submariner while Morag, Old Hamish and the rest of the gang ricocheted around in blind panic. Then lights became visible at the mouth of the tunnel down which this lot had appeared. Flashlights – and uniforms.

Archie Campbell continued his shouted, unintelligible conversation in a language Mike just managed to identify as Gaelic as Detective Constable Kieran McLeod plus half a dozen other police officers swarmed into the cave.

'What the hell –'

In response to Richard's bemused half-question, Mike whispered what he knew about what was taking place, as he watched the undercover operation play itself out mere yards from where they hid.

Burly uniformed police officers grabbed Morag, Hamish and the others by the collars, one in each hand. Kieran himself was making for Archie and the submariner, on whom it was now starting to dawn that he had the only real chance of escape from the police raid. The man hurriedly tried to close the hatch and dive, but two other police officers were already on the deck of the submarine hauling him out. Meanwhile, DC McLeod had grabbed Archie. Twisting the man's arm up behind his back, he cuffed him quickly and efficiently.

'Archibald Campbell, I am arresting you under the Duties and Excise Law, 1984. You do not have to say anything, but anything you fail to say at this point will...'

'Smugglers?' Richard's voice echoed in his ear. 'Then I was right: the photographs Rajiv and I took were –'

'Sabotaged, because you got shots of their submarine.' Mike finished Rick's sentence for him, watching as the rest of the undercover team began to march the culprits back up another tunnel. 'The same way our boat was scuppered, with you on it.' Professor St. Clair's skin was suddenly very hot. 'The same way every one of those bastards has been very keen to distract us from what we're here to do.'

Slowly, the sound of footsteps receded as the party of police officers and their charges made their way from the cavern. Minutes later, Mike and Richard moved out of their hiding place into the body of the once-more silent cave.

Mike's face was still hot. He knew he was blushing – part anger, at his own stupidity, part fear that Richard would find out exactly what form the contraband smugglers' attempts to distract him had taken.

'They led us both a merry dance.' Unexpectedly, Rick's arm slipped around his waist. 'They led you by your dick, me by my own stupid preconceptions about life in the loch.'

A huge sigh of relief escaped Mike's lungs. He laid his head on his lover's shoulder as they wandered towards the mouth of the same tunnel up which the others had recently departed. 'I'm sorry about you monster – I'm sorry it was just some submarine.'

'I'm not.' Dr Rodgers paused, kissing the top of Mike's head. 'I was so obsessed with that bloody thing I couldn't see what was in front of my eyes.'

Michael's stomach flipped over. He half turned, his arms slipping up and around Richard's neck. 'Me neither – I'm sorry, baby.'

'No, I'm sorry. The bloody monster doesn't matter – nothing matters, if things are okay with us.' Rick's voice was low and warm. He moved his face closer to Mike's.

Michael moaned as Richard's mouth brushed his. Then his hand was moving up to behind Rick's neck and he was holding that mouth on his. The kiss deepened. Lips parting, Mike sucked Richard's tongue into his mouth, feeding on it. Both hands in the man's hair, Rick's hands holding his waist, Michael's cock was flexing. He ground his crotch against Rick's groin and lost himself in the kiss.

Neither of them heard the first soft ripples in the pool, a mere yard away. Nor the steady frothing which followed. But when a sudden wave spilled over into the cave and drenched them both, Mike was the first to break the kiss and leap back. His head jerked round.

And his jaw dropped.

At his side, and now also facing the pool, Dr Rodgers's gasp echoed in the dank cavern.

Atop a long, reptilian neck, strangely mammalian eyes regarded them with a mixture of bovine curiosity and something unnervingly human. The great grey head seemed to tilt at the two men. A small mouth opened briefly, exposing rows of tiny, razor-sharp teeth. The creature almost seemed to smile at them.

Then Mike jumped back against Richard as another great wave soaked them a second time.

And the beast was gone.

They stood there, staring at the once-more still surface of the pool. Michael's heart was hammering. His mouth was dry. Beneath his soaked clothes, a warm film of sweat oozed from his pores. And he was shaking. Great shudders racked his body. He reached behind, groping for the solidity of Richard. His lover was the first to speak:

'Did you – ?'

'Yes – oh, man – oh fuck!' Slowly, the enormity of what they'd just seen penetrated his shock. 'Do you realise what this means?' Mike spun round to face his lover and colleague. His mind reeled with the implications of what they'd both just witnessed.

They weren't some gullible tourists or locals with a financial stake in continuing the Nessie myth. They were respected academics. He himself had argued against the Loch Ness Monster's existence for decades. Maybe the marine palaeontology community thought Richard was a crank, but he, Professor Michael St. Clair, would be listened to. Together, they'd write a paper, documenting their discovery. They'd come back with an increased grant, better equipment, a larger boat. They'd find where the creature – whatever it was – had its lair.

Mike's heart was now beating very fast. His head was full of contracts, TV appearances, book commissions, documentary rights. Their discovery would blow the scientific world apart. It was a challenge to Darwinism – a direct riposte to the way they all thought about evolution and species development.

He focused on Richard, whose eyes were still trained beyond him to the pool. Mike gripped the man's shoulders. 'Do you realise what this means? What we have here?' He was shouting now. The cave echoed with his excited voice.

'I do.' Dr Rodgers' response was contrastingly quiet. 'I do indeed.'

Mike laughed and kissed Rick soundly on the lips. 'Wait till Dean Hearns hears about this – they'll be throwing money at us! No more scrimping. We'll come back and we'll –'

'We'll never mention this to another living soul.' Richard smiled softly, a dreamy look in his eyes.

Mike's jaw dropped a second time.

'Jix told me the spirit of the loch could give us treasures beyond our wildest dreams. And hasn't she done just that?' The otherworldly eyes fixed Mike's. 'Hasn't she shown me that work isn't the most important thing in life?'

Michael shook his head in disbelief. 'You've fought for years to convince the marine palaeontology community that such a creature could exist. So now that we know it does, why won't you – ?'

'Because I know what will happen.' Rick sighed. 'We mention one word of this, and the whole area will be overrun by sightseers, research teams, TV crews – the works.' A sadness replaced the dreamy cast. 'They won't give up until they have that wonderful creature in a net, then back at some lab – or worse.'

Michael was about to jump in with logic and scientific detachment, but something in the tone of his lover's voice stopped him. He let Richard continue. 'And I couldn't do that – not when Nessie brought us together again. Not when she let both of us see what we have and were about to throw away.' Rick raised one hand to stroke Mike's cheek.

A shiver of pure arousal shuddered through Professor St. Clair's body.

'Could you? Could you do what I nearly did, and lose what we have because of some stupid professional ambition?'

Mike covered the hand on his face with his own. He tried to take in the man's words. The kudos seeker in him rebelled to the end. 'But – but –'

'We don't even know if she has physical form, in any measurable sense.' Dr Rodgers laughed wryly. 'Jix Tyson called her the spirit of the loch, and if she does possess the kind of power he and Crowley believed her to, maybe she does play with the senses in order to make her point.'

Mike felt his resolve slipping away. He linked his fingers with Rick's, drew the hand down to his mouth and nuzzled the man's knuckles thoughtfully. Droplets of briny water trickled down from his wet hair and dotted the back of his hand. 'Well, something soaked us!'

They both laughed. Standing there, dripping wet, Mike glanced around at the pool one last time. He wouldn't swap the way he felt now for all the academic accolades in the world. He grinned at his partner of ten years, and his new lover. 'Okay – have it your way.'

'Not my way. Just the way it has to be.' Richard chuckled. 'And even if we did tell, they'd probably institutionalise us both.'

Mike laughed. 'So – what do we do?' He stroked the side of Rick's face.

'We find the way back out of here, give our statements to your friend from Grampian Police, track down Lionel and Raji... and return to Oxford.'

'And what about the rest of the summer? What about your research?' Mike's questions were cut, mid-sentence, by Rick's mouth hard on his.

Then they were strolling towards one of the many tunnels and Professor St. Clair, his fist tight in Richard's, felt at peace for the first time in years.

Hundreds of feet above the maze of underwater tunnels and caves, on the surface of the loch, Lionel and Rajiv watched from the deck of the shiny white motor cruiser as dozens of headlights and not a few police sirens swarmed on the far shore.

'What is happening? Where are Dr Rodgers and Professor St. Clair?'

Standing just behind the smaller man, Lionel watched the activity around Boleskin and contemplated a question of his own.

'Has an accident occurred? Someone has been hurt, perhaps?' Rajiv turned away from the streams of headlights and looked at Lionel.

'I'm sure it's nothing to worry about.' Lionel studiously avoided those dark chocolate eyes and continued to watch whatever was going on on the western shore. The past twelve hours had been somewhere between a nightmare and his wildest dreams come true.

They'd talked more. They'd spent more time together. Rajiv had confessed to his crush on Dr Rodgers – something he now admitted was only infatuation and which embarrassed him greatly.

'Perhaps we should not have done this sweep of the loch – perhaps we should have waited for Dr Rodgers and Professor St. Clair.'

'We agreed to do this shift. But we'll take her in soon – just one more length, eh?' He tore his eyes from the headlights and risked a look at the slighter man.

A frown of concern creased the handsome face. But Rajiv nodded. Lionel sighed. Ever since that inflatable monster had been dragged ashore, that afternoon, he'd known they were on a hiding to nothing, research-wise. There was nothing in the loch. At least, nothing of the scale they were looking for. And he knew Rajiv knew this too. They both knew taking the motor cruiser out at all was a waste of time.

Inside his jeans, the lob of semi-hard cock he'd been carrying around all day twitched against his upper thigh. Lionel knew why he was here: he'd do anything to spend time with the guy. What was Rajiv's excuse? He watched the slender man, who was now back at the rail, gazing out over the water as the cruise-controlled boat turned and headed back down the length of the dark water.

They stood there in silence, the soft purr of the engine and the whoosh of the waves the only sound. Finally, Rajiv spoke. 'Perhaps you think I am mad, but this place is like the desert.'

Lionel let the sound of the man's voice fill his head.

'It commands a respect in the same way the great acres of sand which border my country command respect. It is too large – too vast to do anything else.'

Lionel drank in the sound. And, contrary to anything Rajiv might think, he did sort of understand.

'In the past, those amongst my people with questions were advised to make a pilgrimage not to Mecca, but to the Syrian Desert in order to gain enlightenment. When I was a child and I heard those stories, I believed there was some great creature who lived there – like the Sphinx, or maybe this Nessie – who answered all questions and gave the troubled peace of mind.'

Lionel moved forward. His hands rested loosely in the rail beside Raji.

'But then I grew up, I learned the truth.' The handsome, angular face turned. 'It is a size thing.'

Lionel nodded.

'Alone, in that vastness – in that great expanse of emptiness – one loses all sense of ego. And one gains perspective.'

Bottomless eyes gazed into his. Lionel's mouth was suddenly as dry as that Syrian Desert.

'I have never told this to another living soul, my friend – although I think Guro Lee knew, instinctively.'

He was lost in those eyes, as lost as a pilgrim searching for answers in the vast sandy wastes.

'I have always been drawn to those of my own sex.'

Lionel's heart hammered in his chest.

'For years I fought it. I spurned the company of all, both male and female, and sought the answers within me. I was sure if I disciplined my body as my tutors taught me to discipline my mind, I could conquer these urges.'

Lionel's stomach churned. Memories of his own attempts to battle with the bodies of the she-males and the way they made him feel swam in his mind.

'Look around you, my friend.' Abruptly, Rajiv cast a well-muscled arm out over the still waters. 'Look up at the stars.'

Lionel only had eyes for the man by his side.

'In the great scheme of things, what does it matter? Like the great deserts of my homeland, these glens and this loch has been here for thousands of years. Those planets up there – the stars which twinkle at us? They are long dead. We only see the light they have left in the sky.'

His chest tightened. His cock was hard and throbbing against his stomach.

'One twinkle – that's all our lives are. Brief, shining explosions on the surface of eternity. A greater force than our will controls all that, Lionel.'

He was lost in those eyes, lost in the timbre of the man's voice and aware of an echo his words were finding deep inside his quick, down-to-earth, Tynesider's brain.

'And if Allah – or whatever name God goes by – made me this way, who am I to question that?' Rajiv smiled.

Lionel found himself smiling back.

'I have never been with another living soul, in the sexual sense. But you laughed, when I said my body was a temple.' There was hurt in the voice.

Lionel's stomach tightened. He suddenly felt very ashamed of himself. 'Let me worship it, then.' Falling to his knees, his arms clasped around Rajiv's slender waist, Lionel pressed his face against the man's crotch and felt Rajiv's knob flex along his cheek. Long-fingered hands rested lightly on his shoulders. Lionel's lips parted. He mouthed the engorging outline, moaning as it thickened and filled with blood against his sweating face. Each flex of the man's shaft was echoed by a throb in his own groin.

Rajiv sighed a little, his fingers moving up to stroke Lionel's bristly neck. 'But you have been with many, yes? Lain with numerous others.'

The captain of the university First Eleven shivered. 'Women, yes... but no men.' Not if you didn't count Prof St. Clair, and Lionel still blushed at the memory of that fiasco. Tilting his head, his open mouth moved down the stretching ridge of cock beneath the covering of denim. He tightened his lips, drawing them down to the very root of the cock, then raked his teeth back up its thickening length.

The responding sigh was deeper, this time. 'So we are both virgins.' The fingers gripped Lionel's neck.

It didn't matter, none of it mattered. His own hands curled up and over the man's belt, hanging on there as Rajiv began to grind himself against Lionel's face. He was biting now, raking his teeth against the growing ridge, which bucked back at him through the denim. Beneath his knees, engine vibration shuddered up and trembled through his balls.

Rajiv circled his hips, pushing against the mouth on his shaft.

Then Lionel couldn't stand it any longer. His fingers curled around the back of the man's belt, he raked his teeth up to the very head of Rajiv's cock. And took the zip's metal tab between them. It was cold in his mouth, hard between his teeth. Slowly, Lionel leant back and dragged the zip down. Beneath the opening fly, Rajiv's cock bulged out from under its layer of jersey underpants. Lionel moaned and pushed his tongue between the zip's metal teeth, lapping at what he could reach of the thick ridge of flesh. Small whimpers of pleasure drifted into his ears. He mouthed the fabric, drenching it. Taking a section of the underpants between his teeth he drew them into his mouth. He could taste him: taste the sour muskiness of Rajiv's body. His own cock was leaking freely now, oozing clear precum on to his stomach.

Lionel pushed the section of fabric from his mouth, raking his teeth up to the fat swollen head of Rajiv's jersey covered knob. When he could feel the elastic of the waistband, he closed his teeth around it and dragged his head away from the man's crotch. As the folds of fabric ruffled downwards, Rajiv's slender brown cock sprang free and nudged his forehead. It took every shred of strength in Lionel's stocky body not to fold his lips around it straight away. His fingers tightened around Rajiv's belt and he continued to lower the underwear, only pausing when the elastic waistband slid over the man's surprisingly hairy balls and tucked itself underneath.

A groan from above. Then Rajiv's fingers dug into the flesh on his shoulders. Lionel gasped. He found himself hauled to his feet. Then he was staring into huge, chocolate eyes, with Rajiv's cock warm and heavy against his thigh.

The motor cruiser continued its smooth passage back up the dark loch. His gaze never leaving Rajiv's, Lionel hauled off his jacket and sweatshirt. Tossing them aside, shaking fingers moved towards the belt of his jeans. Rustles on the periphery of his hearing told him the other man was doing likewise. Minutes later they stood there naked. Two very different men, two very different bodies.

Lionel tried to steady his breathing but couldn't. Rajiv's face was tight with arousal. He stretched out one arm and curled his fist around Lionel's shaft. A deep, primal moan rumbled deep in the Tynesider's throat. The feel of a man's hand on his cock made his balls clench. The hair on his thick chest sprang to attention. Every muscle in his body tensed. Rajiv slowly moved his fist down the length, then back up to the head, running his thumb across the slit, catching the first ooze of clear liquid. He removed his hand and raised his thumb to parted lips.

Lionel shuddered, watching the man lick precum from his fingers and smear it over his lips. Then those same lips were on his and Lionel could taste his own body fluids in another man's mouth. The kiss was deep and wet. Lionel sucked on Rajiv's tongue, trying to pull more of it into him. His arms hung motionless from shoulders which the other man now held, controlling the movement of his mouth. He was in Rajiv's hands. He widened his lips, feeling Rajiv's tongue explore his mouth. Then the hands were moving from his shoulders, sliding down over his back.

Lionel's spine arched in pleasure, his cock flexing in the air between them. And when those long-fingered hands settled on the cheeks of his arse, the captain of the First Eleven lunged forward, sliding his cock up alongside Rajiv's.

The other man was shuddering now. Lionel's head slumped on to the man's shoulder. He could feel Rajiv's cock flexing parallel to his. A low voice drifted into his ear:

'Your body is beautiful, Lionel.'

His flinched at the alien words. The strong muscles in his thighs clenched, tightening his sphincter instinctively.

'So powerful. So masculine.'

He felt as helpless as a kitten. As weak as a puppy. But something inside him was strengthening by the minute. And when Rajiv's index finger stroked down the length of his hairy crack, Lionel grunted with need.

Pulling away from the man, he spun round. Lionel gripped the rail of the motor cruiser, lowered his head between outstretched arms and spread his thick, hairy legs.

Chapter Twenty Three

His palms slid along the surface of the boat's rail. Feet planted wide apart, he shuddered in the cool air. His balls were full and heavy. His cock fucked the night, curling up from his groin. The tendons in his arms and shoulders ached as he stretched further back, pushing his arse out and up towards the man behind him.

And he waited.

Waited to be fucked.

Lionel Banks squeezed his eyes shut against the need. Pictures danced on his eyelids. Pictures of she-males, dusky and sultry. Billie reared up in front of him, with her perfect tits and her made-up face – and her cock.

Something wet and warm poked against his thigh. Lionel moaned, pushing back against it. It moved away. The moan was filled with longing. Lionel squeezed his eyes more tightly shut. Then soft hands settled on the cheeks of his arse. Lionel tensed. He braced, trying to relax, wanting to open himself to this. But his reaction to Professor St. Clair's finger refused to leave his mind.

Billie's face danced before his eyes. Then the hands were spreading him, opening him up and Billie's face melted into a dark, angular male profile. A wet warmth moved over the surface of his arsehole. Lionel inhaled sharply, momentarily confused. But when Rajiv dragged his tongue down over Lionel's balls, then back up his crack, the stocky Tynesider's cock flexed so violently he had to grip the boat rail more tightly and bite his lip to stop himself coming then and there.

He pushed back, wanting more. The hands held him steady, thrusting forward against his push. And the tongue lapped again. Lionel was grinding now, circling his hips then jutting forward to thrust his cock upwards into the night. The sensation was killing him. The feel of Rajiv's hands holding him open contrasted with the languid, almost laid-back movements of the man's mouth.

Lionel's hole clenched and unclenched, responding to the wet ministrations. Rajiv varied the strokes, sometimes lapping, his tongue broad and flat, sometimes swirling the point around the crinkled hole, flicking against it then diving down to do the same to Lionel's balls.

Just as he thought he couldn't stand it any more, Lionel felt thumbs apply a little pressure, either side of his hole. Chilly air brushed across his arse-cheeks, down into his crack and cooling the man's spit.

Then Rajiv pushed a little harder. Lionel howled. Night air shimmered over his hole. His chest tightened. Then Rajiv's tongue was inside him, licking the rim of his arsehole and pushing on up. His eyes shot open. He stared down at his own cock. A thin sliver of precum hung from the flexing head. He squeezed his eyelids shut once more. Rajiv's tongue was moving over the walls of his arse now, caressing and flicking deep in his body. Lionel fucked the air furiously, thrusting back on to the man's face, wanting more, wanting it all.

His hole was a soaking, drenched mess of spit and sweat. Fingers clenched around the boat rail, knuckles white against the pleasure, he rotated his arse like a whore.

Rajiv was mouthing him now. Lionel groaned at the feel of the man's lips and teeth kissing his crack, slathering his arsehole with spit, nibbling the lips then sucking on them. Then pushing his tongue back inside to lave the rippling walls of his rectum.

Abruptly, it all stopped. Lionel whimpered. The hands which had held him open gripped his tensed shoulders. Rajiv's thighs shadowed his. The man's cock rested in the crack of his arse and warm breath drifted into his ear:

'Lionel...'

His name was more sigh than word. He moaned and continued to grind back, dragging his crack along the length of the man's shaft.

'Lionel...'

The Tynesider's head reared up from between his outstretched arms. Then his neck was craning round and a wet mouth met his. Lionel moaned into the kiss, tasting himself on the tongue which now pushed itself between his parted lips.

He bent his knees, grinding his arse more fervently against the man's cock, sucking Lionel's tongue into his mouth. He was vaguely aware of one hand leaving his shoulder. But the way Rajiv was kissing him, the movement of the man's mouth and the taste of him filled Lionel's mind.

Strong thighs nudged his further apart. Lionel widened his stance, knees bent and another man's body between his legs. A firm, wet pressure settled against the drenched opening to his body.

Lionel's balls knitted together. He knew what was coming: the thing he dreaded and desired more than anything else. He was going to be fucked – to be used by another man in the same way that he had used so many women. The tables were turned. Well, if it was to happen, let it happen. His hands scrabbled around and found his discarded trousers, found the rear pocket and found what he always carried inside it, just in case – a condom in a small foil packet. Holding it between thumb and forefinger, he handed it back to Rajiv, a small token of Lionel's sexual submission and surrender.

The significance was not lost on Rajiv, who was sucking on his tongue now, raking his teeth along it. Lionel inhaled sharply. His cock flexed. The pressure on his sphincter increased. He opened his eyes, gazing at closed eyelids. Rajiv's lashes were long and thick. Lionel moaned at the sight of them. Then a sudden increase in the pressure on his sphincter made him gasp – and Rajiv was in him. The thick, latex-covered head of another man's knob was pushing past arse-lips wet with another man's spit. It felt huge. Impossibly huge.

And wrong.

His head jerked back instinctively. Rajiv's eyes flew open. Another instinct tightened Lionel's sphincter. Still parted from the kiss, Rajiv's lips drew back over his teeth in a low groan of pleasure. He continued to push his cock into Lionel.

And when another man's balls impacted hard and full against the cheeks of his arse, another man's eyes gazing into his, Lionel's knob shuddered violently. What had felt so wrong suddenly felt very very right. Balls churning, chest tight, his hips jutted forward and Lionel shot his load against the side of the boat.

Rajiv fucked him through his orgasm, using short jabbing strokes to bring himself off. Lionel's head drooped down between his braced arms. Mouth open, he pumped slitful after slitful against the side of this boat, his knob flexing again and again.

Then Rajiv's body was shadowing his. The man was biting the back of his neck and the thick hugeness in his arse was throbbing relentlessly. He heard Rajiv's gasps somewhere through the increasing waves of his own pleasure. And when the throbbing became one long shudder and the body behind his tensed, Lionel was coming all over again, with another man's spunk pumping steadily into his arse.

'Yes, Dean – I'm afraid I shall have to admit academic defeat as far as the existence of any palaeontologically significant life in Loch Ness is concerned.' Three months later, Dr Richard Rodgers manufactured another regretful smile at yet another faculty party. 'More wine, Mrs Hearns?' He turned briefly from the Dean and his wife to the table behind, and lifted a bottle of cheap red.

As he did so, Rick caught Mike's eye from in front of the broad shoulders of the new American teaching assistant.

'But you had some excitement all the same.' Behind, the Dean's wife laughed gaily. 'Do tell us all about it, Dr Rodgers.'

Turning back to the head of the college, Rick noticed Rajiv Azad and Lionel Banks, on their own over by the window. They were both drinking mineral water and reading the sleeve notes on the new Jix Tyson CD, which had been recorded in London in an amazing two weeks flat. Entitled Boleskin, and lauded in the music press as the work of a mature genius, the copy now in Rajiv Azad's slender hands had arrived at the university, last month, bearing a Drumnadrochit postmark. No letter accompanied it, but in small typescript on the back of the sleeve notes, the brief acknowledgement 'For Ricky' had touched Richard deeply.

'Well, Rodgers?' Dean Hearns' gravelly voice cut into his thoughts. 'What about it? Are you not going to share your excitement with us?'

To describe it as excitement was to understate it. So much had happened, on that short, four-day field trip. Rick's gaze lingered on Rajiv and Lionel. They were both deep in discussion and only had eyes for each other. Dr Rodgers smiled. He didn't suppose he'd ever get the full story there, but two men who'd hated each other before that ill-fated trip north were now the inseparable best of friends. Emphasising some point in their private conversation, Rajiv briefly touched Lionel's shoulder. The Tynesider's face almost glowed at the gesture. Maybe more than friends, thought Richard. Who knew?

'Yes, Richard,' Mrs Hearns' voice pulled him back to his job as host, and his more oblique role as general whitewash man. 'We read about it in the newspapers. Smugglers, was it?'

Now on automatic pilot, Richard refilled her glass and began the version of events he and Mike had cooked up between them.

Everyone bought it. Parts of their story were backed up by press reports. Himself, Mike, Rajiv and Lionel had indeed given their statements to Grampian Police, in the wake of Archie Campbell and his cohorts' arrest. Richard had confirmed what he and Rajiv had seen. Lionel had eventually decided that what he'd come face to face with on the night of his impromptu swim was more likely to be the underwater lights from the one-man submarine than the gleaming eyes of any monster. And Mike had concocted a tale about Archie Campbell leading him off into the hills on some wild goose chase, as part of the gang's attempts to keep the marine scientists away from the loch.

As he talked on, the Dean and his wife rapt listeners, Dr Rodgers's mind turned back to the evening, six weeks ago, when he'd finally heard the full story from his lover.

Post-sex on the kitchen floor, Michael's face blushing and hot against his chest, Rick had listened as the man had confessed all: the butt plug, Archie Campbell, Morag Campbell – then half the male population of Drumnadochit.

And Lionel!

Jack Dickson

Lying there, listening to it all, Richard had been surprised by its effect on him. Hot on the heels of their own reunion in the underwater cavern, he'd known none of it had any relevance to their relationship. But he'd put off hearing the details, the minutiae of Mike's need for sexual excess – his need to be dominated, abased and used.

But as Mike admitted all the gory details, Richard was semi-appalled to find himself hardening. Sticky and sore from their recent fuck, his cock was soon pushing up through folds of foreskin still tacky from Mike's arse to rub against the hairy skin on his thigh. And by the time his lover had finished, near to tears with his face now buried in Rick's chest hair and begging his forgiveness, Richard only knew one thing: it turned him on too.

Why, he had no idea. The whole thing defied analysis. He only knew that he wanted him more at that moment than he'd ever done. With Mike sobbing, Richard had heaved him to his feet and fucked him over the kitchen table until those sobs turned to moans of pleasure. He'd held him in his arms afterwards. And had never felt closer to another human being.

'So, as you see, our field trip was all rather a waste of time, Dean. However,' Dr Rodgers beamed, 'I have been reading about a lake in the very north of Siberia, where there have been sightings of a similar creature.'

Dean Hearns laughed heartily, patting Richard's shoulder. 'You never give up, do you, Rodgers?'

Rick glanced round at where Mike and the visiting American academic were now deep in conversation. No. He never did give up. Not on himself and not on his lover. He'd been aware of Mike's attraction to the younger lecturer for a few weeks now. Neither of them had said anything, but Richard, at least, knew that accepting past indiscretions was one thing. Staring them straight in the face was quite another.

Returning his attention to the head of the college, Richard joined in the laughter. 'If nothing else, I'm consistent, Dean.' He filled both their glass one last time. 'Now, if you'll excuse me –' And before his courage left him, Richard made his way across the room to his lover and the most recent object of Professor St. Clair's interest.

Mike saw Rick approach. He glanced from the hot American to his lover, then back again. Richard took the signal and paused, a foot or so away – well within earshot, but out of the American's line of vision.

Mike lowered his voice. 'You up for it, Gerry?'

Gerald MacDonald, of the Massachusetts Institute of Technology's Oceanic Department blinked. Then grinned. 'Sure – when?' The tone was conspiratorial.

Mike laughed softly. There was definitely something about Americans. Maybe it was the accent. Maybe it was their up-frontness. Maybe it was this one's strong shoulders. Or that glint of potential cruelty in those cold, academic eyes. 'An hour?'

'Cool.' His back to Richard, Gerry's hand moved to his crotch. He brushed the thick outline Mike had been admiring all night. 'Where?'

'Our place?'

Momentarily startled, the visiting academic's brown eyes creased briefly in confusion. Then Mike reached past the man, beckoning Richard forward. 'Yes, we have a small pied à terre on the west side of the quadrangle.' His voice lowered further, sinking to a hoarse whisper.

Richard moved to his side.

As his lover, unseen to the rest of the room, placed a proprietorial hand on the small of Mike's back, Professor St. Clair's cock shuddered against the fly of his trousers. That tiny gesture spoke volumes. It turned him on as much as the thought of this young American inside him.

'Richard Rodgers – Rick.' His partner extended his free arm. 'Nice to meet you...?'

'Gerry – Gerry MacDonald.' The visiting academic did likewise.

And as the two men who would fuck him and use him shook hands and sealed their bargain around him, Mike knew what he'd found on the Loch Ness field trip truly defied description.

Still waters ran deep – deeper than any of them had ever imagined.

New erotic fiction
by Jack Dickson

Out of this World Out Oct 2001 from Zipper Books

Hard and horny stories of sex between men in the real world, the cyberworld, last year and next century – in their own bedrooms or lost in space.

Jack Dickson's wank-worthy porno tales have been published in US anthologies and all-American magazines like *Powerplay* and *Bunkhouse*. This collection brings together the very best.

UK £7.95 US $12.95 (when ordering direct, quote OUT 634)

And from Gay Men's Press
by Jack Dickson,
the thrilling Jas Anderson mysteries:

FreeForm

A tough Glasgow cop, Detective Sergeant Jas Anderson, suspended from duty for assault, is the natural suspect when his lover and partner in an SM relationship is found brutally murdered.

Dickson has been described as "a weaver of intricate plots which cunningly combine the most gripping elements of the hard-boiled thriller with the most stimulating of erotic fiction" (Gay Times).

UK £8.95 US $11.95 (when ordering direct, quote FRE577)

Banged Up

Detective Sergeant Jas Anderson was the violent anti-hero of FreeForm, expelled from the Glasgow police force. Banged Up starts with Jas being framed by his ex-colleagues. He is remanded to Barlinnie prison, and is forced to share a cell with Steve McStay, sentenced for aggravated assault on two gay men. In this all-male enviroment, inmates don't divide into gay and straight, but rather into who fucks and who gets fucked. Resilient as ever, Jas forms an unlikely partnership with Steve in his fight for survival.

UK £9.95 US $14.95 (when ordering direct, quote GMP 044)

Some Kind of Love Out Sept 2001

Former Detective Sergeant Jas Anderson, the violent anti-hero of FreeForm and Banged Up, becomes emeshed in a dangerous web of intrigue and double-dealing. Working as a private investigator on a routine case, Jas soon finds himself stirring an explosive cocktail of police corruption, sectarianism and murder. Plunged into a world where nothing is what it seems, he is forced to confront the demons of his past. As comforting illusions are stripped away, Jas begins to suspect his boyfriend, ex-con Stevie McStay, of more infidelity. But the truth he uncovers is not only shocking, it threatens the attempt by two damaged men to find some kind of love.

As canny and as readable as any of Dickson's previous thrillers.

UK £9.95 US $14.95 (when ordering direct, quote SOM 311)